Readers love
BRU BAKER

Playing House

"By the highly charged end of the story I loved these men, and it is a testimony to the skill of Bru Baker that I identified as much with Frank as with Warner."

—Prism Book Alliance

Late Bloomer

"…another lovely story by Ms. Baker. I adore her stories so much and this one was no different."

—The Blogger Girls

"…a… cute Christmas story"

—MM Good Book Reviews

Finding Home

"This book is very well written… the journey this book takes on you was enjoyable and interesting."

—Hearts on Fire

"What a sweet, romantic story to read… I really enjoyed this story."
—Love Bytes

By BRU BAKER

All in a Day's Work (Anthology)
Branded
The Buyout
Campfire Confessions
Diving In
Dr. Feelgood (Dreamspinner Anthology)
King of the Kitchen
Late Bloomer
The Magic of Weihnachten
Traditions from the Heart

Published by DREAMSPINNER PRESS
www.dreamspinnerpress.com

KING OF THE KITCHEN

BRU BAKER

Published by

DREAMSPINNER PRESS

5032 Capital Circle SW, Suite 2, PMB# 279, Tallahassee, FL 32305-7886 USA
www.dreamspinnerpress.com/

King of the Kitchen
© 2015 Bru Baker.

Cover Art
© 2015 Maria Fanning.
Cover content is for illustrative purposes only and any person depicted on the cover is a model.

ISBN: 978-1-63476-647-0
Digital ISBN: 978-1-63476-646-3
Library of Congress Control Number: 2015943920
First Edition November 2015

Printed in the United States of America
∞

This paper meets the requirements of
ANSI/NISO Z39.48-1992 (Permanence of Paper).

For my dad, who taught me not only how to cook
but also how to love the kitchen.

Preface

WHILE THE restaurants and cooking shows in *King of the Kitchen* are all fictional, the cooking techniques definitely aren't. The food prepared in the book falls mostly under two broad culinary umbrellas: molecular gastronomy and the slow food movement.

At a glance the two don't share much in common. In fact, in a lot of ways they're polar opposites. Molecular gastronomy uses science and often a slew of chemicals to subvert traditional cuisine and challenge palates through unique flavors and textures. The slow food movement is about using locally and ethically sourced ingredients, showcasing regional cuisines and in-season foods, and using cooking techniques that highlight the freshness and flavor of the ingredients. That dichotomy is part of what made it so fun to write. But when you dig past the surface, both movements come from chefs who are intensely dedicated to the craft and focused on making food more than just, well, food.

Readers don't have to be avid cooks to follow along with the action in the kitchens in the book. Even those who don't know a roux from a rutabaga won't be lost for long, since the cooking scenes are fast-paced and pretty well laid out.

Some techniques used in the book might be unfamiliar, like using a siphon with a nitrous oxide canister to make potatoes into a foam (which is called an espuma). Or using a sous-vide to gently cook something (usually meat) by encasing it in a thin plastic bag and then submerging it in a water bath kept at a continuous temperature, which allows the food to retain all its original fat and juices.

Mostly, though, the food and the differing cooking techniques in *King of the Kitchen* are a backdrop for the chefs who use them. Duncan is every bit as edgy and playful as the food he cooks using his array of smokers, siphons, and chemicals, and Beck is as traditional and classic as his simple, elegant food implies. And when they come together? Let's just say there's more than food sizzling in the kitchen when they're around.

Prologue

July 2006

THE KITCHEN was as hot as a sauna, and the bandanna Duncan had tied around his head had lost its ability to keep his forehead dry hours ago. His feet ached, his hands were chapped, and despite being surrounded by food, he hadn't eaten since breakfast. It was long past the dinner hour, but the flurry of frenetic activity hadn't slowed much at all. People were underfoot everywhere in the small space, bustling around with hot pans and large pots, and no matter which way he turned, Duncan ran the risk of toppling a precariously placed container.

It was perfect.

"Order in! Rancher's omelet, no onions, no peppers, no potatoes, no meat."

Duncan rolled his eyes, yanking the ticket out of John's hand. "So basically they want a cheese omelet? You don't think you could make it easier on us in here and just write down what they actually ordered?"

John grinned. "She ordered the rancher's omelet, dude."

"Without three quarters of what makes it the rancher's omelet? Did you tell her she could order a cheese omelet and save $3.75?"

"I did, but she's not the one paying, and she wanted to stick it to him."

That startled a laugh out of Duncan. John motioned over his shoulder, toward a table, and Duncan leaned through the pass-through, trying to see the couple without being too obvious. He knocked over a battered pot in the process, making most of the diner's customers look up. So much for subtle.

"Them," John said, pointing toward a small table in front of the plate-glass windows near the entrance to the diner. The woman was tall and slender, with dark wavy hair cascading down her back. Her clothing and the purse hanging off the back of her chair screamed money, as did the suit on the man she was with. They weren't the diner's typical patrons by a long shot, but Duncan did have to concede she looked like the type of person who'd be a special order. When business was slow, he and some of the other kitchen staff passed the time by betting on whether the customers who walked in the door would be complicated. He was almost always right.

"What about him?" Duncan asked, jutting his chin toward the man she was with. He could only see him from behind, but from his immaculately cut hair and his ramrod straight posture—difficult in the rickety diner chairs, Duncan knew from personal experience—he looked like a special order as well.

Duncan looked down at the ticket, frowning as he tried to decipher John's chicken scratch. No matter how many times the kitchen complained, John's handwriting never improved. Duncan had worked at the restaurant on and off for more than ten years, and the only constant had been John and his atrocious handwriting. It was kind of comforting, in an extremely exasperating way.

"Seriously? Two eggs over easy, bacon, and whole wheat toast?"

Duncan looked from the ticket to the man, surprised. He peered at him, studying his shoulders and finding himself wishing he could see the mystery man's face. Duncan's culinary profiling rarely went astray. Intriguing.

"They're cousins. It was his week to pick where they had dinner. I'm getting the feeling she's less than pleased," John said.

"Which is why she special-ordered something guaranteed to piss him off?"

"That's just it, though. He didn't get angry. He laughed and told her if she really wanted to pull one over on him, she should have ordered the eggs Benedict, since that's the highest profit margin dish on the menu."

Duncan furrowed his brow. It was true the eggs Benedict was the most expensive breakfast item on the menu, aside from the steak and eggs, but the dish was hardly ridiculously priced. None of the regulars ordered it, but that was more because they had traditional meat-and-potatoes palates.

Francie, the other waitstaff on duty at the moment, broke Duncan's view of the man as she walked up to grab an order off the warmer, and Duncan shot John a mischievous grin before ducking back through the pass-through into the kitchen.

"Duncan," John said, his voice holding a note of warning.

"Order in!" Duncan yelled, ignoring him completely.

Ten minutes later, Duncan got his wish when a plate clanked noisily on the pass-through. He looked up absently, about to scold John or Francie for being so harsh with the dishes, when he realized it wasn't either of them. It was the man in the suit, and even scrunched up in irritation, his face was beautiful. He had a strong, straight nose and full lips—currently thinned in annoyance—and eyes the most interesting shade of blue Duncan had ever seen. He absolutely looked like someone who would special order, and Duncan found himself wishing even harder that he could puzzle him out.

"We didn't order this."

Duncan looked at the plate of eggs Benedict and smiled his dopiest grin, the one that never failed to get him free refills and phone numbers whenever he applied it. He'd sent the guy a free meal along with the breakfasts he and the woman had ordered—could he seriously be pissed about that?

"On the house. I heard you had a particular interest in them."

The man blinked in confusion but seemed to recover quickly, anger clouding his features.

"If you wanted to impress me, you'd have to do a hell of a lot better than a plate of fatty ham and congealing hollandaise. We don't serve eggs Benedict in our restaurants, *Charlie*," he said, eyeing the name on Duncan's chef's whites with disdain and drawing it out like an insult, "and even if we did, I don't appreciate having you encroach on my personal time with your pathetic attempt at a job interview."

Duncan's mouth hung open, and he wavered between outraged and completely confused. What was this guy talking about?

"Listen, buddy. I was only being friendly," Duncan snapped, choosing to go with outraged. He left the plate in the pass-through, pointedly ignoring it—and the man—as he pulled a new ticket off the carousel. "Order in! One deluxe hamburger, one order of chicken tenders, one spinach frittata!"

He turned toward the kitchen to get started on the eggs but was pulled up short by a hand on his shoulder.

"You can't talk to me like that, *buddy*."

Duncan scowled. "Of course, sir. The customer is always right. Yes, the eggs Benedict was part of a convoluted plan of mine to apply for a job cooking for your, what?" He made a point of studying the gorgeous guy's suit. "Office building? Hotel, maybe? I admit, it's always been my life's ambition to run a carving station at a Marriott buffet. How could you tell?"

The man gaped at him and would have responded, but the woman he was with—his cousin, John had said?—walked up behind him and unceremoniously placed her hand over his mouth.

"I apologize for Beck's behavior. Charlie, is it?" Duncan nodded, figuring it was easier than correcting her. He was too busy watching as the man fumed silently behind her hand. "He's a bit on edge at the moment, and he misread your intention in sending the plate. He's used to having dishes we didn't order sent over to our table when we go out, and it's almost always a gesture followed by the chef coming out to ask a favor or chat him up."

She leveled a look at Beck, her sculpted eyebrow arched in challenge as she removed her hand. He huffed ungraciously but didn't resume yelling at Duncan, so Duncan was going to go ahead and call it a win.

"I apologize," Beck bit out, the words sounding forced. "Please add the eggs Benedict to our check in recompense for the misunderstanding."

Duncan was struck by a familiar pang of guilt. He could never hold a grudge against anyone. It was well known among his friends— and often taken advantage of. But he *had* sent the eggs over as a prank, and now he felt bad because he'd obviously ruined their meal. As he looked closer, he could see the designer suit was wrinkled, as if the poor guy had been wearing it all day, and dark circles smudged the skin under his brilliant blue eyes.

"No need," Duncan said, lifting the untouched plate down from the pass-through and setting it aside. He and John were both off shift in twenty minutes; the dish wouldn't go uneaten. He looked over at their table, noting that neither of them had touched their food. "I'd be happy to remake your meals. I'm sure they've gone cold by now."

The man stared at him with an unreadable expression, but the woman chimed in.

"We've had a long day, and I don't think we were that hungry anyway," she said, smiling slightly. She slipped a business card on the pass-through. "I'm Lindsay. I realize you're not looking for a job right now, but if you ever are, give me a call."

Beck looked a bit sour at her parting words, but he followed her silently back to their table, pulled his wallet out, and dropped some cash on the table. Duncan watched them leave, Beck's posture stiff and menacing until Lindsay wound an arm through his and leaned into him. He seemed to melt against her, his shoulders relaxing and his gait less abrupt as they walked down the sidewalk and out of sight.

Duncan looked down at the card on the pass-through, his eyes widening when he read it. Lindsay King, Assistant Producer, *King of the Kitchen*.

"Holy shit," he muttered, staring at the empty sidewalk. The Kings were legends in the restaurant and culinary television worlds. Lindsay's father, Christian, hosted what was widely considered the most popular cooking show on the air, and he had a huge stable of high-class restaurants as well. Duncan had been forced to listen to rants about the evil King empire practically every time he talked to his father.

The rivalry between Vincent Walters and Christian King was epic, which was one of the reasons Duncan had never had the chance to meet Lindsay before. Or Beck, who now that he had a name to go with the face, he recognized as Beck Douglas, Christian's right-hand man. An up-and-coming chef himself, he had a hand in all of Christian's Chicago-based restaurants. Word was he was being groomed to eventually take over the restaurants, and probably *King of the Kitchen*, whenever Christian retired. Duncan had never seen a picture of him because the articles he read about Beck always had shots of the food instead. But damn, he had no idea why a man who looked like Beck didn't plaster himself everywhere. Duncan would definitely watch *King of the Kitchen* if Beck was the one in front of the camera, even though he obviously had a chip on his shoulder as big as his ego.

Duncan's father traveled in the same culinary circles as Beck and the Kings, but their paths rarely intersected because of the feud between Christian and Vincent. Duncan had always assumed he'd meet them someday, but he'd figured it would be at a swanky gala or four-star restaurant, not in the kitchen of the Sunrise Cafe. He'd been steadfast in his refusals to attend events like that with his father so far, or he'd probably have already met the famous Christian and his protégé. Maybe he'd start accepting some of those invitations to have an excuse to ogle Beck's admirable ass.

Duncan's neck heated as he realized he'd just served Beck Douglas a plate of diner eggs Benedict. Hell, Beck had won the James Beard Award last year, one of the youngest chefs ever to take it. Beck knew practically everyone in the restaurant world, thanks to his mentor, and Duncan had insulted him and implied he managed a buffet. Perfect.

"Duncan, I don't know what you said to that guy, but he dropped two hundred dollars on the table to cover a twenty-dollar check. I ought to let you talk to the customers more often, man," John said, grinning from ear to ear as he elbowed Duncan in the side. "You're off now too, right? Let's treat ourselves to some real food, courtesy of Mr. Angry Eyebrows."

"Mr. Angry Eyebrows?"

"They were very expressive," John said solemnly, and Duncan broke out into almost hysterical laughter at the understatement.

"He's training to be a TV chef. I'm sure that involves lessons on how to emote with facial features," Duncan said, unfastening his chef's whites as he and John moved toward the manager's office, where the staff stored their things. The diner was too small to have an actual employee lounge, but no one cared. Especially since the owner and manager, John's mom, was hardly ever there and didn't mind them using her office as a catchall. Duncan had even napped on her couch more than once. Of course, none of the other staff aside from John would dare try that, but he supposed that was a benefit of being pseudofamily.

Duncan had worked at the diner in the afternoons all through high school, and then he'd spent every college break he could at the Sunrise Cafe, helping out. His summers were spent apprenticing in more upscale restaurants, thanks to his demanding father, but he was always happiest in the kitchen at Sunrise. Duncan would be heading back to the University of Chicago to finish his master's degree in biochemistry and molecular biology in a few weeks, which meant an end to his time in the kitchen. He'd already accepted an internship in the research and development department at Kraft Foods for the spring semester. If all went well, he'd be offered a job there come graduation in May.

He'd always picked up shifts at the Sunrise here and there, but he wouldn't have time anymore. His class schedule for next semester was insane, paving the way for him to take the minimum number of credits in the spring, since he'd be spending half the week up in Madison, Wisconsin, at his internship.

There wouldn't be time for marathon sixteen-hour shifts at the cooktop once he graduated, either, assuming he got the job with Kraft. He'd be moving up to Wisconsin, and even though Chicago was only two and a half hours away, it would be too far to pop down to cover line cook shifts when the Sunrise Cafe was in a bind.

He was really going to miss it. And John.

"I can see it. He's pretty enough for television," John said, shrugging out of his own uniform and pulling on a ratty sweatshirt. "So. Pizza?"

"Food of the gods," Duncan agreed, tucking his spattered chef's whites into the laundry hamper.

Chapter ONE

May 2015

"FOR THE last time, Vincent, I'm not taking a position in any of your restaurants." Duncan's tone was the cultivated mix of cold and firm he'd perfected to use on his father over the years, but it didn't deter his father, who kept talking as if Duncan hadn't interrupted.

"Not just *any* of my restaurants. You know I've been saving the executive chef position at Goût for you. Even Henrie knows he's just a placeholder until you're ready—he's been interviewing other places ever since you gave up that ridiculous notion of being a scientist."

The word "scientist" dripped with scorn, and Duncan bit down hard on his tongue to keep himself from responding. Vincent had been fine with Duncan pursuing a university degree instead of going to culinary school. He hadn't gone himself—he had a business degree.

There had been some pushback when he'd enrolled in grad school. His father saw it as delaying the inevitable time when Duncan would take his rightful place as his right-hand man in the Walters restaurant empire.

Not that Duncan had ever professed the slightest desire to do so. He'd even skipped over Vincent's restaurants when he'd done his apprenticeships in college, thinking it would send the message to his father that now he was an adult, he wasn't going to be working for him.

But hope springs eternal, and Vincent was a classic example of that. His head was buried so far in the sand—or up his ass—that he ignored Duncan's plans for the future.

"Vincent—"

His father laughed. "Duncan, please. You lasted… what? Three years in the lab? You were made for kitchens, my boy. God gave you a gift, and you should be using it."

Duncan held the phone away from his ear, rolling his eyes exaggeratedly at his mother, who looked up from the show she was watching and laughed fondly. He hated that she had a good relationship with his father—the man who had left them when Duncan was six because his culinary career was more important than his family.

The accusation wasn't exactly fair. Vincent and his mother had split amicably, and it had more to do with the fact that Vincent needed to be in a big city to keep advancing in his career, and Duncan's mother refused to leave their small town because she was caring for Duncan's elderly grandfather at the time.

Even though the divorce hadn't been contentious, it had been hard on Duncan. As an adult, Duncan was well aware his parents shared the blame for the divorce, since neither of them was willing to accommodate the others' needs. But at the time, he'd been too young to understand that, and all he'd known was that his father had disappeared and his mother had cried all the time.

It didn't help that after the divorce Vincent became radically religious in the worst possible way. Whatever hope there had been of the two of them being close was shattered when Vincent found some fundamentalist church right around the time Duncan realized he liked boys as much as girls. Even their shared passion for food hadn't been enough to bridge the gap that Vincent's constant disdain for Duncan's sexuality had caused.

"It was four," Duncan said flatly. He rolled his neck, praying for patience. Or maybe for a freak meteor to strike his father. No, that wasn't fair. Damn it. He could understand why his father was so insistent he come work for him, but he wished Vincent could exhibit the same level of understanding for why Duncan was so very, very against that.

In the kitchen, they got along fine. Better than fine. They worked seamlessly as long as their whole focus was on the food, as it should be in a professional kitchen. But the second service ended or they stepped out of the kitchen? Disaster.

"I say tomato, you say canned tomato paste. Oh, wait, you don't anymore, because you came to your senses, and you're not in that godforsaken fake-food lab anymore," Vincent snarked, and Duncan sent up another prayer for patience.

"Vincent, I appreciate the offer. I do. But I'm covering for Navien at 134°. She's got another month left on her maternity leave."

Duncan would do about anything for Navien. She was a good friend, and she'd always been willing to let him pop in to take over dinner service for a night or two while his soul had been slowly dying at Kraft. He'd been filling in for her as executive chef at the pretentious-as-fuck steak house for the last three months, and he was itching to move on. The food was boring, as was the concept. Seriously, who names a restaurant after the temperature of a medium-rare steak?

Vincent apparently agreed with Duncan's assessment, judging by his ill-mannered snort. "Haven't you wasted enough time with this traveling chef routine? Settle somewhere, Duncan."

Duncan didn't bother to suppress his sigh. He and Vincent both knew that by "somewhere," Vincent meant "at one of my restaurants."

Duncan had started out as a dishwasher and general dogsbody in the kitchen of Vincent's flagship restaurant the summer he'd turned fifteen, learning the ins and outs of the kitchen. It was more time than he'd spent with his father since the divorce. His father wasn't a bad guy. Not really. He did love Duncan, in his own way. But early on Duncan had realized if he wanted to be in his father's life at all, it had to be on his father's terms. He probably wouldn't have bothered if not for his interest in cooking. His mother had seized on that and sent him stumbling into Vincent's kitchens as soon as he'd been old enough, and the rest was history.

So even though Duncan considered the two of them estranged, he knew his father well.

He was especially familiar with the concept of Vincent never *listening*. Like now, while Vincent was continuing to take digs at the kitchens Duncan had been in lately.

"I'm happy with how things are going, but thanks for your interest," Duncan said before going in for what he knew would be a kill shot. "But if you're that worried about me staying in one place, I suppose I could take Christian King up on his offer to run the kitchen at one of his places."

"The day you step foot in that unfortunately named godless heathen's kitchen is the day I disown you," Vincent said.

Duncan could imagine him frothing at the mouth. "You two call each other the sweetest things. His latest nickname for you is 'that religious zealot,' had you heard?"

Even though Duncan didn't like Christian's food any more than his father did, he did have to give Christian props for reading him so spot-on. Points to Christian for that.

"I'll not have you cavorting with that man," Vincent said, his voice low.

Duncan smirked. Usually that sentence was uttered with a completely different meaning. The conviction was the same, though. Who knew Vincent hated his nemesis as much as he hated Duncan's sexuality?

"I'm hanging up now," Duncan said into the phone before his father could continue his tirade. He quirked an eyebrow at his mother's exasperated expression as he tossed the cell onto the couch cushion next to her, knowing she would pick it up.

His parents' continued friendship remained a complete puzzle to Duncan, but he didn't worry too much about it. Aside from giving Vincent the inside track on what restaurants Duncan was working in—something Vincent was more than well-connected enough to find out on his own, anyway—he knew his mother respected his desire for privacy and didn't disclose much else.

Duncan wandered into the kitchen to get dinner started, while his mother chatted with Vincent and made excuses for Duncan's obstinate refusals.

"He's not that bad, you know," his mother said from the doorway a few minutes later. "You two fight because you're so similar. I wish you could see that."

She trotted this favorite argument out whenever Duncan and his father fought, and it never failed to sting like a bitch. Duncan refused to believe he was anything like his father. He could agree they both shared a passion for food and a talent for making masterpieces in the kitchen, but that was where it ended. Vincent Walters was a slave to his own ambition and intent on finding fame. Duncan simply wanted to cook. The media liked to draw the same kind of comparisons, but those were easier to dismiss. After all, the reporters were strangers. This was his mother. She of all people should know better.

"Sure, Ma," Duncan said, waving her off. Hopefully if he didn't argue, she wouldn't launch into her fifty-point lecture on why it was true and how if Duncan would get to know Vincent better, everything would work out.

"You really should consider your father's offer. I know it's hard for you to see it, but he's so proud of you."

Duncan wrinkled his nose, ignoring his mother in favor of pulling ingredients for a simple dinner of chicken and rice out of the refrigerator. Everyone always assumed that as a food scientist and chef with an interest in molecular gastronomy, he always ate fancy, deconstructed food, but to be honest, he preferred simpler meals. Eating them, at least. Duncan couldn't deny he loved the thrill of taking apart a classic dish and putting it back together in a fresh and modern way. But at home? He was a pizza and burgers kind of guy.

"I've told him again and again. I don't want to work for him," he said, busying himself with dinner prep to keep his annoyance in check. Having his hands busy always helped him keep his temper, which was one of the reasons he was so good in a professional kitchen. Tempers always ran high in them, but Duncan managed to keep a level head by immersing himself in prep and cooking. Outside the kitchen was a different story. More than a few epic showdowns between the Walters men had occurred in Vincent's office over the years.

"But he loves you, Duncan. He wants you to be successful. I know you enjoy moving around, but it's been almost a year. He can actually help you get ahead. Why won't you take him up on it?"

His reasons were legion, and he'd gone over most of them with her untold times before. What this really boiled down to was her getting anxious that he'd move across the country. She liked having him close, and for the most part, he enjoyed being back in Chicago. His last job offer had come from an up-and-coming bistro in Napa, and it was really tempting.

He'd been wandering, a kitchenless nomad, since the last place he'd been executive chef closed in 2014. It hadn't been a terrible blow since he'd only been there six months. Before that he'd had three other restaurant jobs around the country. He'd flitted around through different concept restaurants, going from traditional French bistros, to venues where he could get his mad scientist on with true molecular gastronomy, to things in between, like the steak house. The only thing all the restaurants had in common was the fact that they *weren't* owned by his father.

"Duncan."

He blew out a frustrated breath and shook his head. He was done with this conversation.

He looked over at his mom. "Do you really have to ask?"

Duncan bit his tongue to keep from saying more. His true irritation lay with Vincent, not his mother. She didn't deserve his anger, but the more she pushed, the harder it was to remember that.

His mother clucked her tongue, making the same disappointed noise that had always had him cowering as a child when he'd come home with a bad report card or tales of getting punished for fighting on the playground.

"Don't shake your head at me, Duncan. You and your father both have a stubborn streak a mile wide and enough pride to sink a ship." She sighed, and Duncan felt his anger burn off as guilt replaced it. His mother looked tired and upset, which was the last thing he wanted. "At least let him pull some strings for you and get you in somewhere on a full-time basis, even if it's not at one of his restaurants. You know he'd do that for you."

"I'll have dinner with him this week so we can talk," Duncan promised.

His mother's face brightened, but Duncan put his hand up, stopping her before she could comment. "Not to accept his job offer. To explain in no uncertain terms why I'm *not* accepting the offer. Again. I want to do this on my own, Ma. I don't want to get a job because I'm Vincent Walters's son. I want to get a job because I'm a talented chef with great ideas. I don't want to be indebted to him for anything."

His mother started setting the table, her gaze lingering on Duncan as she laid out the plates and cutlery. Duncan had spent his entire childhood, save the summers he'd been forced to live with Vincent, in this house. He knew every nook and cranny, and he knew his mother did too. Both of them could move around the small kitchen with their eyes closed and not make a single misstep. He was usually grateful for their ability to work together in the tiny space, but at the moment, Duncan felt a bit hunted as his mother's eyes penned him in.

"I know I did you a disservice by not pushing the issue and forcing Vincent to be more active in your life when you were little,

Duncan," she said, and Duncan tried to protest. They'd had this conversation before too, and he'd made it abundantly clear he didn't blame her. Duncan placed the blame for his strained relationship with his father solely at Vincent's feet, and he refused to believe the choices his mother had made had been the wrong ones.

"Can we not, Ma?"

She ignored him, pressing on with another speech Duncan practically knew by rote.

"I did, and every day that becomes clearer. I thought I was doing the right thing for both of you. You're the two men I love most in this world, and I wanted to make both of you happy. Vincent would have stayed if I'd asked him to. I know he would have. He would have done right by us. But he was already a rising star by then, and I couldn't let him give that up for us, like I couldn't force myself to go live in that godforsaken city both of you seem to love so much. I wasn't enough for you while you were growing up. I know you feel like you don't need a father in your life. I think you're wrong on that count, but it doesn't matter."

Duncan's expression was stony as he flipped the chicken in the pan. This argument was unwinnable, and he knew it. He chose to disengage instead, centering all of his focus on the task in front of him. He could feel his mother's gaze on his back as he cooked, but he ignored it. The silence was deafening, making the sizzle of the chicken in the pan seem abnormally loud, and he could practically feel the hurt radiating off his mother the longer he went without responding. Still, the silent treatment, no matter how immature for a grown man to employ, was a better option than voicing what was actually on his mind.

His father's pride in Duncan's accomplishments was more professional than paternal, and it left Duncan cold. Duncan was content with floating at the moment, filling in here and there at friends' restaurants, though he'd have to buckle down and find something more permanent soon. He'd had a few short-term contracts, and they lasted anywhere from a few weeks to a few months. It was a fun way to travel and catch up with old acquaintances he'd worked with over the years, and it calmed both the wanderlust and urge to be back in the kitchen that had driven him out of research and development. Why would he give that up to work for a father he could barely stand?

His mother switched tactics, and Duncan had to suppress a groan when he saw her start to warm up to her topic. "Can't you think of him as a restaurateur instead of your father? You know him, Duncan. Would he be offering you this position if it was purely nepotism? He loves his restaurants, and he takes his career very seriously. He wouldn't be so excited to have you join him if he didn't think you'd earned the job on your own merits."

Duncan had made no secret of his plan to leave the kitchen and go work for a corporation after graduation. The entire purpose of getting a food science degree had always been to work as a food chemist in a large commercial food company's research and development department. Vincent had taken the news that Duncan was going to take a spot at Kraft Foods with grim resignation, and at first life had been good. Duncan had gone to work every day, donned his lab coat, and experimented with compounds designed to mimic the taste of natural ingredients, prolong the shelf life of foods and whatever else was necessary to make packaged foods more appealing and shelf stable.

And he'd hated it. The science had been thrilling, but it had nothing on the sweaty, adrenaline-filled atmosphere of a restaurant kitchen.

After more than four years of spending his vacations working in upscale restaurants in Chicago and New York as a guest chef and sneaking onto the roster to spend his weekends cooking for twelve hours a day at the Sunrise Cafe—showing up to the research lab exhausted and stressed on Monday morning—Duncan had finally admitted corporate food science wasn't for him, and quit his job.

John had taken over the Sunrise Cafe the previous year when his mom retired, and he'd offered Duncan a job as a full-time line cook. As much as he loved working with John, slinging eggs and hash wasn't going to be a long-term solution. So he was putting himself out there, flitting from kitchen to kitchen on short-term contracts, letting the chefs he'd worked with in the past know he was on the market again, so to speak, and looking for a kitchen to call his own. Still fitting in a few shifts at the Sunrise Cafe, of course, because there was something almost Zen-like and soothing about zoning out and frying egg after egg to order. At least, that was the case for Duncan.

Vincent, of course, took Duncan quitting his research job to mean Duncan was ready to "come home," as he liked to say, and start getting serious about taking over the Walters restaurant empire. Naturally, Duncan told him he could take his offer straight to hell, and he'd been repeating that for the entire time since he'd hung up his lab coat and started kitchen hopping.

It was getting harder and harder to turn his offers down, and Duncan hated that most of all. The hiatus he'd taken from professional kitchens while he worked in the lab wasn't a problem. The culinary arts was not an industry that changed rapidly. His skills were still sharp, and he still had a keen eye for trends and pairings. No, it was his "love 'em and leave 'em" reputation in the kitchen that preceded him, and big name restaurants seemed to have decided that while he was fun to date, he wasn't long-term material.

Duncan was having a great time kitchen surfing, but it wasn't a sustainable career option. He needed to find a real job, and soon. Between his student loans and the rent on the apartment that had sat empty for much of the time he'd been traveling, he was in debt up to his ears. A steady paycheck would be quite welcome right about now.

Not that he'd told his mother that. She'd guilt him into taking Vincent's generous six-figure offer, and then he'd be even more miserable.

He forced himself to smile and dished up a serving of chicken, ignoring the concerned look on his mother's face.

"Do you want to eat in here?" He nodded toward the table in the corner. The banquette needed to be reupholstered, stuffing spilling out of a long tear that had started as a series of pinpricks when he'd poked his fork into it in elementary school.

Meals had always been eaten at the table when he was a kid. His mother used the time to talk to him about his day and grill him about homework. Now she used meal times to prod him about his father and his career, and he just wasn't up for it tonight.

His exhaustion must have been written all over his face, because his mother took pity on him. "Your show's about to come on. Why don't we take this into the living room, just this once?"

Duncan rolled his eyes. "It's not my show, Mom. It's just a show that I sometimes watch."

His mother's lips twitched. "A show you sometimes watch, huh? Is that why you refuse to let me delete them off my TiVo until you've had a chance to see them?"

That was just because he didn't have cable. "Not all of them."

She gave him a knowing look and put her plate down on the coffee table. "Well, your man Beck has been hosting more and more often, and it's filling up my list. Soon you're going to have to start deleting some of the earlier ones because I'm not letting your obsession keep me from DVRing *Law and Order*."

"Lies and slander," he mumbled as he picked up the remote control. There were six new *King of the Kitchen* episodes in the queue, and from the descriptions it looked like Beck had hosted four of them. "I just like his dedication to using fresh ingredients."

And the way his ass looked in his well-cut suits, but he wasn't about to point that out. From the snicker his defense earned from his mother, he figured she already knew.

Chapter TWO

"TUNE IN next week, when Christian will be back and we'll have a special guest chef who will be showing us how she makes her signature pasta. Trust me, it's delicious. If you haven't had the opportunity to eat at one of Glenda Abram's restaurants, you're missing out. But don't worry, we've got you covered here on *King of the Kitchen*. We'll get the inside track on how Glenda has captured the nation's heart with her pasta and learn how you can make it in your own kitchen.

"I'm Beck Douglas, and thanks for inviting us into your kitchen today!"

Beck grinned at the camera, his lips curving up into the carefully practiced boyish smile that had made him a hit in households across the country. He kept his face relaxed and his eyes trained on the large placard bearing the countdown, sited behind the camera. Beck waited a full three beats after it reached zero and the red light on the camera clicked off, before slumping against the counter. Within seconds, he lost both his smile and the high-energy enthusiasm that was his trademark on the show.

"You went a little over on the intro today."

Beck didn't open his eyes, his resigned posture unchanged. "We had an advertiser pull a spot at the last minute, so I had an extra thirty seconds to fill."

"Who pulled?" The sharp edge to Christian's voice left little doubt someone was going to be out of a job by the end of the day, and Beck privately wished it could be him. He knew better, though. Christian was grooming him to take over the empire, as he had been for the last ten years. Lindsay had been the obvious choice for mogul-in-training, but she was an absolute disaster in the kitchen. Beck was Christian's nephew, and he'd inherited the position of Christian's protégé. It was awesome and terrible at the same time because Beck loved cooking. He was lukewarm about being in front of the camera, but he did love having the chance to teach people how to create amazing food in their home kitchens.

He hated the trendy food his uncle made him cook. But Christian would never stand for Beck quitting, and what's more, Beck wouldn't dream of it outside of his own silent fantasies. At the end of the day, he was exactly where he wanted to be, even if it came at the cost of a little bit more of his soul dying every time he had to cook something with aioli.

"Agneau," Beck said, keeping his voice level. He knew why the spot had been pulled. He'd even warned the advertising department it might happen, and he'd prepared to cover the time by rehearsing an extended show intro.

For most television personalities, successfully being the host of a live show was due to a combination of hard work and natural talent. Beck had no natural on-screen charm, so he had to work doubly hard for his success. No viewer would ever guess that every bit of Beck's carefree, easy demeanor on the show was scripted, or that for every five minutes of on-screen time, Beck spent about an hour preparing. He worked with a team of writers to preplan jokes and asides, and he spent ages over a range in the cramped test kitchen, perfecting recipes with the development team and learning how to make them effortlessly.

"Did they say why? Agneau has been an advertiser with the show since the beginning."

Beck's eyes slid open, and he stared at Christian with disbelief. "Are you really asking me that? How could they *not* pull after what Felix Cartwright said during his guest spot last week?"

Christian scowled. "That throw-away comment about GMOs?"

"Of course 'that throw-away comment about GMOs.' Genetically modified organisms are a hot topic right now, and Agneau has a huge contract with Monsanto. Most of the corn in the processed food Agneau produces is genetically modified."

One of the things Beck hated about working on the show—and there were many—was being forced to play nice with food distributors he'd never use personally. Agneau had been a sponsor of *King of the Kitchen* way back in the days when Christian was the little-known host of a local cooking show in upstate New York, some twenty years ago. Christian always made a point of using Agneau brand dried pasta on the show, as well as other boxed or canned ingredients that never showed up in his pantry at home. Beck's uncle was the ultimate food snob personally, but professionally he was happy to put his face on pretty much any product that offered a high enough fee for endorsement.

"I'll talk to Rollie. I'm sure a few rounds of golf and an afternoon at the club will change his mind."

Beck leveled him with an incredulous look. "Felix called the company's refusal to label which of its products use GMOs 'irresponsible' and implied Agneau's entire line was unhealthy. Somehow I don't think you playing golf with Agneau's chief financial officer is going to be enough to convince the company to advertise with us again. I'd be worried about them dropping you as a celebrity sponsor, actually."

He didn't flinch under Christian's scathing look, but it was a near thing. Only years of being the recipient of it kept him from cowering like most of Christian's other employees did when he was dressing them down.

"I don't need you to tell me how to manage my affairs, Beck." One of his eyebrows twitched, and Beck braced himself. Christian definitely had a tell when it came to dropping the hammer, and that was it. Anytime there was eyebrow twitching, Beck knew he was in for a tirade. "If I were you, I'd be more worried about finalizing the menu for Brix."

Beck's muscles tightened, dread coiling in his stomach. Christian had promised him he was going to be the executive chef for the new restaurant in the King empire in more than name only; it was going to be his from the ground up. His concept, his menu, his management. He thought he'd been doing a good job, and the focus groups Christian insisted on using for everything agreed.

"I gave the menu to Sarah yesterday. She said she'd slotted in time on your calendar for you to review it."

"And I did, but honestly, Beck. That wasn't a menu. It was a schoolboy love letter to farm food. It was an embarrassment. I can only imagine what your instructors from Le Cordon Bleu would say if they saw it. You're not a bored housewife, Beck. You're a classically trained chef. Act like it. Sarah should be e-mailing you the changes today."

Beck bit his tongue, trying to swallow down his impulse to snap back. No one ever won an argument with Christian King, even if they were right. Still, Beck couldn't keep himself from responding.

"Cooking with simple ingredients doesn't mean the food isn't sophisticated."

Christian snorted. "Pasta with butter?"

"Homemade pumpkin pasta with a sherry brown butter, served with sage and roasted pumpkin seeds."

"At the end of the day, Beck, that's still pasta and butter. People aren't going to pay a premium to eat that."

"You said this was my restaurant. You wanted a wine-focused theme with a casual, upscale atmosphere, and that's what I've delivered."

"It is your restaurant, Beck. But it's my name on the door and my reputation on the line, and Christian King does not serve pasta with butter. Sarah will be in touch. Do make sure the menu gets to the printer by Friday. Send the final design directly to Sarah—she can sign off on it for me while I'm in Atlanta checking in on the restaurant there."

That job was usually relegated to Beck, trekking across the country to do audits on the dozens of restaurants in his uncle's chain. None of them were the same concept, but all of the menus shared one thing in common: They were all overwrought, too trendy by half, and priced accordingly. In other words, everything Beck hated. He'd been busy getting Brix ready for its soft opening in three weeks, though, and Christian had him doing extra hosting shifts on *King of the Kitchen* to up his own personal "brand awareness," as Christian and Lindsay and her ever-present marketing team called it, so the actual running of the empire had fallen back into Christian's hands, at least for the moment. Beck had no doubt that as soon as Brix was up and running, he'd be resuming his old duties as well.

Christian was obviously waiting for a response, so Beck nodded tightly.

"Yes, sir."

No matter how much effort Beck put into the menu or how much backbreaking work he put into Brix, at the end of the day it was his uncle's restaurant, not his. Beck fisted his hands at his sides as he watched Christian stride away, expertly dodging all of the camera equipment and not sparing even a second glance at any of the crew. None of them expected him to, of course. Christian was well known as a jovial, friendly personality on television, but everyone who worked with him knew he was a cold and calculating bastard most of the time.

Not like Beck, who even in his current funk took the time to nod to the boom operator as he walked past.

Despite wanting nothing more than to hole himself up in his office upstairs and sulk over the new menu, Beck didn't take his anger out on the crew. It was the biggest difference between him and his uncle. Beck's success was dependent on everyone who worked with him, from the executive producers and head chefs to the boom operators and the prep cooks who came in at six in the morning for thankless tasks like peeling garlic and chopping a metric ton of *mise en place* for the dinner service chefs to work with later in the day. Whether he was at the studio or at one of his uncle's restaurants, Beck made it a point to at least have a smile and a nod for every employee he came across.

He was almost home free when he saw a cluster of people near the door to the stairs. He sighed and made sure he was smiling as he approached them, though he wanted nothing more than to burst through the door and run up the six flights to his office. He was tense and itchy from the pent-up energy he always felt during filming.

"Carlie, you're a brave woman, bringing a baby onto Christian's set," he said as he greeted the child in question with a silly face that made the nine-month-old gurgle in delight.

"We stayed outside the sound stage until the filming light went out," she said, shifting the baby on her hip when the girl started reaching for Beck. "I'm not suicidal."

He didn't reach out to take the baby since his hands were still covered in aioli from the sandwiches he'd made on air today—seriously, who still used aioli in this day and age? Christian's pander-to-the-middle tastes were killing Beck—but he leaned in and let the child tug on his hair and pull his microphone off his collar.

"Benton will skin me alive if you gnaw on that," Carlie chided her daughter as she grabbed the mic from her chubby little hands and tucked it in Beck's breast pocket.

"Matt sick today?" Beck asked, making a face of exaggerated alarm when the baby tugged on his hair again, setting her off into peals of fresh laughter.

Carlie was Beck's favorite set stager, and her husband, Matt, usually stayed home with their daughter since he was a writer for another network and could work from home. If Carlie had her kiddo on set with her today, it either meant Matt was sick or he was forced to go in for an all-hands meeting at his studio.

Carlie wrinkled her nose. "No, they're up for renewal, and all of the writers had to go in for a brainstorming session. He's been working ridiculous hours trying to get storyboards together for the next sixteen episodes. They're afraid the show might be canceled."

Beck hummed sympathetically. "So you've got Annabelle for the duration, eh?"

The baby squealed again when Beck said her name, and he stuck his tongue out at her.

"Well, I wasn't supposed to be in today at all. But Christian called and was upset because he didn't like the new curtains, so I had to come resurrect the old ones from storage. We changed them... what? Six episodes ago, and he's only noticing now?"

Beck snorted. Christian probably hadn't been in the studio to notice the new curtains in the last six weeks. When Beck had joined the show, he'd been in the background, but over the last three years, his uncle had slowly but surely been pushing Beck into the host role more and more often. He still made enough appearances and hosted enough of the specials and other important shows that the fans knew *King of the Kitchen* was still very much his show, but the day-to-day management and menial hosting was something Christian had passed to Beck and Christian's daughter Lindsay.

"What did you do with the new ones? I liked them."

Carlie pursed her lips. "That's the thing. By the time I got here, he'd already decided he liked the new ones after all."

Not surprising. Christian was pretty fickle. "So why are you still here?"

They'd been filming for three hours, and if she'd come in early enough to do a set change, then she and Annabelle had been hanging out at the studio for nearly four hours.

"Because he told me he wanted to have me on hand in case he changed his mind."

Beck raised an eyebrow. "In case he changed his mind in the middle of filming? So what, we'd either have to reshoot the scenes with the curtains in them or deal with the continuity problem of having two different sets of curtains in the same episode?"

She offered him a tight smile. "Yup."

Beck sighed. "Take your daughter home, Carlie. Make sure you put in for a full day's pay today so you don't waste a day of your vacation on this. Are you out the rest of the week?"

She nodded.

"If he calls again for anything, call me or Lindsay. He shouldn't be asking you to come in on your day off, even if it does mean we get to see this cutie." He pressed a smacking kiss to Annabelle's cheek.

Some of the tension bled out of Carlie's expression. "You're a lifesaver. Normally I'd have told him where to shove it, but with Matt's show on the chopping block…."

"You didn't want to risk Christian firing you. I understand. And I won't let that happen, Carlie. You've been with the show longer than I have. You ought to be able to tell him to have someone else deal with a minor set-dressing problem while you're on vacation."

He leaned over and pecked her cheek, much more sedately than he had Annabelle's, but it made Carlie laugh all the same.

"Enjoy what's left of your day, and I'll see you when you're back in the office," Beck said, infusing his voice with the authority he used when he was managing a kitchen. It wasn't a suggestion. He didn't want Carlie to think her job would be in jeopardy if she refused to let herself be dragged in to work on her day off, her baby in tow.

"Thanks, Beck," she said, both she and Annabelle waving at him as he pushed his way into the stairwell.

He let the door close heavily behind him before he dropped his smile. Filming was exhausting. Beck loved social situations and talking to people, but talking to a camera was infinitely harder. Most people hated live shows, but Beck would rather do one of those any day than have to spend hours going over the same lines and doing the same things over and over until they met Christian's approval.

His on-screen charm might be faked, but in terms of actual interpersonal relations, charm was something Beck Douglas had in spades, and used ruthlessly when necessary. And it was a good thing too. If he and Lindsay weren't so invested in the crew and their lives, most of them would have quit ages ago. They certainly weren't staying out of loyalty to Christian.

King of the Kitchen was a semiclever play on Christian's last name, but Christian treated it like a mandate. He went out of his way to be abrasive and demanding, and it was getting worse as he got older and added products and restaurants to his empire.

Beck indulged in a moment of quiet in the stairwell before taking a deep breath and trotting up the first flight. No one else in the building took the stairs, so they were a bit of a respite for Beck. Especially when he hadn't had a chance to hit the gym yet.

He cracked his neck and stretched, tucking his tie into his waistband before he started sprinting.

Chapter THREE

SADIE'S BROW furrowed as she frowned at Duncan, who was fiddling with the edge of his bow tie. Like all close friends, they'd developed a silent language over the years, and at the moment hers was screaming disappointment.

Duncan knew it couldn't be his suit—she'd helped him pick out the tuxedo years ago, and he'd even let her bully him into getting it cleaned for tonight's opening. It was beautifully tailored, and since he'd bought it on Vincent's dime and not his own, it was designer. Sadie had insisted on a classic cut that wouldn't ever go out of style, something Duncan was grateful for now. The need for black-tie wear went with the job, unfortunately. If you wanted to cook with the big leagues, you had to party with the big leagues, and that meant monkey suits.

"Duncan," she said with a heavy sigh, and Duncan followed her gaze down to his feet.

"Ah, come on, Sadie."

Duncan wiggled his toes in his battered Converse sneakers. He'd even worn the green ones tonight, since they matched the emerald cuff links Vincent had given him when he'd been named to Zagat's 30 Under 30 list a few years ago.

"I know you have a very respectable pair of Cole Haan dress shoes that match your tuxedo perfectly," she said, her eyes narrowed.

"They are also perfectly uncomfortable," he muttered. "It's not like this is a big to-do, Sadie. It's just a restaurant opening. It wouldn't even be black tie if your boss wasn't such a—"

Sadie's hand shot out and covered his mouth. He licked it for good measure, grinning when she pulled away in disgust.

"It wasn't his choice. He wanted to go with a more casual theme, but Christian insisted on keeping it formal."

Duncan made a face but grudgingly toed off his shoes when she brought him the dress shoes from his closet. They were badly in need of a shine, and he took malicious pleasure in that fact as he caught the pair of dress socks she threw at his head. She could force him to put them on, but he'd smile all night looking down and knowing they were hardly more acceptable than his Chucks.

Not that anyone in the media would be surprised to see Duncan show up in Converse. He'd gotten himself a bespoke suit from a thrift store up in Madison, and he'd delighted in wearing it to events. The sneakers were a must with it, and half the time he wore a fedora.

Vincent hadn't been amused the first time he'd told Duncan to dress formally and he'd showed up in the purple suit, complete with his gray Converse sneakers and an understated, but undeniably rainbow, tie. Duncan wasn't sure which part of his outfit had been responsible for nearly making his father stroke out, but he'd put money on it being the tie that sent him over the edge. Of the many freak flags Duncan flew, the rainbow one was the one his father had the most trouble accepting.

Duncan tied his shoes with a flourish and stood, bowing to Sadie. She looked gorgeous in her silk gown, as she should. It was her night to shine, even if it was Christian King's name on the restaurant.

"Shall we?" he asked, holding his elbow out for her to take.

She sent a quick text and slipped her phone into her clutch, taking his arm. "We shall. And you can wipe the smirk off your face, because Corbin carries a spare shoe shoeshine kit in his car. He doesn't trust you to do it right, so he'll be fixing your shoes when we get there."

Damn.

"Are you sure I can't wear the sneakers? No one's going to give my feet a second glance if I'm standing next to your radiant beauty."

She rolled her eyes. "No. Beck would have my head if you showed up in those shoes. Last time you wore something that ridiculous, half the stories the next day were about you and your tongue-in-cheek fashion sense and disregard for the culinary establishment instead of the opening itself."

Well, they couldn't have that. Duncan could only imagine the hissy fit Beck Douglas would throw if he got upstaged at his own opening. Not that the restaurant was really his—everyone knew he was Christian's lackey. He was executive chef of Brix in name only. The menu had probably come from Christian, and all the decor and hard work had come from Sadie. It was more her restaurant than Beck's, in Duncan's mind at least.

He sighed in a put-upon way and bobbed his head. "It does get tiresome being the style icon for a generation," he teased.

His penchant for quirky clothes and his laid-back attitude contrasted pretty sharply with the way Duncan ran a kitchen. The dichotomy, along with how far from his father's traditional French food his own molecular gastronomy masterpieces were, had made him something of a media darling in the culinary press. Interest in him had started back when he was a teenager, since the story of Vincent mentoring his own son in his kitchens had apparently been a heart-warming one. Duncan didn't see what was so inspiring about a man who'd been so obsessed with his career that he'd left the woman he loved and abandoned his child. He supposed it was the other side to it, that Vincent had seen the error of his ways and realized how empty his life was without his son in it (seriously, where did the press come up with this stuff?) and taken Duncan under his wing, welcoming him into the culinary family and publicly doting on him. That Duncan had been some sort of culinary savant hadn't hurt, and before he'd fully understood what was happening, Duncan found himself the subject of media scrutiny and national interest, with gossip columns reporting on what he ordered when he went out to eat with friends, and food magazines clamoring for interviews every time he apprenticed in a new kitchen.

The media even viewed his long-standing status as a chef who couldn't settle in a kitchen long term with indulgent affection; it was actually a bit sickening. His inability to commit to a relationship was painted with the same rosy brush. Duncan rarely dated anyone for more than a few weeks, which the press liked to jokingly point out was shorter than the time he spent guesting in most kitchens. More proof, they said, that like his father, Duncan put his career ahead of his relationships.

Actually, it was proof he couldn't commit to anything. Not a person. Not a job. Not even a career, though by now he'd spent longer working as a chef than he had as a food scientist, so maybe that one had worked itself out.

So when several magazines had run two-page photo spreads on his unconventional gala outfit, with fashion industry "experts" weighing in on how refreshing his youthful brashness was and how they could see Duncan starting a trend of wearing Chucks with formal wear, he'd tossed his better judgment out the window and made a deal with the devil, aka his father. He'd let Vincent spring for an expensive tuxedo and all of the frou-frou that went with it, and in exchange Duncan would toe the line and act more like a dutiful son than a culinary rebel when he was out in public. It had served dual purposes; not only had it gotten the press off his back a bit, since Duncan wasn't as interesting if he wasn't rebelling against his father's rules or sullying his reputation, but it also pleased Vincent enough that he agreed to publicly announce he and Duncan had agreed Duncan's career would be best served if he apprenticed in other kitchens on his college breaks. No one had been willing to steal him away from Vincent until then, so it had opened up a lot of doors for him.

He was still wearing the same tuxedo now, though Sadie had insisted on updating the bow tie and vest with ones she insisted were more *en vogue* at the moment. Duncan hadn't cared, preferring to let her dress him like a doll over having to listen to her arguments and weigh in on them.

Corbin was running around the restaurant when they arrived, uncorking wines and frantically tweaking the cocktails for the night. He was wearing a tuxedo very similar to Duncan's, and Duncan privately thought the coordinated ties and vests made them look like groomsmen in a wedding. He was smart enough to keep that observation to himself. Sadie wouldn't find it amusing, and Corbin was so disgustingly besotted with Sadie he'd probably tattle on him the moment the words left Duncan's mouth.

God, he loved his friends. Even when they were forcing him to schmooze with investors and crappy restaurateurs—in freshly shined shoes.

"Are you sure I should be here? I've only met Beck Douglas once, and trust me, it didn't go well."

Sadie tsked at him. "You have every right to be here, Duncan. You'd have been on the guest list even if you weren't a personal guest of mine. You and Beck are both culinary royalty, you know. It would have been very bad press not to invite you."

"But not Vincent? If I'm royalty, isn't he too?"

Sadie brushed off his question with an irritated wave of her hand. Her gown flowed around her like water, so obviously expensive Duncan knew she couldn't have afforded it on her own. No doubt it was a perk of her new job as Beck Douglas's latest Girl Friday, as Duncan liked to call her. She swore up and down that working for Beck wasn't the nightmare Duncan was sure it must be.

"Everyone knows about the feud between Vincent and Christian, Duncan. Just like they know you and Beck are kinder, gentler versions of them."

Duncan wrinkled his nose at the comparison.

"I've never met Christian, but if Beck's the kinder version of him, then I think everyone should be very, very afraid."

"Duncan, you met him once, and that was on a bad day. Would I really work for him if he was the ogre you claim he is?"

Duncan held her gaze and shrugged. "Probably, if the money was good enough."

Sadie huffed, and Duncan grinned. He hadn't seen much of Sadie or Corbin in the last few months since they'd been working feverishly toward Brix's opening. Looking around, Duncan felt a swell of pride at the knowledge that Sadie was responsible for the opulence surrounding them. She'd spent tireless hours working with interior designers and contractors to get the front of the house in order, since Beck was so focused on the kitchen and menu. He'd had to sign off on everything, of course. But ultimately the attractive, efficient dining room and flawless service were down to Sadie's skill as a manager.

The restaurant was essentially a wine bar that offered a full complement of upmarket food, though Duncan hadn't been impressed by anything that had come by on the opulent silver trays yet. It had all been predictably trendy fare, well executed but still boring. The true star of tonight's opening was the wine, which was no surprise. Corbin had done a spectacular job as Brix's sommelier, putting together a well-rounded wine list that was both innovative and exciting.

For the opening party, Corbin had worked with JT, the head bartender, to create tasting flights of wines and beers that went up a graduated scale of sweetness, playing on the restaurant's name since the term "brix" referred to the scale used to measure a beverage's sugar content. Duncan had enjoyed both of the offerings immensely, even though he usually hated the pretentious flights most trendy places served.

"Are these going to be on the permanent menu?"

Sadie shrugged, following Duncan's abrupt change of topic easily. They'd been friends since college, and Duncan was well aware it took a special kind of person—namely one with deep wells of patience—to be friends with him that long. John was the longest-running, but that was because Duncan had claimed him as a pseudobrother in kindergarten.

"I think so. We're using plastic cups tonight, but Corbin had me put in an order for some mini sommelier beakers I assume are for wine and beer flights. They're really cute."

"Sounds like they'd go well with the decor too."

The entire place was done up like a prohibition-era speakeasy, a theme that could have been overdone to the point of being trite, but Sadie and the rest of her crew had managed it admirably.

"I picked them because they had a kind of alchemical appeal," Sadie said with a giggle. She shot Duncan a sly glance, and he wouldn't be surprised to find a few of those beaker-style wine glasses showing up in his Christmas stocking. He'd met Sadie in a freshman-level chemistry class his first day on campus, and they'd been best friends ever since. Every holiday she managed to sneak in at least one chemistry-related present to further their inside joke, and the beakers would be perfect. Duncan kind of hoped she did steal a few for him.

"I do love what you've done with the place," Duncan said, stepping in close to speak near her ear, since the roar of conversation around them made it hard to hear each other.

"I did all the ordering, yes, but the whole concept was Beck's," Sadie gushed, and Duncan almost groaned out loud. Sadie and Corbin were both head over heels for Beck Douglas, and Duncan couldn't understand how two otherwise good judges of character had fallen so hard for someone who was such a jerk.

It had been almost nine years since Beck had wandered into the Sunrise Cafe and had his ego explosion, but the indignation was still fresh in Duncan's mind. It was hard to reconcile the bitter, angry man he'd talked to in the diner with the suave, charming Adonis on television, but Duncan knew better. Sure, he'd left a huge tip for the waitstaff, but that was probably more of an indication that he was accustomed to buying people off because of his bad behavior than it was a tick in the nice-guy column.

"I'm sure," he said, taking another sip of the beer in his hand.

"It was, Duncan. Christian gave him the basic outline of what he wanted, but Beck really made it all come alive. You should have seen the original menu. You'd have loved it, it—"

"Tut, tut, Sadie. Don't share insider secrets with the enemy," a cultured voice said from over Duncan's shoulder. He didn't have to look to know it was Beck. He sounded just as charming and posh as he did on television.

"I don't see how an unemployed sous-chef is your enemy," Duncan snorted, taking another long sip of his beer. He needed to keep his mouth occupied before he said something he couldn't take back. Beck might be an epic asshole, but he was a very attractive one. His silky voice did things to Duncan he didn't want to admit, which was one of the reasons he kept watching the show. That and the fact that on-screen, Beck was a fabulous guy. He was open and friendly and easy for the guests to talk to, exactly the opposite of Duncan's real-life experience with him. It intrigued him, like Beck's simple food order had.

"I don't see a sous-chef here," Beck said, making a show of looking around. "All I see is culinary prodigy Duncan Walters."

"I wasn't such a prodigy when you were shoving a plate of eggs Benedict in my face at a diner a few years ago," Duncan answered with a challenging tilt of his head. He could see the moment Beck put it together.

"Charlie, wasn't it?"

Duncan grinned, delighted. "I had quite a few sets of whites, and none of them had my name on them. Kind of like wearing bowling shirts from thrift stores. Ironic."

"Ironic," Beck echoed, looking perplexed. "Like slumming it in a sketchy diner?"

"I like the ambiance," Duncan said easily. It was a familiar jab; anytime a chef found out Duncan liked to spend time as a line cook occasionally, they made a point of turning up their noses at it. Duncan didn't see why; he'd gotten a lot of practical experience at the Sunrise

Cafe over the years. Certainly more than he had in the ritzy kitchens he'd cooked in before he'd started garnering attention.

Sadie cleared her throat, edging herself between the two of them. Duncan hadn't even realized how close they'd gotten to each other while they'd been trading insults.

"Beck, I don't know if you've formally met Duncan. Duncan, this is Beck," she said, an undertone of warning in her voice. "This is his restaurant."

"It's very nice," Duncan said tightly, earning an approving nod from Sadie for at least trying to be civil.

Beck didn't take the same cue, though. He was holding himself so rigidly upright that Duncan was tempted to check and see if the crisp navy-blue three-piece suit he was wearing still had a hanger in it. The great Beck Douglas was apparently too suave for a run-of-the-mill black tuxedo. Not that it would have helped him blend in—someone as attractive as Beck would have stood out no matter what he was wearing.

"Have you landed at a restaurant yet, Duncan? I hear your father is eager to get you on at one of his. Though I'm not sure how much of a step up they'd be from the dive diner."

Unlike Beck's first insult, this one did manage to strike a nerve with Duncan, but he clenched his jaw and forced himself to remain impassive. He was sure Sadie knew how much the taunt had affected him, but she didn't do much more than ease a fraction of a bit closer to him, her silk sheathe dress brushing against his hand, warmed by her skin. Duncan wasn't sure if she meant to comfort him or to remind him they were in Beck's restaurant—Beck who was her *boss*—so he shouldn't make a scene.

Duncan pursed his lips, bringing his hand up to stroke his jaw thoughtfully. "Vincent's restaurants are dives? What does that make this place, then? He has more Michelin stars at his flagship restaurant than all Christian's places combined, and Christian has a hell of a lot of restaurants. What does that tell you, hmm?"

Despite his rocky past with his father and the bitterness he felt toward Vincent's life choices, Duncan wouldn't stand for anyone insinuating Vincent wasn't a success. He was. He hadn't gone to culinary school, but he had more awards and accolades than most classically trained celebrity chefs. Certainly more than Christian, who had gone to the same fancy, overpriced school that Beck had.

The press liked to play Christian and Vincent as jocular rivals, but they weren't. They'd both apprenticed for the same chefs as they'd been coming up in the culinary world, and there had been a lot of jealousy and fighting between them even then. It had only escalated as their restaurant empires had grown, to the point that any interaction between them ended in shouting and insults.

The two couldn't really be together for long without fur flying. Kind of like his dealings with Beck, actually. Except with a lot more hostility and epithets.

"No response to that?" Duncan asked.

"That was uncalled for, and I apologize. I do respect Vincent and his culinary ability," Beck said stiffly, and Sadie relaxed beside Duncan. Duncan waited, knowing the other shoe was going to drop soon. "You, on the other hand, cook in a diner. So don't think you can claim any of his gravitas, no matter what the press thinks."

Duncan narrowed his eyes. "That's a big word, gravitas. Are you sure you know what it means? I thought all your education was in fancy French sauces, not mundane things like vocabulary."

Duncan could tell from the way Beck's eyes flashed he'd scored a hit, but for some reason he felt guilt instead of pride. He'd taken the low blow, he knew, and it felt wrong. Duncan blew out a frustrated breath, shaking his head. He wasn't usually this argumentative. Something in Beck seemed to bring it out in him.

"I'm sorry. Friends? Or at least tolerant acquaintances?" Duncan quirked an eyebrow at Beck, who seemed to have been stunned into silence by Duncan's sincere apology. "You have a great place here. It's gorgeous. Best wishes, good tidings, and all that. Congrats." Duncan tipped his now-empty beer bottle in Beck's direction. "Thanks for the drinks."

He nodded to Beck, bowed to Sadie, and turned to move away. Before he could take a step, though, a hand closed over his elbow, stopping him. Duncan's entire body went rigid when he felt Beck lean in to block him from moving. What was it with Beck and grabbing? He'd done it the last time they'd met as well. Duncan took a moment to wonder if Beck made a habit of physically assaulting everyone he met, or if Duncan was special.

Not that Duncan minded having Beck's hands on him, though he'd have preferred it to be for a different reason. Duncan was close enough that Beck's breath tickled against his ear when he spoke, and it sent a frisson of something other than anger sliding down Duncan's spine.

He could see Sadie fluttering nearby and wringing her hands, distressed over what was about to happen. Corbin had materialized from somewhere, as had JT the bartender, and while their postures were relaxed, Duncan could see they were both ready to spring into action and break up a fight if they had to.

Duncan took a deep breath, very aware all eyes in the crowded restaurant were on them. He'd bet more than a few camera phones were recording them now, and at the very least, there would be grainy still photos of Duncan Walters and Beck Douglas published on gossip sites within the hour. He could imagine the headlines if they actually got into a fight. Right now people only knew Duncan and Beck were having an intimate conversation, and it was getting a bit heated. The media would run far enough with that without Duncan and Beck giving them any real fodder.

And really, despite the fact that Beck was baiting Duncan, he didn't deserve to have the opening of his new restaurant—even though it was technically Christian's, everyone knew it was Beck's baby—overshadowed by the news that he and Duncan had taken the famous King-Walters rivalry up a notch into an actual physical altercation.

"I'm not looking for a fight. I get it. You're stressed and amped up on adrenaline because of the opening, and I was a jerk. Just let it go," Duncan said quietly, bringing his hands up to rest lightly on Beck's chest. He wasn't going to try to push him away, but he wanted Beck to know his proximity wasn't welcome. The last thing Duncan wanted was a physical fight. He hated fighting, and beyond that, he knew Beck would wipe the floor with him. Through the thin suit coat Beck was wearing, Duncan could feel his bulging biceps and rock-hard chest. Most of the other professional chefs Duncan knew, himself included, were fairly fit; they had to be, to stay on their feet all day, darting around a sweltering kitchen. But Beck's body took fit to a whole new level, and

Duncan absently found himself wondering where Beck found the time to work out, given his busy production and restaurant schedule.

"If you keep walking into people's establishments and insulting them, you might find one even if you're not looking," Beck muttered.

"I didn't throw anything at you that you weren't throwing at me," Duncan said, unwilling to take the fall for the fight. Beck gave as good as he got; it wasn't Duncan's fault he couldn't take a verbal punch as well as Duncan could.

Beck hesitated, then stepped back, releasing Duncan's arm. Duncan resisted the urge to brush his hand over the wrinkled fabric, not wanting to call more attention to the fact that Beck had been gripping him tightly, not just laying a friendly hand on him.

"I heard you tell the reporter from *Epicurean Adventures* that the food was bland," Beck said, his jaw clenched. "The culinary world respects you and your opinions, whether their adoration of you is valid or not—and I definitely think it isn't—what you say matters."

Beck closed his eyes briefly and took a deep breath. Duncan could tell it was costing him a lot to be so frank, and Duncan appreciated it. And yes, he had told George the food was bland—because it was. But he hadn't done it in an attempt to hurt Beck's restaurant.

"He's an old friend," Duncan said, his lips curving up into a small, apologetic smile. "The reporter from *Epicurean Adventures*. I helped him get that job, actually. He knows nothing I say to him is ever on the record, not unless he specifically calls me for a comment about something. And even then, I usually refer him on up the food chain and have him talk to Vincent, because it's his opinion that matters, not mine. I'm only an ignorant line cook, remember?"

Duncan saw the fight go out of Beck's posture, and without anger lighting his features, Beck looked tired. "You are a lot more than a line cook, Duncan."

Duncan shrugged easily. "I don't get too hung up on terminology. Line cook, sous-chef, whatever. At the end of the day, we're all little more than kitchen minions, doing the bidding of the executive chef."

He playfully bumped Beck's shoulder with his own, drawing a reluctant smile out of him.

Sadie startled both of them when she stepped close, putting an arm around each of their waists. "Beck, you really need to get back to mingling. Duncan, I'm putting you over at the bar where JT can watch you. I don't need you starting a brawl like you did at Tyler's wedding."

"That was you?" Beck asked, giving Duncan a very obvious once-over.

"Hey, I might not look like much, but I fight dirty. I'm wiry, but I'm strong," Duncan said with a grin. It was a total lie, of course. The other guy had tripped, and Duncan had been there to break his fall. The crowd had taken the sprawl of limbs for a fight, and Duncan hadn't cared enough to correct them. But he hadn't realized Beck had been at the wedding. Curious.

"Strong enough to take down Gary? That man is built like a mountain."

"Gary was also drunk off his ass at the time, so I wouldn't read too much into it," Sadie said smartly, leading both of them away from the bulk of the crowd and back toward the kitchen.

"Don't ruin my street cred, Sadie," Duncan pouted, obediently taking a seat on the barstool she'd guided him to. "You street-cred ruiner, you."

Sadie laughed. "Duncan, trust me. I'm pretty sure you're your own worst enemy when it comes to ruining street cred."

"You need a drink, boss." JT had followed them back through the crowd, and he gave them all a sunny smile before he twirled a ridiculously expensive bottle of Glenlivet in the air and tipped it into a shot glass behind the bar. Beck growled at him wordlessly but took the shot, downing it in one go and almost managing to hide his grimace.

"Back into the lion's den," Beck muttered as he nodded at the three of them and then weaved his way back into the crowd, his apparent reluctance catching Duncan by surprise yet again.

He'd have figured Beck Douglas thrived on mingling and charming guests. Beck smiled and chatted his way around the packed room easily, stopping to pose for photos and speak with reporters and well-wishers alike, always with a smile that held none of the exhaustion Duncan had seen in his face earlier.

Beck Douglas was an enigma wrapped inside a mystery, and he was becoming more and more interesting to Duncan with every layer he unearthed.

Chapter FOUR

AS EXPECTED, the gossip columns were abuzz with tidbits about Beck and Duncan's friendly standoff at the Brix opening the night before. Beck couldn't contain his smile as he looked at the photo Lindsay had texted him earlier, a screen capture of a fuzzy snapshot obviously taken with a camera phone from a distance away.

He pulled his laptop out and scanned through the list of links one of Lindsay's underlings had put together sometime during the wee hours. Beck hadn't made it home from the opening until an hour or so before dawn, and he'd fallen into bed without even bothering to take his shirt and suit pants off. They were rumpled almost beyond repair, and he had a private laugh over how debauched he must look. People often said owning a restaurant was like having a particularly demanding mistress, since it took all of your spare time and energy, and though Beck had never been the cheating sort, he could appreciate the sentiment. A casual observer would probably make some very different assumptions about his life if they saw him sitting at the kitchen table in his sunny breakfast nook, sipping coffee and scrolling through the gossip sites, with his hair mussed and his wrinkled dress shirt open at the collar. He found it particularly ironic since his life was so hectic he had no time for any sort of love affair, torrid or otherwise.

The headlines about his altercation with Duncan ran the gamut from close to the truth to ridiculous, and the more ludicrous ones made Beck chuckle into his drink.

"The new Romeo and Juliet? Culinary heirs from warring King and Walters empires share an intimate moment at Brix opening" was his favorite, and the accompanying blurb was hilarious, filled with innuendo and speculation that he and Duncan were in love and hiding their secret affair from Vincent and Christian, who would pull them apart.

The press was clearly underestimating Christian and his penchant for drama if they thought for one second he wouldn't fully embrace a relationship between Beck and the son of his arch nemesis. As Christian was fond of saying, "You couldn't buy this kind of publicity." Beck had already had several e-mails from Christian's secretary—all unread, because even though it was after 1:00 p.m., it was still morning to him, and e-mails from Christian were not to be opened without ample caffeine for fortification—and he doubted any of them were a reprimand.

Most of the articles hit closer to the truth, speculating that the King-Walters feud was continuing into the next generation, making them some sort of culinary Hatfields and McCoys. The media thought that, like the famous feuding Appalachian families, Christian and Vincent couldn't even remember the reason for their long-standing animosity. Beck knew differently. His uncle could—and would—launch into a laundry list of transgressions a mile long if given the opportunity.

Beck finished his coffee, putting it in the sink with a heavy sigh that signified his daily switch from personal time to work time. And make no mistake about it, e-mails from Christian's secretary definitely fit into the work-time category.

He opened the article attached, noting it was different from the ones Lindsay's assistant had sent him. For starters, the byline was one of the more respected writers in the food industry, and it had been published on the web site of one of the major magazines.

"The Heirs-Apparent Come to Blows: The Next Generation of the Food Feud?"

Beck scanned the piece and felt a flash of annoyance at the magazine writer's condescending attitude toward Duncan's credentials. It was well known that, like his father, Duncan hadn't gone to a traditional culinary school. But he'd been cooking professionally for more than a decade in some of the best kitchens in the world, and he had Vincent Walters, one of the most world-renowned chefs alive, as his personal tutor.

Beck had gone to culinary school not because he wanted to, but because he'd *needed* to in order to succeed. Beck had grown up in the kitchen, but he hadn't had the advantage of having his famous and talented mentor work with him the way Duncan had. Christian expected greatness and wouldn't settle for anything less than perfection, but he hadn't had the time to let Beck work with him directly. By the time Beck was old enough to truly apprentice in a professional kitchen, Christian's television show had taken off, and his restaurants were franchised across the country. He'd become more culinary personality than chef, so Beck had been forced to apprentice with the executive chefs in Christian's empire instead.

Going to culinary school had been a necessity, and it had been one Beck had hated. He preferred simple food, but he'd known the key to succeeding with simple ingredients was to know how to treat them, and that meant he'd needed to be put through the paces of all those fancy French sauces Duncan had teased him about the night before. Beck hadn't prepared a *sauce á l'orange aigre-douce* since culinary school; the point was he knew how to do it. The techniques he'd learned had been invaluable. For him, at least. He had no doubt Duncan had mastered the technical part of cooking as well as Beck had, possibly more so. The fact that Duncan had learned his skills in a kitchen instead of a classroom didn't matter.

At least, it didn't matter to Beck. Even though he'd needled Duncan about his lack of formal culinary education, Duncan had a pedigree. He wasn't an idiot, and he wasn't a line cook, no matter how much Beck liked to imply he was.

In fact, Beck was a bit jealous of Duncan's education. He'd never even considered college, not seriously, because he knew Christian expected him to attend culinary school. He'd spent a year working insane hours as every kind of prep chef imaginable in Christian's kitchens before he'd been deemed ready for the next level and promptly enrolled in his uncle's alma mater, Le Cordon Bleu in Paris. Beck would have preferred studying at the Culinary Institute of America, which was almost as prestigious, but Christian had been footing the bill, and he'd shot that down before Beck had even printed an application.

Beck knew he allowed his uncle to have too much influence over his life. The few close confidants he had told him that again and again. But as much as he chafed under Christian's expectations, Beck wanted to be there. He wanted to work with him, with the goal of working *beside* him someday, where he could substantially change the King empire.

Although he hated most of what they made on the show, working on *King of the Kitchen* gave him a platform to educate America about food, and he loved that. And yes, most often he was cooking things that weren't his passion, but every once in a while he actually got to do some good, like not cutting Felix Cartwright off when he'd started talking about GMOs, the way Christian would have if he'd been hosting. Beck had taken some heat for that, yes, but it was worth it. Just like it was worth it whenever he got to cook one of his own recipes on the show.

What would it be like, Beck wondered, to have Vincent as a father and mentor? He was committed to classic cuisine, but from what Beck had read, Vincent had never balked at the unconventional way Duncan approached food. Duncan's passion for molecular gastronomy was worlds away from Vincent's technical and precise French cooking, but Vincent had nothing but praise for his son's innovations when he was interviewed in the press.

Beck hadn't realized Duncan was the chef from the Sunrise Cafe until last night, but he'd followed Duncan's professional career from a distance for years. Truth be told, he was envious of Duncan's ability to fade into the shadows when he wanted and cook at a greasy spoon like the Sunrise Cafe. Beck had no such opportunities; he was always on, always watched by both Christian and the culinary world. Beck had expectations to live up to, and heaven help him if he didn't. He couldn't even imagine having the freedom to cook the way Duncan did, from manning cooktops in a diner to experimenting with molecular gastronomy in ways that both puzzled and delighted even the harshest critics. If a dish Duncan was presenting got a bad review—and with the niche he cooked in, it happened more often than not—Duncan shrugged it off with a smile, leaving the culinary world admiring his resilience and his dedication to experimentation.

But if Beck got a bad review, it was completely different. The stakes were higher for him, not only because Christian was his boss and mentor. Beck didn't cook innovative food like Duncan did; Christian wanted the King empire to focus on the classics, veering modern for trends but only after they were time-tested and general-public approved. There were no solid sauces or juxtapositions of temperatures or flavors in the food Beck cooked. Not that he'd want there to be. He could appreciate Duncan's ingenuity and the true talent it took to come up with the off-the-wall things Duncan made in the kitchen when he was indulging in his molecular gastronomy, but that wasn't Beck's cup of tea. Neither were the foods Beck did get to cook, though. Duncan had called Brix's menu boring and predictable, and he'd been right.

Beck didn't necessarily want to use liquid nitrogen to flash-freeze sauces or experiment with chemical reactions as a means of cooking food. He was happy to leave that sort of kitchen alchemy to Duncan and his colleagues. But Beck did want to cook innovative food. He wanted to be at the forefront of cuisine, blazing a trail away from trendy, ridiculous dishes and toward actual food. He'd never categorized himself, since it seemed pointless to attach himself to a specific food movement when he knew full well Christian would never allow him to do anything outside the norm, but Beck did have a special affection for the Slow Food movement.

When Cartwright had expounded against GMOs on the show, Beck had silently been cheering him on. He didn't like cooking with genetically modified ingredients, and he avoided them whenever possible. Christian hated what he called Beck's "micromanaging," but whenever Beck started up a new restaurant in the King empire, he always paid special attention to sourcing produce as locally as he could. If he was truly opening his own place, Beck would serve as many locally grown products as he could, from organic vegetables to artisan cheeses, meats, and breads. Food was meant to be savored slowly, and Beck firmly believed it should be cooked that way, too, with reverence and care and attention to bringing out the natural flavors, not covering them up with heavy sauces and seasonings.

The ping of a new e-mail had Beck looking up at his laptop, grimacing when he realized he'd gotten yet another message from Christian. This time it had been important enough to come from Christian himself, without the help of his secretary, which couldn't mean anything good. Beck opened it, wincing as if he were hearing the words in his uncle's scathingly condescending voice. In a few terse sentences, Christian managed to get his point across very clearly. Beck hesitated before following the link to the popular online magazine his uncle had included. It was a well-respected site, which meant anything it reported would be taken seriously.

Jocular rivalry was one thing, but Beck had no doubt his and Duncan's exchange had crossed the line—he'd known it when it had been happening, and he was pretty sure Duncan had too. That's why they had both ended up apologizing. With Duncan's general good humor— toward anyone other than Beck, that was—and big cow eyes, Beck could tell the apology he'd gotten from Duncan hadn't been knee-jerk. Duncan had an incredibly expressive face, and guilt had been written all over it after he'd landed the sharpest jabs.

Those apologies hadn't made it into the article, though a few quotes from their hostile banter had. Christian was demanding to know whether or not they were true—and threatening to unleash the legal team if they weren't. But Beck knew they were without glancing at them a second time. He came off as an incredible ass, and Duncan didn't fare much better. The most damning part, however, was the accompanying photo, which had been captioned "Food fight? Culinary empire heirs nearly come to blows at Brix opening."

The picture wasn't from a camera phone. It didn't have any of the grainy blurriness of the others Beck had seen; instead, it was professional in its clarity, probably snapped by the web site's photographer, who had been on hand to cover the opening. Beck supposed he should have expected this. There had been several professional photographers at Brix last night; he doubted this would be the only publication to run with the story.

And whereas the camera phone shots had been from odd angles and blessedly fuzzy, this one left no question that Beck's hand on Duncan had not been friendly. The picture was so clear Beck could count the wrinkles on Duncan's sleeve if he wanted to, and there was no way anyone who looked at it would think they were friends exchanging banter the way most of the gossip sites had played their confrontation.

From the tight expression on his face, Beck looked about ten seconds away from hitting Duncan, though the slighter man looked every bit as irritated and angry. They were relatively matched in height, but Beck had to have twenty pounds of muscle on Duncan, so even though they were equally culpable, Beck was the one who came out looking like the bully.

"Fabulous," Beck hissed when his phone rang on the counter. It was either Christian or Lindsay—everyone else he knew would still be sleeping off their hangovers, like he should be doing. Deciding that knowing his fate wouldn't make it any harder to take, he answered without looking at the caller ID.

"Beck Douglas."

There was a muffled laugh on the other end, then a beat of silence. "Of course you answer your phone like that. Why wouldn't you? You're Beck Douglas, after all. Why would you bother with a greeting or pleasantries like the rest of us mere mortals?"

Beck blew out a breath, his stomach jumping with something that felt perilously close to excitement.

"Do I want to know how you got my number, Duncan?"

"Beck, you do realize we share a lot of the same friends, right? I was there at the opening as a guest of several of them, remember?"

Beck swallowed, uncomfortably reminded of Duncan's jab from the night before. "I thought I didn't have friends. They're all just employees, right?"

Duncan made a frustrated sound, and Beck heard him muffle the receiver with something and hold a brief but fierce whispered conversation in the background. Beck couldn't tell what Duncan was saying or who he was talking to, but it wasn't a pleasant exchange.

"Stop sulking and come to brunch," Duncan said when he'd lifted whatever was muffling the phone. "We need to talk about how we're going to deal with all this media attention."

"I wasn't aware we were going to deal with it at all," Beck sniped, inexplicably stung that Duncan was only inviting him to brunch so they could talk about how to salvage their reputations as media darlings.

"Well, we are. Campbell thinks it's best if we talk to each other before we talk to my father and your uncle, and I agree."

Beck frowned. Duncan couldn't mean *his* Campbell, the Campbell who had been his best friend since they'd been in diapers. He'd know if Campbell was friends with Duncan, wouldn't he? He'd complained about Duncan to Campbell enough times to have given Campbell the chance to pipe up with that information.

"Campbell? Campbell Grange?"

"How many Campbells do you know? It's not exactly a common name. Yes, that Campbell," Duncan said, exasperation clear in his tone. "He's already heard from Christian about a dozen times since he's been here—shut up, Campbell, it's not really an exaggeration—and my father has left me about four messages, all of which I've deleted without listening to them. Campbell says we need a strategy, and I trust Campbell."

"You know *my* Campbell?"

"Oh my God, Beck, yes! Campbell Grange, middle name Allen. Employed by the King Corporation as a producer and business analyst but spends most of his time down in the test kitchens flirting with the sous-chef, Joanna."

Beck heard Campbell's unmistakable growl, followed by a sharp squeal from Duncan.

"That was uncalled for," Duncan muttered, presumably at Campbell. Beck could sympathize; he and Campbell had both grown up with Lindsay, spiteful pincher extraordinaire, and Campbell had learned retribution at her knee. His pinches were brutal.

"So let me get this straight. You want me to come have brunch with you and Campbell, who is somehow a close enough friend of yours that he's already at your place on a Saturday morning, and talk about what we're going to do about these articles?"

"I'll have you know I am Campbell's top choice for a dog sitter when he goes out of town. Snuggles stays with me whenever Campbell has to traipse across the country checking the books at all of Christian's restaurants, which he'd do well to remember is *often*, so he needs to stay on my good side." Duncan paused, and Beck assumed he was staring Campbell down, probably still smarting over the pinch. "Also, it's not morning. It's almost one thirty. And he's here because he always has breakfast with me on Saturdays, even when we're eating it in the afternoon because we got horribly, horribly drunk the night before."

"Wait, Campbell has a *dog*?"

Duncan sputtered incredulously, and Beck let him hang for a beat longer before he laughed. Teasing Duncan came so naturally, Beck found it hard to resist. Rendering the usually talkative Duncan speechless was a bonus.

"Yeah, you got me," Duncan said, sounding resigned. Beck could hear Campbell laughing in the background. "Just come over. I'm going to text you my address, and you're going to show up in forty-five minutes. Otherwise the frittata is going to be overcooked, and I'm going to be even crankier than I already am."

Chapter FIVE

"HE'S ON his way."

"I told you he'd come," Campbell said, snorting with laughter when Duncan's only reply was to stick his tongue out at him.

Duncan hadn't been exaggerating when he told Beck Campbell came for breakfast almost every Saturday. They'd met through Corbin three years ago, bonding over a deep and abiding love of breakfast foods. Campbell was one of the only people he'd met who, upon hearing he enjoyed working as a line cook in a diner, had truly understood why. Campbell wasn't a chef by any means, but he did love to cook. He'd nodded, sagely said "eggs are awesome," and promptly been named Duncan's friend for life.

They usually ate at Duncan's, but only because he bemoaned how poorly stocked Campbell's kitchen was. It wasn't Duncan's fault if he was accustomed to certain luxuries, like the restaurant-grade espresso machine he was currently petting fondly as it brewed, while Campbell looked at him like he was insane. Not that petting appliances was anywhere outside the norm for Duncan; Campbell really shouldn't have been surprised.

Even though the majority of Duncan's friends were chefs, Campbell was the only one he allowed to cook in his kitchen. No one else understood that Duncan stepping back and letting someone else manhandle his beloved pots and pans was a privilege, but Campbell always treated them with the respect they deserved. He was also the only person other than himself who Duncan trusted to make him a fried egg, which in Duncan's estimation was just about the most perfect food on the planet—if it was done right. Sadly, even most of the Michelin-rated chefs he knew couldn't consistently get the yolk to achieve that moment of not-quite-a-liquid, not-quite-a-solid Zen, but Campbell could.

"Is there anything I need to know about Beck before he gets here? The way he takes his coffee? His stance on bacon, crispy or chewy? And most importantly, Spice Girl crush?"

Campbell laughed. "He's not as cold as you seem to think, Duncan. He's actually a really good guy. I wouldn't be friends with him if he was an asshole."

It was a rejoinder Duncan was getting tired of hearing, and he gave Campbell a flat look, prompting more laughter.

"Okay, you're right. I would be friends with him even if he was an asshole, because apparently I have a type and assholes are it," Campbell said with a sunny smile.

Duncan swatted at him with his spatula, then made a face when he realized he was going to have to wash it now. "Go on," he prompted.

Campbell gave him a put-upon look but complied. "He likes his first cup of the morning ridiculously sweet and milky, but after that any coffee throughout the day is taken black. His view on bacon changes based on how it's being served—"

"As it should," Duncan said, nodding.

"—and he had a style crush on Ginger Spice when we were younger, even though his real crush was reserved for one of the guys in 98 Degrees. Don't ask me which one because they all looked alike to me."

Duncan pondered his answer for a moment and then nodded in approval. "Probably one of the Lachey brothers. Solid choice. It was the biceps," he said, a faint smile curving his lips as he remembered his favorite boy bands of the nineties.

Campbell shook his head in what Duncan liked to think of as fond annoyance. He had no idea why Campbell put up with him, since he seemed to vacillate between that and outright annoyance whenever they were together, but somehow the dynamic worked for them. Duncan figured someone who worked so closely with a fuddy-duddy rule follower like Beck needed comic relief from time to time, which was probably what he was to Campbell. They were either joking around or working in silence together, and that was exactly what Duncan needed on occasion. And they never talked about Beck. It was rule number one after Campbell had nearly taken Duncan's head off for casually insulting Beck once.

Duncan grabbed his phone and started searching Spotify for boy bands, but Campbell cut his plans for a welcoming serenade for Beck short by clapping his hands together and heading for the kitchen. "Frittata?"

Duncan gave his phone a longing glance but put it aside. He had a firm rule about electronics in the kitchen. It was unsanitary, for one—most people had no idea how dirty their phones and other gadgets were, but as a microbiologist, Duncan had seen for himself how much disgusting shit phones picked up, sometimes literally. For another, it wasn't a good place to be distracted. And the likelihood of dropping an expensive piece of technology into the sink or soup pot was too great.

He knew a lot of chefs who liked music when they cooked at home, but he wasn't one of them. He liked the quiet, since it was a nice respite from the noisy professional kitchens he spent so much time in.

Campbell understood that. It was another of the reasons he was allowed in Duncan's kitchen.

They worked together silently, with Duncan raiding the fridge for leftovers he dutifully handed over to Campbell, who had set himself up at the cutting board with one of Duncan's favorite knifes. That was true friendship, right there. Letting someone else in his kitchen was big, but he wouldn't even let his own mother touch his knives.

He hadn't been home much over the last week, so the pickings were pretty slim. Luckily frittatas were a very forgiving medium. He'd seen a *King of the Kitchen* where Beck called it refrigerator Velcro, and even though Duncan was loathe to admit a TV chef could be right about anything, Beck absolutely was in this case. Wilted veggies? Throw 'em in. Almost expired dairy? It's all good. Frittatas were amazing. There were a few different foods that could successfully help you clean out your stash of leftovers, but frittatas were Duncan's favorite.

Campbell made a face when he opened up a container that had gone fuzzy inside. Duncan wrinkled his nose and tossed it, Tupperware and all, into the garbage.

"You should—"

Campbell quieted when Duncan narrowed his eyes. He recycled when he could and did his best to minimize waste of all sorts in the restaurants he worked in, but he drew the line at cleaning out moldy things. He'd forgo a plastic bag next time he stopped in at the convenience store on the corner and call it ecologically even.

Campbell shrugged and went back to chopping the ham Duncan had brought home from his mother's earlier in the week. He'd inherited every ounce of his cooking prowess from his father. His mother could barely boil water, and she'd exist on Lean Cuisines if Duncan let her. So whenever he was in town, he made the hour-long trek out to her place once a week to cook her a good meal and set up some easy-to-microwave meals for later in the week. She hadn't liked the wasabi-soy rub he'd put on the ham, though, so he'd brought it home with him.

Duncan grabbed the eggs last and started cracking them into a bowl, beating them with a fork until they were nice and frothy. He seasoned them lightly—one mistake cooks made all the time was too much seasoning in eggs, since it was so easy to overpower the flavor of the eggs themselves—and put them aside so he could get a pan heating on the stove.

Campbell scraped the onions and garlic he'd chopped into it as soon as the oil began to shimmer, and the smell of sautéing aromatics filled the small kitchen. Duncan was pretty sure heaven smelled like sautéing onions. Or bacon.

Speaking of, he'd better get that started too. He liked it crisp, which was sacrilege in some circles. He'd once almost brought a restaurant reviewer to tears—not the good kind—by making a bacon-fat foam and calling it bacon on the menu. It hadn't gone over well, and he'd learned an important lesson in making sure menu descriptions were thorough. Especially when it came to much-beloved things like bacon.

Duncan slipped around Campbell, who'd started sautéing the veggies with practiced skill, and grabbed his huge cast-iron skillet from its spot of honor hanging next to the stove. He'd found the skillet at a garage sale a few years back. It had been a pain in the ass to drag home on the El, but totally worth it. It was blackened and seasoned to perfection, probably thanks to someone's grandmother who'd likely cooked three meals a day in it for years before the idiot he'd bought it from inherited it and sold it for five dollars. The joke was on that dude, because a well-seasoned cast-iron skillet was worth its weight in gold.

Most people thought a hot pan was the way to go, since bacon had a lot of fat to be seared off. But they were wrong. The secret to perfectly crispy bacon was to start it in a *cold* cast-iron pan. It took a little more patience, but it was so worth it. Once he had the bacon situated just so, he turned on the heat.

"Do you have any parm?" Campbell asked, his head mostly hidden inside the refrigerator.

Duncan took a peek at the sauté pan, nodding in approval when he saw Campbell had added the ham and arranged everything in a nice even layer across the bottom.

"I have aged Mizithra."

When Campbell eased his head out of the refrigerator and stared at him blankly, Duncan snorted and moved around him to dig into the cheese drawer, coming out with a small block of hard white cheese.

"Kind of a Greek parm," Duncan explained, unhooking his microplane from its spot on the hanging tool rack. He grated a generous portion into the eggs and gave it another stir with the fork before pouring it over the mixture in the pan. It sizzled and bubbled, and Duncan gave the pan a hard shake to help the eggs evenly distribute.

"If it's like Parmesan, then why not just buy Parmesan?" Campbell asked, squinting at the cheese Duncan had left on the counter.

"Because I wanted Mizithra, not Parmesan?"

He was pretty sure Campbell was making rude gestures at him, but his back was turned so he could flip the bacon, so Duncan couldn't tell for sure. He set about making a huge pile of toast—they *were* hungover, after all, which practically demanded carb overloading—and kept a close eye on the eggs, watching them until they were semiset and ready to be popped under the broiler.

The doorbell rang as he closed the oven, and he waved Campbell off to get it. He was Beck's friend, after all. And Duncan didn't like leaving things broiling in his kitchen without his own direct supervision.

THEY ATE brunch in companionable silence, all three of them still nursing enough of a hangover that the quiet was enjoyable rather than awkward. After the last of the plates had been cleared away, though,

Beck was all business. Duncan noticed the exact moment Beck shifted from Beck to Beck Douglas; it involved his shoulders actually straightening and his face taking on a pinched expression. Duncan didn't favor the change at all.

"I think all we need to do is issue a statement that the comments were taken out of context," Beck said after they'd shuffled through all the printouts and used Duncan's laptop to scroll through a few new pieces that had popped up since they'd taken a break to eat.

Beck had brought a tablet, too, but Duncan had refused to give him the Wi-Fi password, partially out of spite and partially because he wanted an excuse to sit close to Beck. Both of them using the laptop worked, though it had the consequence of forcing poor Campbell to squeeze in on Beck's other side. Beck didn't question why Campbell hadn't sat between the two of them, and Duncan wasn't sure if it was because he hadn't noticed or because he actually wanted to sit next to Duncan.

As it was, Duncan was having trouble concentrating, with the warmth of Beck's thigh right next to his. It was distracting. He shifted away slightly, trying not to let his libido run away with him. This was important—he could draw hearts around Beck's name in a notebook later.

"A statement? Who are we, Exxon explaining the Valdez?" Duncan snorted, shaking his head. "I think calling attention to it validates what they're saying. Even if we say 'no, no, that wasn't what happened,' us issuing statements is going to make us look like they got it right."

"They did get it right, Duncan," Beck said with a sigh. "We both actually did say those things. I know Christian is hoping to hear I was misquoted, but I wasn't. And I won't lie and say I was."

Duncan quirked a brow at him. "Keep your shirt on, Mr. Man. I wasn't saying we should lie. I'm saying if we give a press conference or any sort of official statement, it will make what we said even more damaging."

"You need to change the story," Campbell said. Duncan looked over Beck's shoulder and smiled at him.

Beck threw his hands up in exasperation. "I just said we aren't lying! We can't change the story."

"Not like that," Campbell said, a bit of steel underlying the patience in his voice. It was one of the things Duncan appreciated about Campbell; he was a bear of a man, but people respected him not because of his size but because he radiated quiet authority. Clearly Beck needed someone like Campbell in his life to keep him grounded, and Duncan could see why they were such close friends.

"We need to change their focus to something else," Duncan said, wrinkling his nose at Beck when Beck rolled his eyes.

"I hardly think we can call hoping some big news event happens and distracts everyone a plan. I know we aren't well known enough for the mainstream press to be interested, but it's all over the culinary press. Even some of the purely gossip sites have picked it up, probably because of *King of the Kitchen*."

"I'm not saying we wait for some other news event," Duncan said, shaking his head. Campbell was smiling. That had to be a good sign, so Duncan forged ahead. "I'm saying we control how this story plays out. Sure, a bunch of people saw us get in a high-profile argument. And yes, you grabbing me—no matter how innocent it was, Beck—don't look at me like that—might have made it seem like there was a physical aspect to the fight. But if we do the opposite of what they're expecting, the story fizzles before it even takes off."

Campbell must have sensed how frustrated Beck was getting since he jumped in. "You go out and make sure you're seen around town with Duncan, Beck. You two go have dinner at whatever trendy spot is impossible to get reservations for now. You meet for drinks out somewhere. Hell, you go feed the pigeons together at the park. Whatever. But you do it in plain view of everyone, and you do it with a smile."

"See? This way we don't need to say 'we're actually friends, it was a good-natured argument that got taken out of context.' We *show* them that."

Beck squinted, and Duncan had to admit he'd finally found an expression that didn't look gorgeous on Beck's face. It was a little comforting to know someone as attractive as Beck Douglas could be a bit ugly at times, even if it was only when he was gawking incredulously.

"But we aren't friends."

"If you keep saying that, eventually I'll be hurt, Beck," Duncan said, holding a hand over his heart. "You never write, you never call. You're always washing your hair when I suggest we go out. Tell me, Beck, is this all one-sided? Are you going to leave me to waste away here in my apartment, pining for you?"

It was uncomfortably close to what Duncan feared could become the truth if they hung out much more, but Duncan played it with earnest innocence anyway.

"Oh, screw you both," Beck said, glaring at them. "This plan is ridiculous."

"But it isn't, Beck," Campbell interjected. "Think about it. No one would bat an eye if you and I'd had that argument. We have to find a way to convince them you and Duncan aren't the arch enemies the culinary world likes to make you out to be."

Beck scoffed. "We aren't arch enemies. We don't even know each other."

"Exactly!" Campbell crowed, a grin splitting his face. "You don't know each other. You definitely don't hate each other. You have no intention of continuing the feud Christian and Vincent have going, right? So what do you have to lose here?"

Duncan watched Beck size him up, like he was weighing the pros and cons of being seen out in public together against the bad publicity that would ensue if they didn't fix the situation. Duncan barely restrained himself from a victory fist pump when Beck sighed in resignation.

"Fine," Beck huffed. He crossed his arms over his chest, the picture of hostility. "But there are going to be ground rules."

"Ground rules? Like what—we only eat at five-star restaurants and can't be seen drinking anything that wasn't barrel aged?"

Campbell snorted at Duncan's retort, but Beck's stony expression didn't change. He was clearly serious.

"Like topics that are off-limits, Duncan. I don't care what you order or what you drink, as long as you don't get sloppy drunk and expect me to drag you home."

Duncan couldn't help but imagine what it would be like to be drunk and draped over Beck. He wouldn't even think about

Beck taking him home—that way lay madness. Or at least a very inappropriate erection.

"That's actually a good idea," Campbell said, pulling a notebook and pen out of his pocket. "Obviously, you shouldn't talk about Duncan's father or Christian. I'm assuming your restaurants are off-limits too?"

Beck nodded. "Same goes for the television show."

"And no potshots about culinary school," Duncan said, giving Beck a pointed look.

"That's a good start for now. I'll e-mail this to you two. You'll be fine if you keep to neutral topics."

Duncan wasn't sure what topics were left. His career was his entire life, and he was certain Beck's was too. If they couldn't talk about their restaurants, what did that leave? Somehow he doubted Beck would want to talk about the indie music scene Duncan loved, and Duncan sure as hell didn't care enough about the sports Beck might follow to have a conversation about them.

"That leaves us… what? Gossiping about you?" Duncan asked, earning himself a swat from Campbell.

Beck gave him a look of disgust. "I'm sure even someone with your background could come up with something more interesting than Campbell to discuss. The nutritional value of Hot Pockets, perhaps?"

"Hey! You're already violating the list."

"What?" Beck sounded affronted. "I am not."

"You are too! You took a jab at my lack of a fancy culinary education."

"I did not! That was aimed at your general ineptitude, not your education. Besides, no self-respecting chef would wear that shirt."

Duncan looked down at the soft cotton T-shirt he was wearing. It was one of his favorites; John had given it to him several birthdays ago. The words "I'm kind of a big dill" were superimposed over a large pickle.

"What's wrong with my shirt?"

Beck gaped at him. "What's wrong with your shirt? Are you five?"

They stopped bickering at the sound of Campbell's head hitting the table.

Chapter SIX

FOR THE third time in twenty minutes, Beck cursed the fact that Campbell had access to his personal calendar. It made scheduling sports practices and bar crawls easier for them, since Campbell usually took point on arranging anything Beck did outside of work. It was sad, when Beck really stopped to think about it. He virtually had no social life that didn't involve Campbell. There wasn't much time to do anything outside of work, especially since Beck essentially worked two full-time jobs. He spent his mornings prepping and filming *King of the Kitchen* and doing paperwork for Christian's restaurants, and he spent many of his nights floating around the three Chicago-based restaurants—four, now, with Brix open—filling in wherever there was a shortage. He wondered what Duncan would have thought of him last night, when Beck had put his two years of culinary school to use to be a prep chef in Christian's most popular fine dining restaurant. Duncan would have laughed his ass off seeing a Cordon Bleu-trained chef chopping carrots and straining sauces, but Beck had no problem rolling up his sleeves and jumping in wherever he could help.

He didn't have an ego when it came to dinner service. He very much did have one when it came to getting stood up by Duncan on their very first PR date.

Campbell had arranged for Beck and Duncan to have the first of what Beck steadfastly refused to call a "bro-date," no matter how insistent Duncan was, at a trendy bar near the center where Beck and Campbell had a standing monthly racquetball game with Christian and Georges Lapin, another chef on the network that aired *King of the Kitchen*. If Duncan didn't show up soon, they weren't going to have the chance to even have one drink together before Beck had to dash off for the game.

Then again, that might not be a horrible thing. As much as Beck hated to admit it, he was the slightest bit anxious about meeting up with Duncan without Campbell there to referee. Something about Duncan put

Beck on edge; try as he might, Beck couldn't seem to avoid putting his foot in his mouth with Duncan. Most people would describe Beck as charming. It was an image he worked hard to cultivate. Duncan, he was sure, would not be one of those people.

Beck looked up at the door in irritation, wishing he could somehow force Duncan to appear. He felt like an idiot sitting at the bar waiting for him, and Beck was sure the bartender was not amused that he'd been nursing the same gin and tonic the entire time he'd been taking up valuable real estate at the bar.

"I got caught up in the back, sorry!"

Beck didn't fall off his barstool at the surprise of having Duncan come up behind him and clap him on the shoulder, but it was a near thing. He turned around, scowling when he saw Duncan standing there in an apron with a sheepish look on his face.

"I was in the area for a consultation, so I got here a little early. Abe saw me and pulled me back to the kitchen—their sous-chef has appendicitis, so they're short tonight. I was helping them get past the happy hour rush."

Beck hadn't even known the bar served food, but now that Duncan had drawn his attention to it, he realized almost all of the tables tucked into alcoves around the bar were filled with people eating.

"Anyway, I'm yours now," Duncan said. He slid onto the empty stool Beck had been guarding with his sports coat, garnering him many angry glances from his fellow patrons at the crowded bar.

Beck couldn't hold back a disbelieving snort at that, which only served to make Duncan's grin grow. He felt his cheeks heat, his attraction to Duncan beating out years of television and media training that had all but eradicated Beck's tendency to blush.

"Well, that's interesting," Duncan drawled, and Beck's ears started to burn as well.

He fell back on his best defense mechanism, cool arrogance. "I've spent most of the time I'd allotted for our appointment sitting here alone. Not much interesting about that," Beck snapped.

His terse tone didn't seem to affect Duncan at all, though. He sat there and smiled mildly, like Beck was talking to him about the weather or the latest trade that was sure to tank the rest of the season for the Bears.

Duncan always seemed to have him off balance, and the only way Beck knew to address that was with sarcasm and irritation. It undermined the entire plan, but it was better than letting Duncan realize Beck was attracted to him.

The bartender put a bottle of lager on the bar in front of Duncan, and the smile he gave him was much friendlier than the one he'd given Beck when Beck had arrived. Beck tried not to be jealous, but that didn't stop a hot swirl of it from sweeping through his stomach when Duncan winked at the bartender and exchanged a complicated handshake with him.

Beck's glare must have caught the bartender's attention because he turned to him and motioned toward Beck's empty glass. "Another, buddy?"

Beck shook his head. "I have to go play racquetball after this."

Duncan snorted. "Give him a tumbler with soda water and a lime, Gage." Before Beck could protest—who did Duncan think he was, anyway, ordering for him? And how well did he know this bartender?—Duncan leaned in close to whisper conspiratorially. "Gotta keep up appearances, don't we? Can't share a friendly drink together if I'm the only one drinking."

Duncan's breath was hot against Beck's ear, and his loose-limbed sprawl on the barstool suggested he'd already had a few in the back. Beck was certain that was just for show because Duncan was never anything but a consummate professional in the kitchen. He'd never drink while he was working. Beck wondered why Duncan was putting on such an act.

"You've only got me for ten more minutes, and then you'll have to find someone else to keep you company while you get buzzed in the afternoon," he muttered.

Instead of reeling back in offense at the insult as Beck had expected, Duncan leaned in closer, chuckling against Beck's neck as he wrapped him in a clumsy one-armed hug. "Smile or the guy in the corner is going to get a photo of the two of us fighting again," he muttered.

And there was the reason for the display, apparently. Even though he'd known there had to be a reason Duncan was all over him, Beck couldn't help but feel a little disappointed it was entirely for show.

Swallowing back his discomfort, Beck returned the awkward hug and then jovially pushed Duncan back onto his own barstool. "Seems like I have some catching up to do," he said with a mirth he didn't feel. He must have sold it, though, because the tight line of Duncan's shoulders eased a bit as he resettled himself on his seat.

Beck watched out of the corner of his eye as Duncan tipped his beer back. It looked obscene—from the way his full lips wrapped around the neck to the way his throat worked as he swallowed. Beck tore his gaze away, focusing on the drink the bartender put down in front of him. Beck didn't like the guy's knowing grin as he nodded in Duncan's direction, one eyebrow raised. He didn't want to bond with the bartender over how obnoxiously hot Duncan looked drinking a beer. Hell, he didn't want to think about Duncan like that at all. He couldn't let in any distractions right now—it was a crucial time in his career, and getting involved with Duncan could only lead to trouble.

"So you're going to kill me, but I want you to know this wasn't my fault," Duncan said without preamble, pulling Beck out of his internal debate.

Beck's fingers tightened around his glass of soda water, and he deliberately waited a beat before responding. "What have you done now?"

"I didn't do anything. That's what's important for you to know," Duncan said. He drained the last of his beer and plunked the bottle on the bar. The bartender protested when Duncan dug out his wallet and threw a twenty next to it, but Duncan waved him off. "I know mine was on the house. That's for his and putting up with his scowl. I owe you one, man."

Beck glowered at the two of them as Duncan stood and repeated the complicated handshake with the bartender, though this time it ended with Duncan pulling the guy in close for a hug. It should have looked ridiculous with the bar between them, but Duncan made it look graceful somehow.

"My stuff's in the office. Come on back," he said to Beck.

"I have to get going—"

"Yeah, I know. It's like… what? A couple minute walk to the club?"

Despite his confusion, Beck found himself sliding off his barstool and following Duncan deeper into the restaurant. Several people called out a greeting to Duncan when they pushed through the swinging doors into the kitchen, but he just waved as he ushered Beck into a small office in the back.

"I figured we'd undo any good press we'd managed to get if I told you out there, but you need to know Christian called my father." Duncan blew out a breath, his gestures agitated. "Apparently, we're not doing enough to save face, so they've decided to get involved. I was summoned to play racquetball with you."

Beck's eyes narrowed. "Christian never plays doubles with anyone other than Georges."

"Well, today he's playing with you. Against me and Vincent."

Duncan sounded about as enthused as Beck felt, but that didn't stop Beck from lashing out at him. He hated it when Christian meddled, especially when it was with something as ill-advised as this. There was no way Vincent and Christian would be able to be in the same room together without an explosion. They were worse than him and Duncan.

"Have you ever even held a racquet?"

Duncan pulled a duffel bag out from behind the desk. There was a racquet tied to the side, and he clutched at it, wide-eyed. "You hold the big end, right?"

Beck's lips twitched into an unwilling smile. "This is where you tell me you're some sort of racquetball savant, isn't it?"

Duncan's grin turned vicious, which made Beck's stomach swoop. "Well, I'm not on the US Olympic team or anything."

"There is no Olympic racquetball team."

"Exactly." Duncan winked at him, and Beck laughed. The tension that had held his posture ramrod stiff eased, and he felt himself relaxing. Maybe he and Duncan really could be friends.

"Walked into that one," he said ruefully.

Duncan hefted his bag and shepherded Beck back through the kitchen and out the side door. "Be still my heart. Does Beck Douglas actually have a sense of humor? I thought that was the product of good script writers."

Beck hated it when Duncan said his name like that, like he bought into the idea Beck was an empire, not a person. It bothered him whenever anyone did it, but even more so when it was Duncan.

It wouldn't do to let Duncan know that, though, because Beck knew the teasing would only increase if Duncan knew it was getting to him.

"Is that an admission you watch my show?"

Duncan's denial came too quickly for it to be real. "No."

"You do!" Delight bubbled up in Beck's chest. He hadn't felt this light and free in a long time. People around them on the sidewalk were turning to look at the two of them as they bickered good-naturedly, and Beck could care less. For once he wasn't thinking about his image. "You probably have them all on DVR and watch them over and over again."

"Like I'd want to watch you making panna cotta."

It hadn't been Beck's favorite dish to make by a long shot, and the recipe had been uninspired, but it didn't change the fact that Duncan had watched the latest episode. "Ha! How would you know that if you hadn't tuned in?"

Beck pointed an accusing finger at him, and Duncan swatted it away. "Shut up."

"Admit it! You're a fan!"

"Put your finger in my face again and lose it," Duncan warned.

"You wouldn't want your favorite celebrity cooking host to lose a finger."

Duncan looked around. "Allen Jones is here?"

"The more you deny it, the truer it is," Beck said smugly.

Beck held the door to the club open for Duncan, using the opportunity to discreetly check out his ass. He was wearing another pair of jeans that looked like they were held together with fairy dust and hope. The denim was soft and frayed in a way that could only come from repeated washings and age, no matter how much manufacturers tried to replicate it. He had a feeling the rips in the thighs of Duncan's jeans hadn't been artfully torn into the cloth by a machine; they'd been worn hard and abused.

That line of thinking wouldn't lead him anywhere good, so it was just as well Vincent and Christian were waiting for them in the lobby. From the drawn look on Vincent's face and the tight lines around Christian's mouth, things had gone about as well as Beck had predicted, so far.

"Success, I assume? You wouldn't be smiling if you hadn't managed to get some good publicity in the bar."

Beck flinched at Christian's cold assessment, but he didn't contradict him. The last thing he needed was his uncle realizing this friendship with Duncan was something Beck actually wanted. He'd find a way to use it to his advantage somehow, if he knew, and Beck didn't need Christian interfering more than he already was.

Duncan's smile had thinned a bit, and Beck wondered if all the good inroads they'd made in the last half hour had been trashed thanks to Christian's comment.

"We live to serve," Beck said tightly.

"Shall we get to the court? We only have it reserved for another forty minutes," Christian said, his smile so fake it pained Beck to look at it.

"My boy and I hardly need that much time to thoroughly rout you and your protégé," Vincent said with a smirk that looked eerily similar to the one Duncan had on his face half the time.

"Actually, I wondered if we ought to split the other way," Duncan said. "I mean, this is all about us healing the so-called rift between our families, right?"

Beck gaped at Duncan, who was smiling like the cat who ate the canary. That conniving bastard. "What happened to besting me with all your Olympic prowess?" he asked.

Duncan shrugged. "As fun as the thought of handing you your ass is—and it's a very nice one—I figured maybe it would play better in the press if Christian and Vincent teamed up and took the younger generation on. It doesn't get more good-natured than that, right?"

Christian looked like he was going to protest, but Vincent latched onto the idea with vigor. "If you think we'll go easy on you just because you're younger and less experienced, you've got another thing coming."

Duncan's smile turned sharper at his father's taunt. "It would be a hell of a time to start, wouldn't it, Vincent?"

The zinger obviously hit home, from the way Vincent's back straightened. Beck had never spent any time with the two Walters men together, but they weren't anything like he'd assumed. Vincent was always so effusive in his praise when he was talking about Duncan, and Beck figured they must have a great relationship. Standing here with them and feeling the tension roll off both of them in waves had him questioning that. It seemed like every assumption he'd had about Duncan was being disproven.

"I'm used to playing against Christian, so I'm in," Beck said, trying to draw the mood back to something more appropriate for a public place.

"We'll meet you on the court, then," Christian said, brushing some invisible lint off his pristine white shorts. He and Vincent were both already dressed in their racquetball clothes. He gave Duncan's jeans a distasteful look. "Do hurry."

Beck wondered if he and Duncan should take turns changing just to have one of them on hand to act as a buffer between Vincent and Christian, but Vincent spoke before he could suggest it.

"I'll head to the court to make sure they don't give our reservation to someone else," Vincent said. He sneered in Christian's direction, his chest puffed out like a peacock. "Perhaps you could wait in the café. I believe they're selling that brand of glorified tap water you've been hawking."

Christian's face went puce. "I only put my name on the very best brands," he sniffed. "Not that you'd know anything about being judicious."

Beck grabbed his uncle's arm when Vincent took a step toward them. "Didn't I see Arnie in the café on my way in? When I was in last week he asked me about placing an order for some premade dinners from Brix to sell here. Maybe you should go touch base with him about that. We'll meet you on the court in five."

Duncan snickered. "Yeah, save it for the court, old men."

Christian glowered but held his hands up and stepped away. "I'm always happy to discuss new business ventures."

"Expand or die, isn't that your motto?" Vincent muttered, but he turned and headed down the corridor toward the courts when Duncan cleared his throat menacingly.

"This is such a bad idea," Duncan said.

The photographer from the restaurant was just outside the plate-glass window, so Beck slung his arm around Duncan's shoulders and gave him a sunny smile. "The absolute worst," he said through gritted teeth.

Chapter SEVEN

"HE SAID he was sorry." Duncan even thought it was possible his father had meant the words when he'd said them. It might have been the first time Vincent apologized and actually meant it.

"He broke Christian's nose!" Duncan had heard that level of exasperation from Beck enough in their last few interactions to be able to perfectly picture it, even without the benefit of being able to see Beck.

The racquetball game had gone poorly from the start, with both Vincent and Christian playing too aggressively. It had been funny, watching the two men work themselves up into a ridiculous frenzy, right up until Vincent's racket had smashed into Christian's face on a particularly hard backhand. He'd sworn it had been an accident, and Duncan even believed him. Mostly.

Duncan figured it was a good sign Beck had even bothered calling him with an update from the hospital. He wouldn't have blamed Beck if he'd wanted nothing to do with Duncan after Vincent's stunt.

"There are already pictures up online," Beck said. He sounded exhausted and resigned, but that was to be expected after spending two hours in the emergency room with Christian. That man could push buttons and rile up even the calmest person under the best circumstances, and having his nose reset after it was broken by his most outspoken rival was definitely not the best circumstances.

"I've seen them. Campbell keeps texting me links." The stories were all pure speculation, but that hardly mattered. The photographer who had been watching Duncan and Beck at the bar had gotten the shot of the two of them heading to the locker rooms all smiles, but apparently he'd waited around after that. The shot of Christian climbing into a car with a bloodied towel held up to his face had already been picked up by several news organizations and a score of food blogs.

"He's released a statement saying it was an accident. I guess he and your father are going to claim they meet up for games every so often and this was the first time anyone has been injured."

It was the same thing he and Beck were doing, but it seemed so much more disingenuous. Duncan didn't know the story behind their feud, but he did know the animosity between Vincent and Christian was real. It was different from the playful flirting he and Beck were engaging in. Even when one of them took things too far, he and Beck tried to play by the rules. Vincent and Christian had no such boundaries.

"Why are they bothering? I didn't think either of them minded everyone knowing they hate each other."

Beck sighed. "That would be our fault, according to Christian. The press has taken a new interest in their so-called feud now we're involved, and it's starting to cast them in a poor light. So the new plan is for all of us to get along, like we've buried the hatchet."

"The wrench in that plan is I don't get along with either of them." He didn't point out he'd have no problem mending fences with Beck. That should be fairly obvious, and if it wasn't, he didn't want to press the issue. Beck seemed to run hot and cold, and Duncan didn't want to corner him and make him choose. He had a feeling cold would win out. "So what are we supposed to do now? More bro dates?"

Beck let out a pained noise. "I've asked you to never call them that again."

Duncan snickered. "But we're bros. Going out together. A bro date."

"I am not a bro," Beck snapped. "And no, it's gone too far for that. Lindsay and Campbell have come up with another plan, and unfortunately for us, Christian has already signed off on it."

Duncan didn't like the sound of that. "Which is?"

Beck's silence was not a good sign. "Well?" Duncan prompted, a curl of dread growing in his stomach the longer the quiet stretched on.

"I honestly don't know. They're going to tell us together. You need to be at the studio tomorrow at seven. I'll text you the address."

"Can't. I have a shift at Bar Rio that starts at six." Abe's chef would be out for a few days at the very least, leaving the kitchen scrambling to cover his shifts. Duncan had agreed to pick up a few since he was between jobs at the moment, now that Navien was back from maternity leave.

"In the morning, Duncan. Seven in the morning."

That was just plain ridiculous. "Aren't you working tonight?"

Beck made an impatient noise. "Yes."

"So you're going to be at Brix till God-knows-how-late and then show up across town at the studio by seven?"

"It's what I do every Monday, Tuesday, and Wednesday."

Duncan wondered if Beck's mood swings were due to sleep deprivation. Beck managed most of Christian's restaurants, and even though Duncan liked to tease him about how micromanaged he was, he knew that meant a lot of work. And now with Brix under his purview as well, Duncan doubted he finished up until well after midnight. To turn around and head back to work a few hours later was madness.

"Assuming I show up, and that's a big assumption because do you know how early that is? Jesus. Anyway, assuming I come to your swanky studio, why does Christian want me there?"

"He didn't say. He just told me to make sure you were there for the weekly producers' meeting."

Beck sounded too resigned to not have any idea, but Duncan didn't think he was going to get any speculation out of Beck at the moment. He was obviously tired, and if he was working, his night was only beginning. Duncan didn't want to be responsible for putting any more stress on Beck. Odd that he used to take pleasure in winding him up, and now he wanted to help wind him *down*. Maybe in front of Netflix with a bottle of wine or some good chocolate. Duncan had never wanted to do that with anyone before, and it was honestly a little bit scary.

Duncan decided not to be an asshole this once. This wasn't Beck's fault, so he'd let him off the hook.

"Fine. Maybe Campbell will give me a ride in. I'm not waking up at ass o'clock to take the train."

"Lindsay said she'd send a car. Campbell and I usually go in together, and you're all the way across town. Besides, she said Campbell told her how well you function in the morning. I wouldn't trust you to get there on your own. Wear something professional."

Duncan could hear the judgment in Beck's voice, but he couldn't protest. He hated mornings. Campbell knew that better than most, since more often than not he was to blame if Duncan was out of bed before nine. Those mornings rarely went well.

"That's fair, actually," Duncan said, and he heard a muffled laugh across the line. He felt a little better knowing he'd lightened Beck's mood a bit. Still, this wasn't something he was looking forward to. "I'm not going to like this, am I?"

"Neither of us are."

DUNCAN KNEW Beck was expecting him to either miss the meeting or show up with bedhead and pillow creases on his face. The car was scheduled to pick him up at 6:30 a.m., which was only five hours after he got in after his shift at the bar. Thank God it was a weeknight. He'd have been there till the wee hours if it had been a prime weekend night. The bar's menu was drastically reduced after 11:00 p.m. on weekends, but it still served basic tapas and other snacks until 2:00 a.m. on Fridays and Saturdays.

Duncan made his car easily, with the help of three extraloud alarms and spite. Proving Beck wrong was a strong motivator, and it wasn't until Duncan was tucked away in the back of the studio's car with his tumbler of exceptionally strong coffee that he realized that had probably been the reason for Beck's snarky comments in the first place.

At least he hadn't caved to Beck's demand that he dress up. Or rather, he had, but in his own way. He'd thrown on his nicest jeans and a tailored sports jacket over his favorite graphic T-shirt. Duncan had even scrounged through his closet to find a pair of Chucks that John hadn't drawn all over. Beck would undoubtedly roll his eyes at them, but at least the canvas wasn't covered in sketches of penises.

He'd even brushed his hair.

Duncan sipped at his too-hot coffee, ignoring the way it seared his tongue in favor of getting as much caffeine into his system as possible. If Christian King was anything like Vincent—and Duncan would bet good money he was after spending a very uncomfortable half hour playing racquetball with the two of them—then he was going to need it. Arguing with Beck was fun; arguing with Christian was going to be a different story.

At least Vincent wasn't going to be there. Duncan had confirmed that with Lindsay when she'd called with information about the car. She had been as close-lipped as Beck with details about the meeting, but she'd sounded a lot more gleeful about it than Beck had. That didn't bode well.

He'd finished most of his coffee by the time the car dropped him at the studio. A receptionist from the lobby had even escorted Duncan upstairs, which he thought was overkill. She'd greeted him by name the moment he'd walked into the building, which had been a bit freaky.

Duncan was considering going to find more caffeine when the elevator opened and Beck stepped out.

He stopped short as soon as he saw Duncan. "You've got to be kidding me," he said with a scowl. "You're really wearing that?"

Duncan looked down at the shirt. "What, this shirt? It's one of my favorites."

It had the outline of a bottle of wine with the words "I cook with wine; sometimes I even add it to the food" underneath it.

"It's ridiculous. You look like an idiot." The words didn't have much heat to them, and Duncan wasn't offended. Beck was decked out in one of the crisp shirts and tailored suits he likely owned dozens of, pressed and ready to go in his closet. That wasn't Duncan's comfort zone at all, but he could appreciate how well it worked for Beck. Today's light gray suit and pale lavender shirt accentuated the green flecks in his eyes and made his broad shoulders even more delicious.

Duncan arched into an exaggerated preen. "This is about as dressed up as I get."

Beck didn't look convinced. "I've seen you in a tux, Duncan."

"A memorable sight, eh?" Duncan teased. He was thrilled to see Beck's cheeks flush slightly.

"Only because I was amazed you owned anything that didn't come from Gap," Beck said, but his lips were curved into a small smile.

"Please. Like you could find a beauty like this one at Gap," Duncan sniffed dismissively.

"Maybe Gap wouldn't have butchered the quote," Beck shot back. The lines bracketing his mouth had eased a bit, though, so Duncan didn't think he was wrong that Beck enjoyed their flirting. It was definitely something Duncan wanted to explore more.

"'I love cooking with wine. Sometimes I even add food,'" Duncan quoted. "See? I know it."

Beck rolled his eyes. "And having it wrong on the T-shirt is some sort of ironic statement, then?"

Duncan grinned. "No, it's just a misprint. But I like the shirt anyway."

"You would," Beck muttered. His shoulders visibly tightened when a door down the hall opened and, a moment later, Christian walked out. Suddenly all traces of humor in Beck's expression were gone, replaced with a detached professionalism Duncan didn't care for at all.

"Gentlemen, if you would. I have a meeting with a supplier at eight, so we need to get moving." Christian's tone was easy, but there was something about his manner that made it clear it wasn't a request.

Beck practically snapped to attention at Christian's words, and he immediately moved toward the room. The quelling look he gave Duncan when he glanced back over his shoulder promised violence if Duncan didn't follow suit, and Duncan had to suppress a huff of laughter. There was no question who was in charge here.

He'd been expecting Christian, Lindsay, and Campbell, but when Duncan entered the room, he saw half a dozen other people seated around the large conference table. Christian was at the head, of course, and Beck sent Duncan an apologetic glance before settling down in a seat next to Christian's. Lindsay and Campbell were already seated as well, and Duncan's only option was to squeeze in between two men he didn't know.

"Bob Cook, head of programming," the man to his left said when Duncan had scooted his chair in. He held out his hand, and Duncan shook it awkwardly. He was horrible with these types of situations. Duncan could work the front of the house flawlessly, chatting with diners and touching base with servers and hosts, and he'd never met a kitchen staff he couldn't charm within minutes. But formal situations like this one were different. Duncan's forte was casual conversation, and he didn't think there was going to be much of that here.

"Duncan Walters," he said, taking the man's hand.

"This is Andre Guestes. He's in charge of our test kitchens here at the network," Bob told him. Duncan dutifully shook Andre's hand as well, but he was saved from further introductions when Christian cleared his throat and started the meeting.

Someone put a sheaf of papers down in front of Duncan. His name was prominently featured in the text he was able to skim, and Duncan's hands twitched with the effort of not tearing into them. His impatience was one of his biggest faults, but he had the feeling opening the packet before Christian wanted him to would cause more trouble than it was worth.

Now that he was closer, Duncan could see Christian had a black eye and some pretty severe bruising around his nose. It looked painful.

"As most of you know, I had a bit of an accident on the court recently," Christian said, and the room laughed on cue as he motioned toward his face. Lindsay and Beck didn't join in, and Duncan couldn't tell from their blank expressions if it was because they were upset about him getting hurt or something else.

"We've been filming a week in advance this season, so we're covered for the next episode. The coming weeks pose a challenge, though. I can't go on air looking like this," Christian said. He turned his gaze on Duncan, and Duncan had to fight not to squirm in his seat. "That's where you come in, Mr. Walters."

Duncan didn't like where this was going, especially since Beck was no longer looking in his direction at all. He also didn't like the almost predatory gleam in Christian's eyes. "Call me Duncan, please," he said, hoping to take Christian's ego down a peg with the interruption. "Mr. Walters is my award-winning father."

It worked, from the scowl it earned him. "Duncan, then. Your public fight with Beck has garnered quite a bit of press in the last week. This latest situation doesn't help things." He broke eye contact with Duncan and smiled as he surveyed the rest of the people in the room. "His father is the one who did this. The man's clumsy with a racquet," Christian said conspiratorially, and Duncan's stomach rolled. The other shoe was about to drop.

"I'd like to propose a mutually beneficial arrangement, Duncan." Christian nodded to the stack of papers in front of Duncan, and Duncan took it as tacit approval to start going through them. The wording was formal and intricate, but from what Duncan could tell, it was a contract. "My doctor tells me it could be more than a month before I'm back to normal. Obviously, I can't appear on *King of the Kitchen* until the bruising and swelling goes down."

Christian's smile looked menacing, but Duncan couldn't tell if it was the effect of the black eye or if he always looked mean. "Beck has hosted the show plenty of times, but with me absent, viewers expect celebrity guests. He will take over my duties as host, and you'll be his guest host for the first week, Duncan."

"Christian, that—"

Christian cut Beck off with a raised hand. "I've already talked it over with Bob, and he agrees it's a good move. Lindsay?"

Lindsay's lips were pursed like she disapproved, but she nodded. "From a public relations perspective, it would really help put the rumors about the so-called feud to rest." She looked over at Beck and gave him a small smile before turning back to Christian. "And I agree you appearing on the show like that is a bad idea. We'd need to have the scriptwriters work in dialogue about the injury, and I think it's going to be too hard to pull it off without fueling more rumors."

"And him disappearing for a month won't?" Beck asked incredulously.

"No because we have a new format for the next month that will explain it perfectly. The studio will issue a press release that laughs off the injury as coming at a fortuitous time because we've had this special guest segment planned for months."

"No one is going to buy that," Beck deadpanned.

"They will, because the new format is genius," Andre put in. "You and Duncan have very different cooking styles. We'll be having you two go head-to-head reinventing a classic dish. We have two other chefs lined up for the rest of the month in case Duncan can't hack it on camera, but assuming he can, he'll be guesting all month."

That sounded interesting, Lindsay's not-so-subtle dig aside. Duncan kept flipping through the huge contract in front of him. Most of it centered around nondisclosure agreements and rules about what he could and couldn't say about anything he learned on the set of *King of the Kitchen* and at the studio itself. It was all pretty standard. He'd signed scarier things when he'd been at Kraft.

"You said this would be mutually beneficial," Duncan said as he put the contract down. "So far I only see how it benefits you."

Christian gave him an approving look that made Duncan feel a little dirty. He didn't want a shark like Christian to be impressed with him.

"Maybe you're more suited to the business world than your father after all, Duncan." He paused, but Duncan kept his mouth shut, not responding to the dig against his father. Christian's smile grew a bit more at that, and Duncan couldn't help but feel like he'd passed yet another of Christian's tests. "As I thought," he said cryptically.

"You'll be compensated for your time, of course. Rather generously. And there's also the intangible benefit of getting your name and face out there. You're already something of a hot commodity in the food world, but this exposure can ratchet that up. I wouldn't be surprised to see you get a cookbook deal out of this."

"Or a spin-off show," Bob said, sizing Duncan up. It made Duncan feel like a piece of beef on display.

"Back to the compensation," Duncan said, slouching in his chair a bit to make himself less visible. "Exactly how generous?"

Christian laughed. "You'll make more for the week in your contract than you would in a month of hopping around to different restaurants like you've been doing."

Duncan raised an eyebrow at the confidence in Christian's tone. While it was true he moved around a lot, he did pretty well for himself. It wasn't the salary he could pull down if he settled in at one of the restaurants, but it was enough to keep him in Converses and student loan payments. Mostly. If he ate almost all his meals for free at the restaurant.

"Ten thousand for one episode," Christian said, and Duncan couldn't stop his lips from parting in shock. That was insane.

Now Beck's designer suits made a lot more sense. Duncan turned to gape at him. "Is that what you make? Seriously?"

Beck shifted in his seat. "It's really not appropriate to—"

"No, he makes more. Plus bonuses," Lindsay interrupted. She seemed to delight in the glare Beck sent her way. "We have a very large fan base and some pretty big advertisers. The show is the network's biggest earner. Ten thousand is our standard guest-host rate."

"I'd advise you to take the offer," Bob said, leaning in to tap his pen against the contract. "Go ahead and take this to your attorney if you like, but everything in there is fair."

Duncan was tempted to sign the thing right there because he knew it would annoy Beck, but he resisted. He didn't have an attorney, and there was no way he would be taking it to his father's because Vincent would be apoplectic if he knew Duncan was going to appear on his rival's television show. Honestly, it was a bigger draw than the money. From Christian's reactions, Duncan was sure he knew that as well.

"When do you need an answer?"

Duncan could practically hear Beck's teeth grinding from halfway down the table. His ears were red, and he looked furious. "Is anyone going to ask *me* about this? Because it's a terrible idea."

Lindsay put her hand out to rest on his sleeve. "Beck, it's a good plan."

"It's a terrible plan! He's never been in front of the camera before. What if he's awful? What if he can't stay on script? And we're expecting the test kitchen to come up with all these recipes with, what, a week's notice?"

Andre cleared his throat. "We've been asked to sit that part out. We're resource-prep only on this one."

"This is where the new format comes in," Bob explained. "We'll give you a dish to recreate, and you and Duncan will have a week to come up with your take on it, and then you'll give your recipes to the test kitchen so it can be prepared for the show."

The room was quiet for a long beat before Beck spoke. "You're letting me design my own recipes? In my own style? No oversight and no vetoes?"

"For the next month, yes," Christian said.

Beck gave him a speculative look and then relaxed back into his chair, spreading his arms wide. "Then, I'm in."

Duncan wondered what was going on there. He thought Beck helped design all of the recipes on the show, but that exchange indicated he didn't. No wonder he'd reacted so badly when Duncan teased him about being Christian's minion. The thought made his stomach sour. He hadn't meant to actually insult Beck with his jokes, but Beck's overreaction made a lot more sense now.

"We need to start filming in three days. You can have until tomorrow morning to get us your answer, Duncan," Bob said. He gave Duncan a hearty pat on the back. "Looking forward to working with you, kid. Your dad's a legend. I've tried for years to get him to work with us."

Duncan held back his instinct to snarl at the familiar compliment. If there was one thing he hated more than being compared to his father, it was having someone use him as a way to get to Vincent. "He's going to hate this. Don't plan for any father-son bonding on your show."

Bob laughed. "We already have the family slot filled," he said, nodding between Christian and Beck. "You're the one I'm interested in wooing over to television now. You'll go over well with our target demographic."

Duncan felt uncomfortable under Bob's appreciative gaze, and he folded his arms across his stomach defensively.

"That would be women ages thirty to forty-five," Campbell clarified, and Duncan jumped a bit. He hadn't seen them come up, but all three of them were now behind his chair.

"Don't scare the new talent, Bob." Campbell squeezed Duncan's shoulder and offered him a genuine grin. "He's right, though. You're funny, personable, and not hard on the eyes. They're going to eat you up."

"Not hard on the eyes?" Duncan parroted. "Something you need to tell me?"

"Yes, your graphic T-shirts and gorgeous mud-brown eyes have converted me," Campbell said dryly. "Seriously, though, the test group we pitched this to last night loved the idea. They'd all been following the news about you and Beck in the tabloids. I think we're even going to be drawing in viewers who don't usually watch cooking shows."

"This is the perfect move to dispel all the gossip," Christian said.

"Until you and Beck start flirting on screen," Lindsay added. Beck elbowed her, but she grinned. "Oh, get over yourself. You're both consenting adults. Have a little fun. It'll be great for ratings." She pointed at Duncan and gave him a stern look. "Don't break his heart in the next month, okay? That's bad for on-screen chemistry."

Christian's lips twitched, and he shrugged when Beck turned to him, outrage all over his face. "You're a grown man. Outside of filming, what you two do is up to you."

Campbell gave Duncan's shoulder another squeeze before he and Lindsay filed out, taking Christian with them. Duncan looked around and realized he and Beck were the only ones left in the conference room.

"So that happened." Duncan pushed back from the table and gathered up his contract to stuff in the satchel he'd brought.

Beck waited until he was ready to leave the room before speaking. "I know you don't owe me anything, but I'd really like you to sign on for the show."

Duncan ducked his head to pull his satchel on. "I thought you couldn't stand the idea of working with me? You were sure quick to voice your disapproval there at the beginning."

Beck made a frustrated noise as they walked out of the conference room. "I just—I don't have anything against working with you, okay? But television isn't as easy as it looks. It's a lot of work."

"So it was concern for me wrecking your show's reputation, not a problem working with me?"

"Something like that," Beck muttered. He ran a hand through his hair, leaving the usually immaculate strands standing on end. Duncan liked the look on him. But that wasn't a surprise—Duncan liked *every* look on Beck.

"And what Lindsay said about us flirting? Is that something that's going to continue?" Duncan stopped, and Beck made it a few more steps down the hallway before he realized Duncan wasn't next to him anymore. "I'm on board with that, by the way."

"I'm not."

"Really?" Duncan drawled. He didn't buy it for a second.

"Really. You can barely stand me. You've already got the job—you don't need to pretend to be into me, no matter what Lindsay said."

Duncan frowned. "I really do like you, Beck. You're fun under all that propriety and snobbishness."

Beck huffed out a laugh. "You're a real charmer yourself."

Duncan sighed. There was no middle ground with Beck; they were either fighting like cats and dogs or sharing inside jokes, which was ridiculous, since they hadn't known each other long enough to have those. At least, they shouldn't have them, but Duncan had to acknowledge they definitely did. Something about being with Beck was instinctively easy. Duncan found himself enjoying the snark, even though it was sharper-edged than the banter he exchanged with John and his other friends.

"Look, I get that this is a great opportunity," Duncan said, hoping Beck could hear the sincerity in his voice. "I'm not doing *anything* to screw this up. Do you have any idea how much this will piss Vincent off? That alone is gold, and on top of it, I'm getting paid a freaking fortune compared to what I'd be making in a kitchen. So yeah, I'm all in. I'll sign the contract right now if that convinces you."

Duncan met Beck's gaze, the challenge hanging heavily between them, and Beck cracked the tiniest of smiles. He looked down and busied himself with packing up the notebooks and papers he'd brought, fidgeting with a pen.

Normally, he wouldn't pursue someone like Beck. Duncan preferred guys—and women—who were as averse to strings as he was. He'd only really known Beck Douglas for a week, but he could already tell Beck wasn't one of those easy flings. Beck was the kind of guy who wanted relationship discussions and Sundays in bed instead of quick fucks and nebulous promises to call later that neither Duncan nor his partner of the moment ever intended to follow through on.

Duncan was always given to dramatic moments, so he grabbed the contract out of his satchel and snatched the pen out of Beck's hand. He flipped to the last page and started to sign, but Beck's hand closed over his wrist, stopping him.

"Don't."

Duncan looked up questioningly, his heart thrumming in his chest. Don't what? Sign the contract? Flirt with Beck? Maybe Beck was right. Getting involved with him right now would be messy, and this contract would tie the two of them together for at least the next month.

Beck squeezed his wrist and let it go. "Don't sign it until you've read it. Have Campbell or someone else go through it too. Your father probably has lawyers on retainer. Use one of them. The network is looking out for itself, not you. Make sure it's a deal you want to take."

The tightness in Duncan's chest eased, replaced with a warm feeling. Beck was looking out for him. This was definitely a side of Beck he'd like to know. Beck was his own person, not the stereotype Duncan had cast him as. The more he got to know him, the more Duncan wanted to peel away layers and find out more.

He dropped the pen in Beck's breast pocket and leaned into Beck's space, hovering there for a long moment, silently asking permission. Duncan could be an aggressive dick sometimes, but he wasn't going to take this choice away from Beck. He also knew Beck wasn't the type to act impulsively or take chances, and this might be the only way to shock him into taking things to the next level. Duncan put the ball squarely in Beck's court.

He was close enough to see Beck's pupils dilate and his Adam's apple bob as he swallowed. Just when Duncan was about to back off, Beck closed the last bit of a gap between them and kissed him.

It wasn't the light, teasing kiss Duncan had been expecting. Beck's lips were firm and insistent, and there was no trace of the vulnerability or hesitancy that had shown on his face moments before. Apparently when Beck decided to do something, he was all in. Duncan could relate to that.

A nearby office door opened with a bang, sending the two of them flying apart. Duncan felt a hot blush spread across his cheeks. He hadn't let himself get caught in a compromising position like this for years. He'd managed to forget they weren't alone. They were standing in Beck's workplace, and it was likely going to be his own soon, too. Temporarily, at least. Duncan needed to remember that.... He wasn't here to make out with Beck. He was here to work.

Duncan whirled around, but the person who'd come out hadn't seemed to notice anything was amiss. The janitor was going around the rooms emptying the trashcans. He headed into the conference room and started clearing the debris from the breakfast Duncan and most of the other meeting participants had been too keyed up to eat.

Duncan took a breath and chanced a look at Beck, who was flushing even worse than he was.

"Let's not do that on the air," Duncan joked weakly.

"Ratings would soar," Beck said hoarsely, and both of them burst into laughter.

They headed toward the elevators. Duncan assumed Beck was at work for the day, and he himself was planning to go home and catch a few hours of sleep.

"Listen, maybe we should—" Duncan began.

"Do you want to get lunch?"

Duncan blinked at Beck's interruption. He'd been about to tell him they should be careful about workplace flirting, especially since Beck seemed so hung up on being proper and professional all the time. But this was good. Better than good.

"Later, I mean," Beck said, and he sounded nervous. Was Beck nervous? The thought made Duncan grin as Beck continued to babble. "Obviously. It's barely breakfast time. But do you want to meet up around one or so? I'm in meetings until then, but I don't have to be at Brix to start signing for deliveries until three."

"Sure," Duncan said, his lips curved into a lazy grin. "Somewhere around here, or do you want to hit up a place near Brix? Or I could whip something up at my place."

Beck's expression soured, which was the opposite of what Duncan had been going for with the teasing invitation.

"Duncan, I—maybe you got the wrong idea."

Duncan raised an eyebrow at him. "You mean when you kissed me? What sort of idea was I supposed to get out of that?"

Beck rubbed a hand over his neck and looked away for a second before meeting Duncan's gaze again. "Can you be serious for once?"

"I wasn't aware lunch was a serious meal. My mistake. No more joking here."

Beck sighed. "Forget it."

This time Duncan was the one reaching out and grabbing Beck to stop him from walking away, a juxtaposition of the first two times they'd met. "Wait. I'm sorry. I'm not good at this, okay?"

Beck looked unimpressed. "I should have known better. It's not like I hadn't heard about your reputation."

"My reputation?"

"For sleeping with food groupies. I thought this might be different."

It was. God, it was. Duncan never mixed business with pleasure. He'd learned that lesson the hard way, and he'd been scrupulous about it ever since. The culinary world was pretty small, truth be told, and he couldn't afford to make enemies or alienate potential coworkers or employers because he couldn't keep his dick in his pants.

But this was different. He was attracted to Beck. Ridiculously so. But getting to know him and hanging out with him was more important than sleeping with him, and Duncan didn't want to mess that up.

"Beck, stop. I wasn't inviting you to my place for sex." Duncan blushed harder than he had when the janitor had walked in on them.

That stopped Beck dead in his tracks. His mouth hung open a little. "You weren't?"

"No! I thought we might have more fun eating in because it means we can just be us. We don't have to worry about cameras and rumors. I swear, that was it. I'm not going to jump your bones the second you walk in the door. Give me some credit here. Besides, I don't fool around with people I work with. It's too messy."

Beck still looked skeptical, but he nodded. "All right. I'll see you at one. No bones will be jumped."

Duncan couldn't help himself. He snickered at the turn of phrase, and Beck cracked a smile, too, before waving and heading off down the hallway.

He looked at his watch and grimaced. It was barely eight thirty in the morning, and instead of going back to bed like he'd planned, he was going to have to pry Sadie and Corbin out of bed and put himself at their mercy for advice about how to ignore this growing crush of his.

He'd better stop for coffee and donuts on the way.

Chapter EIGHT

A TWELVE-HOUR workday was a long one no matter what your profession. But twelve hours on your feet in a hot and often crowded kitchen? That was a special kind of torture.

Especially with Duncan by his side. Beck had done his best to curb his too-long glances and flirting, but it seemed like Duncan was doubling his efforts in response. He'd been driving Beck crazy all day, and Beck doubted Duncan even realized it. That was the worst part. It wasn't just Beck he'd been joking around with—he'd been that way with the entire prep kitchen staff. Kiss or no kiss, his interest in Beck didn't seem any different from his interest in everyone else at the network, and that stung.

He watched Duncan pull his sweaty T-shirt away from his skin, revealing a trail of dark hair leading down to his obscenely tight jeans. Duncan sniffed at it, making a face. "It's going to be a fun El ride home," he said darkly.

Beck snorted. "We have showers in the staff locker room. There's a supply of chef's whites down there too."

They weren't the first chefs to burn the midnight oil at the studio. Beck had made use of the showers downstairs multiple times, mostly when he was too exhausted to make it home after a day of episode planning and messing around in the test kitchen until the wee hours, like today. A lot of the celebrity chefs let their sous-chefs do all the testing and recipe development, but Beck was dead set against that. He'd helped plan the majority of *King of the Kitchen*'s recipes for the last four years, and he'd be damned if he was going to stop now he was getting to cook the kind of food he actually wanted to.

Cooking the prop food for filming? That was different. He was happy to let some culinary drone do all the work on that. But the recipes? Even the ones he wasn't proud of—which would be most of the things they cooked on the show, actually—were 100 percent his. He took his job seriously. Beck had never really wanted to be in the television business, but he was damned if he was going to settle for being the talent. He was more than a pretty face. Maybe after this set of challenges with Duncan, viewers would get to see that.

"Chef's whites?" Duncan asked, scowling. "Why the fuck do you wear those here? It's not like you have to worry about health code violations or what diners think of you in the test kitchen."

"A lot of the sous-chefs are right out of culinary school," Beck said with a shrug. "I think it makes them feel more comfortable if they're dressed in the traditional whites."

He didn't wear them when he was testing, but he understood why people would want to. Cooking was a messy business, and he'd ruined many a set of clothes thanks to grease spatters and splashing sauces. There was only so much an apron could cover.

Duncan snorted and shook his head. "I wouldn't figure a cooking channel would be so formal. I mean, they don't even make food for people to eat! It's like the tree falling in the forest. If you don't feed people, are you actually a chef?"

"You're not as funny as you think you are. Don't be an ass."

Duncan followed him down the dark hallway, laughing. "That's pretty much an admission that I am, you know. Funny," he elaborated when Beck raised an eyebrow in question.

Beck didn't have the patience to wait for the elevator, and the locker room was only three floors down anyway. They could take the stairs.

He and Duncan hadn't had any time together that wasn't spent working since their lunch a few days ago. He was beginning to curse himself for not falling into Duncan's bed when he'd had the chance. This whole waiting thing was crap. If Duncan was really only interested in a one-night stand, then all Beck was doing was delaying the inevitable. He needed to trust Duncan—if he said he was all in and he wanted to try dating, then Beck should take him at his word. He wasn't doing either of them any favors by doubting him.

Prepping for the new show segments had eaten into what little free time Beck had, and the result was he hadn't been to the gym all week. He ached to hit the treadmill and run until his mind went blank, or maybe slip into the pool and swim laps until his lungs were screaming. Instead he settled for taking out some of his pent-up energy on the stairs a few times a day.

As a bonus, running the steps helped him manage his sexual frustration, which had to be at an all-time high. The worst part was Duncan really had no idea how provocative he could be purely by being himself—even when he wasn't flirting and playing at being seductive, Beck wanted to push him up against the nearest hard surface.

He took a breath and forced the thought out of his mind. Stairs. That would help.

"You go ahead and go down. It's on level six, and there's a sign as soon as you get onto the floor. It shouldn't be locked. I'm going to run upstairs for a minute, and then I'll join you."

Being in the locker room with Duncan was the last thing Beck wanted, but avoiding it would call even more attention to his growing attraction to Duncan. Beck felt shy about admitting how caged he'd been feeling, especially when a lot of it was due to Duncan's presence. Duncan seemed oblivious to Beck's stupid schoolboy crush on him. Or else he was being chivalrous and ignoring it for Beck's sake.

God, he hoped that wasn't it. How humiliating.

Though to be fair, Duncan really didn't have it in him to be selfless. If he thought he had any sort of dirt on Beck, he'd use it to tease him mercilessly. Small favors, Beck figured. The fact that he wasn't getting teased about his crush must mean Duncan didn't know about it.

He hadn't mentioned last week's kiss, and Beck hadn't either. He chalked it up to the heat of the moment. If it had been more, surely Duncan would have said something about it later, right?

"Do you want me to come with you?" Duncan asked, poised on the top step, his expression expectant.

"No," Beck said, "it'll only take a second. Go ahead and get started. I'll show you where the reserve whites are after we shower."

Which meant he'd be treated to a view of Duncan's naked chest, but it couldn't be helped. The showers weren't set up with any sort of shelves, just hooks for towels. The shower curtains were flimsy, so the towels ended up getting half-soaked most of the time; any clothes hung on the hook would be even worse off.

The studio provided towels and soap, but the brand was floral and made Beck sneeze. He tossed Duncan his locker key. "Towels are on the shelf, and you can help yourself to my toiletry kit if you like."

The offer had nothing to do with Beck wanting to know what his soap smelled like on Duncan. Nope. Not at all. It was the friendly thing to do, saving Duncan from smelling like someone's elderly grandmother.

"I could wait—"

Nope. Beck definitely didn't want to suffer through showering next to Duncan, knowing he was naked and wet and only a thin shower curtain away.

"Nah, you said you felt gross. Go ahead and shower. I'll be back down in a few."

Duncan studied him for a long second like he was going to protest again, but then he shrugged and trotted down the stairs toward the sixth floor.

Finally.

Beck took the first two flights at a measured pace, in case his steps echoed and gave him away. But as soon as he made it up to the ninth floor and was reasonably certain Duncan couldn't hear him anymore, he let loose.

The soles of his wingtips weren't great for running stairs, but he made do. He kept one hand on the railing, and it was enough to stop him from face-planting every time he slipped. He made it up nine flights before his thighs started to burn, and the exhilaration of getting his blood pumping sent him roaring up ten more. He'd have to turn around in another floor since the top floor was locked, but it felt good to be out of breath. Focusing on the burn in his muscles and the drag of his breath kept him from thinking too much about Duncan, and it was a welcome relief.

The situation Beck was in was entirely his own fault. Everything between him and Duncan was a competition, and it seemed they were forever trying to one-up each other, even now that the animosity was mostly gone. He'd let himself settle into an ease with Duncan he felt with very few other people, and it was going to lead to disaster.

It was hard to adjust to being attracted to someone every bit as stubborn and challenge-oriented as he was. Beck hadn't ever analyzed his dating choices before, but what he felt when he was around Duncan was so different that it wasn't hard to see he'd gravitated toward lovers who would let him be the dominant partner. Not that he'd ever flaunted that over them—he hadn't. Beck was devoted to making sure he and his boyfriends were on equal footing, but he could see in hindsight that while he'd considered them equals, his past boyfriends had all had a tendency to want the same things Beck did. There hadn't been the same fire he had with Duncan, and he and Duncan weren't even dating.

It was ridiculous, is what it was. He was half-crazy over a man who barely considered him a friend. Sure, they were great at bantering and flirting. It even carried over into rehearsals, and everyone had been pleased to see Beck ad-libbing and keeping up seamlessly with Duncan's antics in the run-through. He had no doubt it would go just as smoothly during filming tomorrow.

But professional camaraderie was all this was to Duncan. The way he was steadfastly ignoring any mention of their kiss proved that. And one thing everyone agreed on was that Beck Douglas was the consummate professional. The argument with Duncan that had started this entire mess was the exception to that rule, and he wasn't going to let the way Duncan got under his skin hurt his career.

Besides, once the show aired next week, he and Duncan wouldn't have to be seen together out in public anymore. The official PR story Lindsay's office was working up would be that they'd been meeting to plan Duncan's guest spot on *King of the Kitchen*, so once that was over, there would be no reason for the two of them to see each other anymore.

If you didn't count the fact that apparently they shared most of the same friends and a lot of the same interests. Along with Beck's growing attraction to Duncan, and the way he felt at ease around him.

Which Beck didn't count, because that way lay madness. He didn't have time for another stair sprint, and if he thought too much about all the reasons he and Duncan should still see each other after tomorrow, then he'd undo all the good he did with the first set.

Beck trotted down the last flight of stairs, getting his breath back. He knew he looked a mess, sweaty and flushed and very obviously coming off some sort of physical exertion. Hopefully, Duncan was already in the shower and wouldn't see him.

He could hear the water running when he opened the door to the men's locker room, and a bit of the tension eased out of his shoulders at the sound. His locker was closed, but his keys were on the counter by the sink, so he opened it up and grabbed a fresh set of clothes to drop on the bench for afterward. He detoured to the supply closet for a pair of chef's whites for Duncan, guessing at his size. He hoped Duncan didn't think it was creepy Beck had checked him out enough to be able to make an educated guess.

A *very* educated guess, thanks to how tight Duncan wore his jeans and T-shirts.

Beck sighed and ran a hand through his sweaty hair, pushing it back from his face. He had to get through the next few weeks, and then he didn't need to have any professional contact with Duncan. He could go back to the way his life had been before a two-minute fight with Duncan had turned it upside down. He'd have time for the gym again, and probably even a few hours a week to spare for recipe writing. That would have been enough a few weeks ago, but now it felt empty. He'd rather spend that time bantering with Duncan, writing recipes with Duncan while leaning over his shoulder and criticizing every addition.

"Was that you coming in, Beck?" Duncan called from the showers.

Beck shook off his uncharacteristic introspection and tossed the chef's whites on the bench next to his own change of clothes.

"Yeah, I put something for you to wear on the bench out here." A thought struck him, and he flushed. "No underwear or socks, though. Sorry. The studio isn't quite that thorough."

Duncan's reply had Beck stumbling as he eased his way out of his trousers. "Eh, who says I was wearing any to start with?"

Christ. That was not a mental picture Beck needed.

He stripped out of the rest of his clothes without further incident and grabbed a towel. He'd have to make do with the floral soap since he wasn't about to ask Duncan to pass him his soap through the curtain.

The shower room steamed, billows clouding the small space that held three shower stalls, all separated by curtains that didn't quite reach the floor. Duncan's bare feet made Beck's heart skip a beat. He shouldn't be turned on by something as innocuous as *feet*, for God's sake. It was like being fourteen all over again, averting his gaze in the high school locker room after gym class.

Beck had barely started the water before his curtain was yanked back, revealing Duncan wearing nothing but a lascivious grin.

"I'm not misjudging this, am I?" Duncan asked as he crowded into the small stall. Beck shuffled back a few steps until his back touched the cold wall.

Uncertainty flitted through Duncan's eyes, but he shut the curtain behind him and held Beck's gaze. "You're into this, right? Because you've been driving me insane all day, and I really want to get my mouth on your dick."

"I thought you never mixed business with pleasure."

Duncan grinned and shrugged. "I don't, but I'm also fond of the adage 'never say never.' I'm awash in contradictions. So, what do you say?"

Beck made a strangled noise, his eyes wide as he watched Duncan close the small distance between them. Was this actually happening, or had he fallen on the stairs and this was some coma dream?

Duncan's hands hovered a few inches away from Beck's shoulders. "Beck?"

Beck swallowed hard and nodded.

"I'm going to need actual words. Consent is the new sexy and all that," Duncan said, his tone back to its usual indolent confidence.

Of course Duncan would be his normal irreverent self even during sex.

"Yes," Beck managed. His throat felt dry, like he'd been running lines all day instead of cooking.

Duncan was on him before he'd finished saying the word. Duncan was warm from his shower, and he felt delicious pressed against Beck's body. Beck had been right about how Duncan would smell after using his body wash and shampoo too. Duncan smelling like him was heady. Beck indulged himself burying his face in Duncan's neck and taking a long sniff, licking water droplets off the warm, firm skin while he was there.

"Yeah, this is definitely a good idea," Duncan muttered.

"The best," Beck answered before he sucked a mark onto Duncan's neck.

Duncan moaned, tilting his head to the side to give Beck better access. Beck was halfway into another bruise before he realized how stupid that was. They'd both be on camera tomorrow, and the makeup department would give them hell if they showed up with hickeys.

Beck pulled away with a regretful frown, diving in for a kiss when Duncan furrowed his brow at him in question.

"No marks."

Duncan made a disappointed sound and nipped at Beck's bottom lip before wiggling away and twining his fingers through the wet hair at the nape of Beck's neck, urging him down again. "Yes, marks. Duncan likes marks."

And God, he was even sexy when he was talking about himself in third person. How was that possible?

Duncan's heavy-lidded look caused Beck to shiver, and his cock twitched eagerly against Duncan's hip.

"No marks unless you want to be the one to explain to the makeup department why they have to use a metric ton of concealer on you," Beck said, grinning when Duncan's eyes shot open in understanding.

"Right. So. No marks where anyone can see," Duncan said with a nod. He followed it up by ducking his head and licking Beck's chest, which made Beck stumble and flail against the wall in surprise. Duncan snickered, his fingers snaking their way down Beck's body until they were cupping his ass, kneading the flesh like dough.

Beck had always enjoyed sex, and he loved giving pleasure as much as he liked receiving it. In his experience, though, sex had been mutually fun but not playful. Easy, but serious…. He should have known it would be different with Duncan.

Duncan approached sex like he approached everything else— full of energy and determined to wring out every last bit of enjoyment he could. His hands were as talented as Beck had imagined they'd be when he'd studied Duncan's knife skills. He personified animal grace when dancing around the kitchen, and he brought that same rhythm and innate sense of movement to the act of sex.

In short, Duncan was killing him, and they hadn't really gotten started.

Things like this didn't happen to Beck. His life was planned out to the nth degree. There wasn't time for spontaneous sex or one-night stands.

Which begged the question—was that what this was? A bit of stress relief after a long day in the kitchen, coming on the heels of a few weeks of flirting and fighting? Beck wasn't wired like that, but he was loath to stop Duncan to ask. He was afraid of what the answer might be. Duncan personified freewheeling laissez-faire—hell, he couldn't even commit to a kitchen and stay on at the same restaurant for more than a few months. He was probably the same way with his relationships.

Could he do this if it was just a lark? Beck bit back an oath when Duncan worked his way back up to Beck's mouth and started kissing him with renewed vigor. Duncan's hands were everywhere, and they were amazing.

Yes, was the short answer. There was no way Beck was going to call a halt now. He'd deal with the fallout later, and hope against hope it didn't affect their on-screen chemistry for the filming tomorrow.

They'd only been at it a few minutes, and Beck was already on the verge of coming. Duncan's lithe hands were a menace, and his mouth should be declared a goddamn national treasure. He worked Beck over with frightening skill, considering how well he seemed to be able to intuit all of Beck's favorite spots.

With anyone else, he'd give himself over to the pleasure and let himself come. But this wasn't just anyone. This was Duncan, and Beck knew Duncan would be smug and annoying if he managed to make Beck come like a freight train with a bit of kissing and rubbing.

Beck tilted his body away from Duncan's a bit, which didn't help since Duncan followed the motion with his hand and wrapped his long fingers around Beck's cock.

Beck broke their kiss, leaning his head back against the tile. "Duncan—"

Duncan smirked at him. "Have something different in mind?" He stroked up Beck's shaft, and Beck's hips jerked of their own volition, betraying his eagerness. Duncan swirled his thumb over the head, his expression thoughtful. "Hmm. I did say I'd been dying to get my mouth on you, didn't I? Because I have been, all day."

Beck bit back a sobbing moan when Duncan stroked him again. It seriously wouldn't take much more before he'd be coming.

"Though maybe we should save that for when you have a bit more stamina," Duncan said knowingly, the amused curve of his lips getting more pronounced when Beck shuddered through a particularly rough stroke.

"You're sure of yourself, aren't you?" Beck bit out the words, his teeth clenched to hold back his groans.

Duncan laughed, looking absolutely delighted. "We'll see. I don't suppose you'd want to wager on it? A friendly bet," he said, ending on a down stroke and wrapping his thumb and forefinger around the base of Beck's cock, holding him tightly. Beck didn't want to admit how much that helped.

"Is there anything you don't make into a joke?"

Duncan shook his head. "Nope."

He held Beck's gaze for a few more beats, before Beck broke. He really wanted Duncan's mouth on him. "Fine. What are your terms?"

Duncan's grin was electric. "You and Christian want me in a suit tomorrow. I want to wear my usual T-shirt and jeans. You come before, say, six minutes have passed, and I get to wear whatever I want. You make it that long, and I'll let you dress me up like a Ken doll."

Beck choked on a laugh. Duncan certainly did keep things interesting. Normally six minutes wouldn't be a problem, but Beck had been amped up all day, and the teasing in the shower had him more than a little aroused. It would be a challenge, but everything with Duncan was, right?

"Fine."

Duncan didn't need any further encouragement. He released Beck's dick and stepped back out of the shower spray while he unfastened the battered waterproof watch and set a timer. Apparently he was dead serious about this.

His confident swagger was firmly in place, which had Beck worried. A few seconds later, Duncan was on his knees in front of him, and Beck was splayed out against the tile again, holding on for dear life while Duncan did his best to suck Beck's brains out through his dick.

There was no finesse to Duncan's technique. No teasing touches or kitten licks. He jumped in full force, swallowing most of Beck's length down without warning.

Shit.

This was going to be an agonizing and wonderful six minutes.

He had to make it. If Duncan chose his own clothes for tomorrow's episode, he would no doubt appear in a T-shirt with some pithy—if not downright obscene—slogan and jeans that would have Christian frothing at the mouth.

How hard could it be to stave off coming for six minutes? Normally, Beck had no problem with stamina. Then again, normally he didn't have Duncan Walters on his knees in front of him, either.

Beck held back a whine when Duncan's tongue laved over the head of his cock. Water beaded on his eyelashes, and he blinked it away so he could get a better view of Duncan on his knees on the shower floor.

Christ on a crutch, what had he been *thinking*? No, scratch that. He hadn't been thinking. He'd been preoccupied by the thought of what Duncan's gorgeous lips would look like, swollen and cherry-red as they stretched around his dick.

The sight was every bit as enticing as he'd imagined, if not more so. Beck's cock throbbed. That line of thinking was not helping his current situation.

Duncan seemed to know exactly how seeing him on his knees staring up at him was affecting Beck.

Beck groaned, the sound loud even against the backdrop of the water beating down on the tiles. He rested his head against the wall and closed his eyes, more out of self-defense than anything. Duncan looked obscene.

Duncan's tongue twirled across his head and dipped teasingly into his slit, and Beck choked on his own saliva.

Fuck, Duncan really was trying to kill him. Beck looked down again and watched as Duncan picked up the pace, his head bobbing furiously now. He held Beck's gaze, and the challenge was clear in the sparkling glint of Duncan's eyes. How much longer before he could come? Duncan's watch was on the floor next to him, and Beck squinted at it, trying to make out the numbers upside down. It didn't work.

He'd guess a good three minutes had passed, but he also wouldn't be particularly surprised to find it had only been one.

Beck gritted his teeth, his toes curling against the tile floor after a hard suck sent shivers of need up his spine. He felt his orgasm building again, hot and heavy in his belly. This was going to end quickly if he didn't do something, but fuck if he knew what he could do to take his mind off what Duncan was doing.

Duncan hummed, and the added sensation of the vibration made Beck squirm. Duncan glanced down at his watch and flashed four fingers at Beck. Did that mean four minutes had passed or four minutes were left? It had to be the latter. Beck could do this. Four minutes was nothing. Four minutes was—

He slipped deeper into Duncan's mouth, and Beck swore he could feel the soft skin of Duncan's throat rubbing against the head of his cock. Sweet fucking *Jesus*. No one had ever taken him that deep before, and Beck's balls tightened convulsively. His thighs trembled with the effort of staying upright. Beck was one good suck away from losing control, and he knew Duncan could tell.

Beck scoured his mind for a distraction. *Any* distraction. He thought about the old joke about guys going through baseball statistics in their heads for stamina. He'd never been so regretful he wasn't a sports fan.

Sauces. He could do that. What are the five French mother sauces in alphabetical order? He latched onto the train of thought like a lifeline, straining to remember any facts or figures that could distract him from the ridiculous things Duncan was doing with his tongue right now.

Béchamel. His hands clenched so tight he could feel his nails digging grooves into his palms. Roux whisked with milk or cream, or any dairy, really. He'd been experimenting with using goat's milk and olive oil instead of the traditional cow's milk and butter, and—

Duncan hummed again, bringing Beck's mental vacation to an abrupt halt. *Jesus.* Duncan raised an eyebrow in challenge and held up three fingers.

What was next alphabetically? It was a challenge to think because usually the sauces weren't arranged that way. Concentrating on that helped back down some of Beck's urgency. Espagnole. That was next. Dark roux as a thickener, added to dark stock like veal or beef, browned mirepoix, and tomato puree.

Oh God. Duncan cupped Beck's balls, tugging on them a little too roughly, sending sparks of sharp pleasure up Beck's spine. Two fingers this time. Two minutes. Beck could do this.

Next was… fuck, he couldn't remember. Beck's concentration slipped as Duncan pursed his lips into a tight ring, gripping the shaft of Beck's cock even harder as he slid his mouth up and down its length. *Oh, fuck. Fuck, fuck, fuck.*

Hollandaise! That was next. The only mother sauce that didn't involve roux, since it was thickened by an egg yolk and butter emulsion, with citrus juice to brighten it, and heavy cream. It was the sauce on the eggs Benedict Duncan had sent out to him at that ratty diner years ago. A lot of restaurants used powdered hollandaise sauce because the real thing was so delicate, but now that he knew Duncan, he doubted that's what it had been.

Duncan's fingers moved from caressing Beck's balls to pressing against the skin behind them. Beck writhed against the wall, simultaneously trying to move away from Duncan's talented fingers, and get closer. He couldn't take much more of this. His skin tingled unbearably, the pleasure so great it almost hurt. He was close to the point of no return, but he was determined not to let Duncan win. Especially not with barely a minute left.

Okay. Sauces. Velouté. Right? No. There was one before that. Sauce Tomat was next. Was he forgetting one? The flat of Duncan's tongue swept over the head of Beck's dick again and Beck's knees actually buckled this time. If not for Duncan grabbing his hips and steadying him, Beck would have sprawled on the shower floor. Fuck it, did the order really matter?

Sauce Tomat was one of the simplest French mother sauces. Tomatoes cooked down with pork and aromatics, thickened with a roux.

Beck struggled to keep his eyes open and glued to Duncan's watch even though he couldn't see it well enough to read the time. For all he knew, Duncan's countdown was just a way to psych him out. He could be giving him false cues for a competitive edge. It seemed like the kind of thing Duncan would do.

It had to be down to seconds now. *Fuck, fuck, fuck.* Which sauce hadn't he done yet? Velouté. Light roux for that one. Whisked with a clear stock, like fish or chicken, for a sauce that was velvety smooth and tasted like the protein used.

Ugh, this wasn't helping anymore. Thinking of velvety sauces made Beck focus on how slick and soft Duncan's mouth was.

He was scrambling for more things to list when Duncan's watch alarm chimed, marking the end of the six minutes. He was coming before the last of the chime faded, his entire body shuddering as the rigid tension he'd been holding back flooded out of him with his orgasm.

Seconds after Beck's dick stopped twitching, Duncan pulled him down to his knees on the shower floor. Beck went willingly, though he wasn't so far gone he didn't have a brief moment of panic at the thought of sitting on the communal shower floor. Still, he sank down obligingly. His bones felt like jelly, and the cleaning crew was in here every night anyway.

Duncan was so hard the head of his cock was stretched and shiny, veins standing out along his length. His chest was flushed a mottled red, either from the heat of the shower or arousal, Beck didn't know which. It hardly mattered. There would be time later to learn the details of Duncan's body. For right now, Beck was desperate to get his hands on him and return some of the pleasure Duncan had wrung out of him over the last agonizing minutes.

Duncan seemed on board with that plan, his body bowing up off the floor when Beck wrapped his hand around Duncan's straining cock. His own fingers still felt tingly from his orgasm, but he flexed them to bring back feeling—making Duncan groan out loud at the tight squeeze—and started stroking him off.

It was exhilarating, since Beck had no idea how Duncan liked to be touched. That exploration was always fun when his partner was as responsive as Duncan. His moans and gasps left no doubt Beck was on the right track.

Duncan started moving impatiently, trying to speed up Beck's strokes. Beck leaned forward and kissed him, shuddering as he tasted himself on Duncan's tongue. Letting Duncan suck him off without a condom went against everything he'd ever been taught about safe sex, but in the moment, Beck hadn't cared. He felt a little guilty about it now, even though he knew he was clean. He hadn't even checked that Duncan was. God, he hadn't lost his head like that since he'd been a teenager.

Duncan pressed into the kiss, letting Beck's tongue sweep into his mouth as he kept thrusting his hips up into Beck's fist.

Beck kept his grip firm as Duncan moved, his free hand bracing against the floor so they didn't slide on the wet tile as Duncan pushed into the tight ring of his fingers, his hips jerking. Floating high on his own orgasm—and victory—Beck deepened the kiss and rolled his wrist to graze his thumbnail lightly over the head of Duncan's dick on the next upstroke, pulling a strangled moan from Duncan's throat.

Duncan didn't last long after that, an irony Beck decided he would manfully not point out. A few strokes later, Duncan leaned heavily against him, pressing Beck into the tiles as he came. Beck let the movement carry them both over onto the floor, germs be damned. Even after the brief amount of time he'd spent kneeling on the ground, his knees were aching, and he wondered how Duncan had stood it for all that time. Between the unforgiving floor and the six-minute blow job, Duncan had to be aching like mad.

"My suit is from the thrift store," Duncan said inanely, his voice raspy. How positively like him to avoid admitting he'd lost. At least he was still honoring the terms of the bet. "And I don't wear ties."

Beck smirked, satisfaction flowing through him at the thought of seeing Duncan in a suit again. It wouldn't be as dashing as the tuxedo he'd worn to the Brix opening, but if it even came close then Beck very much approved.

"Fine, but don't think I'll forget. You're not getting out of this. If you show up for filming tomorrow without the suit, I'll have a production assistant go to your apartment and get it. Don't think I won't."

Duncan laughed hoarsely. "I can't believe you made it," he said, rubbing his jaw. "I'm impressed."

Beck hadn't technically showered, but he struggled to his feet and turned the steaming spray off anyway. His fingers were pruned and his skin felt sensitive and overheated. Washing could wait until tomorrow morning. He'd rinsed off the worst of the sweat, at least.

Duncan accepted the hand Beck offered him, and Beck hauled him up off the floor. He tossed a towel to Duncan and then wrapped another around his waist.

"So where are these illustrious chef's whites? I told Corbin I'd meet up with him after he closes at Brix tonight. There's a poker game somewhere."

Beck's stomach fell. So this was a one-off.

"I left them on the bench for you."

"Thanks. I'm going to catch hell for showing up looking like this, but the guys will get a good laugh out of it." He ran the towel roughly over his hair and then started drying himself quickly. "So do—"

"Hey, I never actually got to wash, so I'm going to do that," Beck interrupted. He really didn't want to hear about how Duncan planned to spend the rest of his night. He dropped his towel and stepped back into the shower. No reason to make this more awkward than it already was, right? Avoidance was always the answer. "I'll see you tomorrow? We're in the studio at one, but we'll have a read-through of the script and a dry run, with switch-outs starting at nine."

"Are you—"

Beck turned on the water, the rush drowning out whatever clichéd letdown Duncan had been about to use on him. Beck could handle being a one-night stand, but he couldn't handle being fed some line like he was one of Duncan's groupies.

Duncan's inscrutable expression was the last thing Beck saw before he closed the shower curtain, cutting off his view into the locker room. It was cowardly, but it was better than watching Duncan walk away.

God, he was an idiot. He could only hope it didn't make things strained between them on the show.

Chapter NINE

"THANKS FOR tuning in to *King of the Kitchen* today! We're going to be switching things up here for the next month. Our executive producer, Bob Starden, is here to tell you about it," Beck said, smiling woodenly at the camera with the blinking light.

Duncan watched from offstage, waiting for his cue to go on. Something was off about Beck today. Maybe it was nerves about the new show format. He'd flubbed his lines more times than Duncan could count on the read-through earlier this morning, and he'd actually dropped a pan during rehearsal. He'd never seen Beck with anything but rock-steady hands before, so something must be up.

This was why he should never break his no-sleeping-with-colleagues rule. One night of sex wasn't worth weeks of awkwardness. He chanced a glance over at Beck, who even managed to look gorgeous when he was flustered. And damn, the sex had been great. Maybe Duncan would be willing to do it again, which was mind-blowing since Duncan studiously avoided anything that even casually looked like a relationship.

Lindsay gave him a hard nudge, sending Duncan sprawling forward a few steps. He looked up, startled, when he realized Bob was motioning to him from the set. He must have zoned out for his entire introduction. Shit.

Duncan trotted forward, pulling at the front of his suit jacket. He'd skirted the letter of their agreement, wearing the suit but pairing it with a favorite T-shirt, both for comfort and to give him a bit more confidence. He was out of his element enough filming a television show—he damn well wasn't going to do it without his security blanket.

Beck had taken one look at the shirt and scoffed, but Lindsay had appreciated it. Even Bob had laughed. Duncan had left his sports coat unfastened so the graphic was visible: a silhouette of a pig with the caption "Bacon is murder. Tasty, tasty murder."

"Thanks for joining us, Duncan," Bob said, reaching out to shake his hand.

"Happy to be here," Duncan answered, keeping his smile wide and easy. If he focused on Bob and Beck, he could almost forget the camera. "I'm excited to be working with Beck on *King of the Kitchen* since I've been a fan of the show for years." He ignored Beck's quiet snicker, the first sign of actual life from Beck he'd heard all day.

"That's always good to hear," Bob said after a beat when Beck didn't respond. "So we've explained to the audience that you and Beck will be facing off each week, reinventing a classic dish. What we haven't told them yet is they will be the ones voting on the winners—and that voting is going to aid some very special causes. You'll be letting your checkbooks do the voting each week. Duncan?"

Duncan steeled himself with a deep breath and faced the camera. Lindsay and Campbell had stationed themselves on either side of it, and Duncan relaxed in relief. They were geniuses. He grinned at them. He had this.

"As Bob said, we'll be competing to raise money for our charities. I've worked with Healthy U Foundation for years, and I'm proud to be representing them here today. They work with at-risk inner-city children from kindergarten through high school, helping them learn about making healthy food choices with partnerships in schools and some really fabulous summer camps, where kids get to learn how to not only prepare healthy foods, but also get to grow some of their own."

"You've worked at a few of those camps, haven't you, Duncan?" Bob asked.

They'd edit in a montage of photos of Duncan at various Healthy U events and camps after filming, so Duncan turned to Bob and answered him directly, knowing it didn't matter if he was looking at the camera or not.

"I have, but only on the cooking side of things. Most people hear 'microbiologist' and think I'll be good at growing things, but most of my experience with that involves petri dishes. Pretty much everything I know about gardening has come from sitting in on sessions at Healthy U. It's a wonderful charity that has done so much good work here in the city. And the kids love learning about urban gardening. It's amazing introducing kids to fresh vegetables and seeing how much they enjoy eating the things they've cooked."

Bob slapped him on the back, using the motion to turn him back toward the camera gently. Duncan took the hint and looked up, smiling at Campbell and Lindsay again.

"I think most of our viewers are already familiar with the charity Beck is competing for. It's something you've been active in for quite a while, and we've had segments on the show about it before," Bob said.

"Yes, I'm competing for the Danowski Foundation's Waste Not, Want Not program, which mobilizes area restaurants and grocery stores to donate their excess stock to food pantries and homeless kitchens around the city. It's a big undertaking, because we have to ensure that food is handled properly. We have eight kitchens that serve hot meals twice a day, every day, around the city, and this year we've started a mobile food cart to bring cold meals like sandwiches to people on the streets who aren't able to make it in to one of the kitchens. They're doing great work, and I'm humbled to be a small part of it."

Bob laughed. "I'd hardly call you a small part of it. For anyone who doesn't know, Beck was one of the founders of the charity. He's too modest for his own good."

Duncan hadn't realized that. How had he managed to get such a narrow view of who Beck was? Had he really let one run-in with him shape his entire opinion? Beck had an ego, that was for sure, but he really was a nice guy at the heart of things.

"I'm not doing anything special," Beck said. "The people who really make Waste Not, Want Not thrive are the ones who are out there every day, coordinating food pick-ups at the wonderful restaurants and stores that participate, and the volunteers who cook, serve, and deliver the meals. They're the ones who work tirelessly for the cause, and I'm so happy to be able to help them in any way possible."

God, who knew modesty and charity could be hot? They were, though. On Beck, at least. Duncan wanted to climb him like a tree.

But they had food to cook, and that was almost as good.

"I'm going to let these two get to the meat of things—cooking today's challenge!" Bob said, clapping his hands together. "You'll have the opportunity to vote by making a donation to one of the charities at the end of the show. For now, we'll let them get started."

Bob patted both of them on the back and slipped out of the shot, leaving a big hole between the two of them. Beck gave him a slightly exasperated look and then stepped in, closing the distance. Oops. The script had called for Duncan to be the one to move. He needed to start paying better attention.

Beck pulled a plate out of the warmer, sitting it on the counter between them. The camera came forward, zooming in on it, and Duncan had to force himself not to take an instinctive step back. Filming television was hard.

"We're taking on brussels sprouts today. They get a pretty bad rap, but when Duncan and I are done with them, I think you'll see they're a flavorful and nutritious addition to any dinner table.

"I'll be going the more traditional route, slow roasting my brussels sprouts with grape tomatoes and finishing them with a balsamic reduction." The camera panned over the ingredients a stagehand had set out moments before.

"And I'll be bringing some chemistry into the kitchen and showing you how to make a bacon foam that will complement my crunchy smoked brussels sprouts perfectly," Duncan said. He'd brought his smoke gun and his whipping siphon, and both had caused quite a stir in the prep kitchens. He held them up now. "These probably aren't tools you'll find in your home kitchen, but there are plenty of affordable models out there for the home cook. They look a little intimidating, but we'll talk through the process today. You'll find science in the kitchen can be fun and tasty."

Both of their dishes took a long time to make, which was why Andre and the prep kitchen had supplied them with multiple switch-out dishes so they could show the cooking process to the audience as they went. Some of Duncan's steps couldn't be prepared in advance, though, like setting up the smoke gun and preparing the siphon to make the foam.

He was more than a little nervous about things not working as they should, but everything moved along seamlessly, aside from a minor spill when he and Beck collided.

"And that's why you always call out 'behind' in a professional kitchen," Duncan joked, brushing off the balsamic vinegar he'd spilled on his coat. "It's also why no one but Beck wears these monkey suits while we're cooking."

He put his pot down and peeled off his sports jacket, handing it off to the stagehand, who darted forward to take it. Having all this off-screen help was nice. Kind of like what he'd imagined having Thing would be like when he'd watched *The Addams Family* as a kid.

"Ah, that's better."

Beck sighed and shook his head, but Duncan laughed it off. "My shirt is very topical, because now that we've deep fried our brussels sprouts and gotten them in our countertop smoker to soak up all that wonderful flavor, we're going to start on the bacon foam."

He angled toward the camera and let it pan over his shirt. "Pigs are delicious, folks. Don't ever let anyone make you feel bad for eating bacon," he said, wagging his finger at the camera.

Beck held his hands out placatingly. "I'm not judging the bacon. I love bacon. And there have even been recent studies that show bacon in moderation can be part of a healthy diet because it's rich in niacin. *My* problem is with his shirt," Beck said, making a face at the camera. "He's got an endless supply of ridiculous culinary T-shirts. I don't think I've ever seen a repeat."

Duncan puffed his chest out. "Wear 'em loud, wear 'em proud," he teased.

Beck sighed. "While he's getting his beloved bacon chopped up and into that big stew pot, I'm going to be starting my balsamic reduction. Basically, that's a fancy way of saying we're going to take something and cook it down until it has lost enough moisture to thicken up. That concentrates the flavor and, in this case, gives it a texture that will help it coat our roasted brussels sprouts, making sure we get some of the sauce in every bite."

Duncan didn't actually have to chop more than one slice of the thick-cut bacon. He had an entire plate of perfectly cubed bacon in the small fridge under the counter, along with bowls of the chopped onions and the herbs he was going to use. The wonders of television.

The director pointed at Duncan, and he smiled at the camera. "So we're going to cook this bacon for a good long time in some chicken stock so it renders all its fat and flavors the broth, which we'll be using to make our foam."

He looked up, startled, when he heard the sizzle of olive oil hitting a hot pan. Beck was at the range, getting the stockpot ready. "I figured I'd help out, since my glaze is reducing and my brussels sprouts are still in the oven," Beck explained.

"As long as you don't try to sabotage my foam," Duncan said, arching an eyebrow dramatically.

"I'm not even sure how one would go about sabotaging a foam," Beck said with a grin. "Got any tips?"

"Well, there are a lot of ways. Basically, we're talking about an unstable foam here. This is going to start falling, or degrading, as we call it in a lab, as soon as we make it. A foam relies on a lot of air to give it height. And short of permanently setting that foam, there's nothing we can do to stop it. So always make your foam right when you're ready to serve it. I recommend you have your dish plated and ready, and then apply the foam at the dinner table for extra oomph. There's that great wow factor when you're using a siphon."

"That's the fancy whipped-cream container?" Beck asked, winking at the camera.

"You joke, but yes, it can be used to make whipped cream. It uses nitrous oxide to help make a foam, the same way canned whipped cream is made."

Duncan tossed his bacon into the hot fat on the range, letting Beck be the one to watch that while he gathered his stock and the herbs he'd need. "So while Beck browns the bacon—which is an important step, and you shouldn't skip it because it adds a complexity of flavor that we'll definitely be able to taste, plus it helps render that fat—we're going to get everything else ready. Once the bacon's browned, we'll add in the stock and some thyme and garlic, and we'll let it simmer over low heat for a good two hours or so.

"After that, the mixture needs to be strained and then cooled in the refrigerator. We're talking good and cooled, a few hours at least."

Beck took the pot off the burner and handed Duncan one that had been simmered properly. "He's going to strain that, and while he does that, let's check on my brussels sprouts and tomatoes."

Truth be told, Duncan hated tomatoes. But the ones Beck pulled out of the oven looked pretty good. They were caramelized and looked like they'd be a good soft counterpoint to the crunchy leaves from the roasted brussels sprouts. He had to admit, Beck knew what he was doing.

"See how much color and crispiness the roasting gave them? These are definitely not your average boiled brussels sprouts," Beck said, using a spatula to move them around the pan. "We're going to toss these in with the balsamic reduction, and then we'll be ready to plate. How's it going over there, Duncan?"

Duncan had been too busy watching Beck work to stay on script. Luckily, someone had pulled the strained and chilled liquid out of the fridge for him.

"The brussels sprouts should be fully smoked now," he said, lifting the lid. Fragrant smoke drifted out, and he retrieved the plate. "And we can fill our siphon with our cooled bacon liquid to finish it off. There's a nitrous oxide cartridge in here, like we talked about earlier, and we'll use that to give our foam its oomph." He poured some of the liquid in and capped it. "Like I said, this foam isn't going to be stable, so I'd wait until right before serving to do this."

He held the siphon up and pulled the handle, layering the delicate foam on top of the brussels sprouts. Just because he could, he turned and held it up to Beck's mouth, looking at him expectantly.

"You're such a child," Beck said, shaking his head. He opened his mouth anyway, and Duncan shot a bit of bacon-flavored foam into his mouth.

"Oh my God," Beck murmured as he swallowed. "I had my doubts, but that actually tastes like bacon."

"Cool, right?" Duncan grinned. He took one of the foam-topped brussels sprouts and popped it in his own mouth. They'd turned out pretty well.

"Okay. So now that we've plated," Beck said, carrying both plates to the front counter so the camera could zoom in on them. "It's time for us to sample each other's creations."

Duncan took a forkful of Beck's brussels sprouts. The balsamic reduction was a great counterpoint to the soft flavor of the roasted tomatoes, and the brussels sprouts were flavorful in their own right. "'S good," he said as he chewed.

Beck laughed. "So eloquent." He took one of Duncan's brussels sprouts, and Duncan actually held his breath for a moment when he ate it. He was pretty good at letting criticism roll off his back, but he really cared what Beck thought.

"It's—I can't quite...." Beck frowned. "I'm having a hard time describing it because I haven't had anything with these textures and flavors before. It's delicious, but I can't quite find the words for the mouth feel. I taste bacon, and I expect to have the chewiness of the bacon, but it's not there. And the crunch of the brussels sprout is nice, but the smokiness is almost meat-like."

"That's what molecular gastronomy is all about," Duncan said, spreading his arms. "We take the normal and make it abnormal, and that creates a whole new flavor and texture profile your brain isn't sure how to process."

"Well, you succeeded on that front," Beck said, elbowing him. "Now for the fun part. Which dish did you like the best, viewers? The information for my charity, Waste Not, Want Not, is on the bottom left, and the information for Duncan's charity, Healthy U, is on the right. Remember, you're letting your dollars cast your vote on this one. We're asking for a one-dollar donation per vote, and you'll be able to do that either by phone tonight or on the charities' web sites up until Thursday."

He shook Duncan's hand, which took Duncan off guard even though it had been in the script.

"It's been fun cooking with you today, Duncan. I definitely learned a few things, and I hope everyone at home did too. Thanks for inviting us into your kitchen. We'll be back next week with the next challenge."

Beck dropped Duncan's hand the minute the red light went out on the camera. Duncan took a step back, a little stung.

"So that went well," he said, frowning as the easy demeanor Beck had adopted during the show dropped and he tensed up again.

"It did. I didn't expect to, but I really did like your dish."

"Yeah, I—"

"I have to get to Brix. It's my night to oversee the kitchen. We'll have a meeting tomorrow to go over how things went and start prepping for next week. Lindsay or Campbell can give you the details."

Duncan stared after him as Beck shot off the set.

Well, hell. Beck really *was* avoiding him.

Chapter TEN

"So the audience ate you two up, just like I thought they would," Lindsay said, perching on the end of Beck's desk.

He'd missed the morning meeting, despite the heads-up he'd given Duncan about it yesterday. It couldn't have been helped, though. The day manager at one of Christian's boutique restaurants was out sick, and there had been a delivery to sign for at nine thirty. He couldn't be in two places at once, so he'd opted to go take care of that since it was more important.

He hadn't orchestrated it—Rachel really was sick. But he'd jumped at the chance to head down there and do it instead of asking someone else to, even though he'd known that was the coward's way out.

And now he was going to pay for it.

Lindsay crossed her arms. "So spill. You never miss postproduction scrum. Never."

He shrugged. "I had something else to do. Unlike you, I work more than this job."

She shook her head. "Try again."

He sighed. "Did I miss something earth-shattering? Are you here to tell me you really *did* need me at the meeting, and it wasn't just the tech guys reporting on how editing went? There couldn't have been much to do—we shot it like a live show. All they had to do was add in the graphics later and do the fades for the commercial breaks."

"No, that went fine. But we also talked about the format and Duncan made a very impassioned plea to drop the script, which was accepted because you weren't there to provide a counterpoint."

Beck's throat went dry. "Drop the script?"

She nodded. "He said you two were off of it more than you were on it dialogwise, which was true. I've never seen you ad-lib like that before. It was good."

Beck rubbed a hand over his neck. "That was all him. I was just responding to his questions." He pushed away from his desk and stalked over to the window. If he stretched and squinted, he could almost see the river. "Seriously, though? Christian let him get away with ditching the script?"

"Christian didn't have much of a say because Bob jumped all over it. All he could do was gush about the chemistry you two had and how well it played with the focus groups. And he's right. You two tore it up, and the audience loved it."

"How's voting going?"

Lindsay beamed. "Like gangbusters. Best idea ever, seriously. We're getting so much good press out of pairing up with the charities that even if we didn't raise any money for them at all, we'd be golden."

He glared at her, and she backtracked. "Not that I'm saying I don't care if we don't raise any. I do. Obviously. And we are. So far there's something like three or four thousand dollars in the pool between you two."

"Seriously?"

"Yeah, I think it could be big."

"Any word on who's winning?"

"Nope. And voting goes right up to next week's show, so we won't know till then. I don't think Bob's planning on telling you guys who won till you're filming the next one."

That did sound like Bob. Maximum dramatic effect.

He turned back to face her and leaned against the window. The glass was cool through his thin shirt, which helped a bit with the nervous sweat that had sprung up as soon as she'd mentioned ditching the script. "So what are we doing, if we don't have a script?"

She waved away his concern. "You'll have the actions scripted, so it'll still have all the time counts and the switches planned out. But your dialogue will be ad-libbed."

"Completely?"

"You can still write your own script for your stuff if you want. I know it's a big part of your preparation for filming. But there won't be any scripted banter between you and Duncan because the things you two come up with on the fly are tons better than anything our writers can do."

Beck didn't know if that was a dig at the writers or a compliment. He didn't care.

"I'm not comfortable with that."

"Take it up with Duncan. Oh, wait," she said, widening her eyes. "You can't because you're not talking to him."

"Don't be ridiculous."

She pinned him with an unimpressed stare. "He told me so himself, and I admit I thought he was making a mountain out of a molehill—I mean face it, you can be kind of an asshole, so it would be easy to make the mistake—until you didn't show up for scrum."

"I told you, I had somewhere else to be. I assure you I didn't go give Rachel the flu just so I could miss a goddamn meeting."

Her smile didn't reassure him at all. In fact, he had the sinking suspicion he'd somehow unwittingly played right into her hands. "And now you're getting defensive, which I know means you're upset. Tell me what's going on. Duncan said it was personal. Did you two get into a fight again? Tell me you at least had the good sense to do it in private."

He choked on a laugh. It had been private, though only because it had been late enough that no one else was in the building.

"Of course we didn't," Beck muttered tersely. "And it's none of your business."

"It's definitely my business since I'm in charge of managing your image. Remember? I need to know what's going on between you two so I can take care of any rumors that pop up."

Beck shrugged, nervous energy making him feel restless. He was still hung up on how Duncan had dismissed him after sex. Pleasant, but detached. Like they'd gone for a run together instead of exchanged orgasms.

"Okay, I get it. I'll butt out," she said, holding up her hands. "*Unless* it hits the press or you two fight on camera. Then we're going to revisit this. Got it?"

He nodded. "Yeah. He didn't seem to know why I was avoiding him?"

"No, he had no idea. Or maybe he's a really good liar, I don't know. But he seemed genuinely surprised when you left so quickly after we wrapped yesterday, and he was shocked you weren't there this morning."

Beck processed that for a moment. If Duncan didn't know, then he could still make a friendship work between them. He just had to find a way to let go of his crush.

"So tell me what you're making," Lindsay said, leaning over and rifling through the papers on his desk.

Bob had called earlier with the next episode's challenge, asparagus in hollandaise. It was a classic dish that was already simple; Beck had no idea how he was going to revamp it.

Usually, it would bother Beck to have someone look at his notes before he'd set a menu, but he was eager for feedback on this one. It wasn't often Beck got to bring his own food onto the show—or into any of the restaurants. Even Brix, which was supposed to be his, didn't feature the food he liked to cook.

"So you're going with the slow food thing?" she asked, squinting at his scribbles.

Beck scowled. "It's an actual food movement, you know. And I don't know—kind of. I'd like to focus on seasonal food and local ingredients and maybe bring some of the principles of the movement into it. Simple food, high taste value, that sort of thing."

Lindsay pushed the notebook back across the desk. "I like it. You're thinking quiche?"

"It's probably too trite." Beck needed to be in the kitchen, not at his desk. But Duncan was down in the test kitchen right now. Beck heard he'd breezed by with Andre in tow after dropping off his contract for the next two shows an hour ago, headed for the kitchens to "experiment," as he'd called it, until it was time for his shift at the bar.

"So figure something else out. What's Duncan doing, do you know?"

"I don't think we're supposed to know. Not until the recipes are final, at least. It's a competition."

Lindsay kicked him again. "It's not *really* a competition. That's only to garner a little more viewer interaction and interest."

Beck raised an eyebrow at her. "So we're not really having the audience call in and vote on which dish they think is the best?"

"We are."

"So it's a competition."

She laughed. "In the weakest sense of the word, yes. You won't get anything if you win. I think it's fine if you and Duncan want to collaborate on recipes. It would be bad TV if the two of you were both making the same dish, you know."

That wasn't likely to happen, not with them being given free rein. It was true Duncan had a reputation as a bit of a culinary chameleon, since he was able to copy practically any style of cooking. But his area of interest was molecular gastronomy. The way he treated food was the polar opposite of Beck's philosophy. He had to hand it to Christian and Bob; pitting the two of them against each other like this would make a good show. And he was curious about how Duncan would approach the rest of the challenge. Just because he didn't use that particular cooking style himself didn't mean he wouldn't be able to enjoy whatever Duncan came up with. The level of ingenuity required with molecular gastronomy was mind-blowing.

"You could make it interesting," Lindsay said, her tone coy. Alarms went off in Beck's mind. Nothing good came of Lindsay plotting. "Wager something between the two of you. I've already talked to Duncan, and he's game."

That didn't sound devious enough to merit her pleased expression. "What, make ourselves a trophy?"

"No, whoever wins is getting one of those anyway on the show. Shh, don't tell Bob I let you know," she said sotto voce. "I think he's hoping to make this an annual thing, actually. But I was talking about a private wager between the two of you for whatever you want." Her grin grew when Beck groaned. "I'm sure you can think of something to make it interesting."

"Let me guess. Duncan was fine with that part too."

Lindsay hummed in agreement, looking far too smug for Beck's liking. "I'll leave you to decide those terms with Duncan on your own."

"How kind of you," Beck said dryly.

She laughed when Beck caught her kick to his shin and squeezed her toes through her shoes. She stuck her tongue out in retaliation. "Andre said he's got your area prepped if you're ready to go down and start testing. You'll be on your own for recipe testing, but once you have a plan, you can give him your breakdown of steps so his people can get it all camera-ready."

Andre spearheaded all the recipes and menu planning for the show. Beck gave input from time to time, but if he was down in the kitchens, it was as a grunt, not a chef. He liked the big open kitchens, though, so he went down to help out the prep staff often. He doubted Christian even knew where it was, despite the fact his name was the one on all of the recipes that came out of it.

They'd worked with Andre for their first challenge dishes, and Beck had figured that was going to be par for the course. He didn't mind—not exactly. He'd gotten everything he'd wanted menuwise last week, and Andre was letting them have a lot of leeway, if Duncan's bacon foam was any indication.

"So we really do get autonomy? I figured after the first show Christian would start poking around, now he's back in the studio." He knew he sounded earnest, but he didn't care. This was a big opportunity for him, and Beck was afraid Christian was going to pull it out from underneath him at the last minute.

"You really do. That was the one change Duncan made to the contract, you know. He had it written in that you both had free rein on the recipes and preparation of the food." She hopped down from his desk and gave him a serious look. "He had Campbell go over it with him to make sure everything was fair, and Campbell said that was Duncan's own suggestion. He said you seemed excited about the opportunity, and he wanted to make sure if he signed on, you got to do your own thing, so to speak."

Duncan was scarily perceptive. And Beck found himself grateful for that at the moment. He couldn't believe Christian had signed off on that contract rider. "That's surprising."

"That he cared enough to make sure you got what you wanted, or that Christian let him?" She shrugged. "He took the contract to Bob. He's technically the boss around here. It was a done deal by the time it came across my father's desk."

Beck winced. "That's going to be fun."

"Oh, I've already gotten an earful, but I told him when he pitched this idea that Duncan is a live wire. He's getting his just desserts as far as I'm concerned. I hope Duncan turns everything on its head."

She had been fighting for quite a while to get Beck more editorial control on the show, and he appreciated it. It wasn't purely family loyalty, either. As the show's marketing director, she kept a close eye on the demographics and audience feedback, and for the last year it had been pulling in the direction of a different type of food and atmosphere. Christian had pushed back against that forcefully, but maybe things were starting to change.

"Be careful what you wish for," he warned. Duncan seemed to be good at causing chaos.

"Right now I wish you'd get over yourself and ask him out. You two would be cute together."

"The only thing I know about his personal life is that he's always unattached. He usually brings a friend instead of a date to all the industry parties he attends. I have no idea what he's like when he's dating someone, or if he even dates." Beck picked his pen back up and started doodling in the margins of his notebook. "And I'm not looking for anything right now, Lindsay. I have the restaurant—"

"You're always going to have a restaurant or a show or a whatever," she said dismissively. "The great thing about Duncan is that he'll actually understand when you cancel dates because a sous-chef is out sick or a menu needs to be revamped. It won't be like the others."

Beck had a history of choosing poorly when it came to relationships. He'd only had a few serious ones, but they'd all ended badly because he was too focused on his career to be fully present with a partner. That wasn't likely to change anytime soon. Beck's career was important to him. But Lindsay was right; that might be something Duncan would understand. At the very least, he wouldn't complain when Beck used him as a sounding board for new recipes.

"Maybe."

Lindsay seemed to sense she wasn't getting anything else out of him because she left shortly after that without any more haranguing. Beck figured it was his cue to head down to the test kitchens. He'd put it off long enough. He had to leave for Brix in a few hours; if he didn't get some time in now, he wouldn't be starting until tomorrow.

Duncan was still there when he walked in. He'd set up on the right side of the room, and Andre was there helping him. Though from the looks of things, Duncan didn't need any assistance. Andre was perched on a stool next to the counter, and Duncan was giving him a crash course in something.

Beck had been planning to dive into his own recipe testing, but he was too curious about what Duncan was doing with a large stockpot and a strange black device.

"It's not as impressive with asparagus as it is with, say, a chicken breast, but you get the idea," Duncan was saying as Beck made his way over.

The water in the pot was roiling, and Beck could see a temperature gauge on the black thing partially submerged in it. "Is that a portable sous vide?" He'd never seen anything like it.

"Yeah, isn't it cool?" Duncan beamed. "It's an immersion circulator. It's not quite as powerful as a traditional sous vide, but it gets the job done. Especially if we're talking small batches instead of commercial quantity."

"And you carry it with you?"

Duncan grinned and patted the satchel propped up against the wall at the back of the stainless-steel countertop. Beck cringed at having it so close to the food prep; it was unsanitary. Beck was surprised Andre had allowed it. They were every bit as meticulous in the test kitchens as Beck was in the restaurants. Then again, it was pushed back and out of the prep space. He should give Duncan more credit than that. He was well trained enough he wouldn't introduce something that couldn't be sterilized into his actual workspace.

"I almost always carry it with my knives. You never know when you're going to need to sous vide something. Case in point," he said, nodding toward the pot.

"What exactly are you making?"

"Eh, I don't know. Usually I'd wing something like this, but Andre needs a detailed plan from me to make the television magic happen," Duncan said with a shrug.

The transitions that looked effortless on television were actually the product of a lot of carefully orchestrated hard work. Recipes had to be broken down into stages so the audience could follow along, but prepped enough that there were no awkward pauses while something cooked. They'd barely touched the surface of how the prep kitchen worked when he and Duncan had been setting up for the episode

Duncan had guest hosted. That had been setting up recipes and figuring out which of Duncan's tricks could be replicated in a home kitchen. It had been tame compared to what they'd be asking the prep cooks to do now that Duncan wasn't limited to the kind of ingredients and equipment a home cook would have.

Not that Beck didn't have every confidence it could be done. Andre's staff was very good at figuring out which parts of a recipe were crucial for viewers to see. Sometimes they made dozens of prop dishes to show the various stages of cooking. They'd make Duncan's recipes work, though it was definitely going to be harder than usual.

Duncan's reluctance to plan out his dialogue put a major wrench in things. The prep staff used the script to figure out the pacing of the food, which told them how many of the steps they had time to showcase and how many different prop dishes they'd need along the way. If Duncan went way off script, that would mess things up for them. What looked like magic when the show was edited and aired was actually a lot of painstaking work.

The thought of being in front of the camera without scripted dialogue made Beck's neck prickle with nervous sweat. The shows weren't going to be live, but time in the studio cost money, and the producers were sticklers for getting things done in as few takes as possible. It took a lot of work to reset a scene—the entire *mise en place* had to be redone, as well as any prop dishes that had been used in it. It was why they were so meticulous about their prep and action scripting.

"Hey, it'll be fine," Duncan said, and some of the tension spreading through Beck's shoulders eased. "Did Lindsay tell you I'm not going to let them script our dialog again? I kept missing cues."

"It'll get easier."

"It will, in that it won't be happening again." He shook his head. "Bob signed off on the no dialogue thing. But he said I have to meet with the writers to talk about pacing and what kinds of things I should be talking about. Why do they have to meet so early, though? I thought writers were supposed to be nocturnal, like chefs. You people and your morning meetings are going to kill me. I don't know how you do it all the time."

Beck smiled. "A lot of caffeine." And the occasional nap in his office, but he didn't want Andre to know that.

"Dude, I've already had so much today I'm practically vibrating," Duncan said. "Honestly, we're trying the sous vide because I'm afraid I'd chop off a finger if I tried any knife work."

Beck cringed at that lovely image. He liked Duncan's fingers where they were.

"Well, I'm here now. I'll be happy to pitch in with any knife work you need done," Beck said. He had an urge to swoop in and press a quick kiss to the side of Duncan's mouth, but he stopped himself. This entire thing felt domestic, but it was a sham. They weren't cooking dinner together in Beck's kitchen—they were at work. And they weren't dating, anyway. It had merely been a casual thing to blow off some steam.

Duncan threw him a flat look. "Don't you need to be working on your own recipe?"

It had been what he'd come down to do, but standing around with Duncan was more interesting. He was so different from Beck, and that was attractive.

"I'll spend some time on it later if we get a lull at Brix. I probably don't have enough time to get too far into it here anyway." Which was true. He was thinking about roasting the asparagus, which would take more time than he had at the moment.

"All right," Duncan said with an easy grin. "Andre, thanks for showing me the ropes, man." Duncan held out his hand and shook Andre's, and Andre gave Beck a hearty pat on the back and a wink as he excused himself.

"So now you've got me all to yourself in this cavernous kitchen," Duncan said, waving his spoon around, "what's up?"

Beck busied himself with clearing the mess on the counters. "Lindsay said you had a wager for me?" he said, changing the subject.

"Ah, yes. The public challenge is fun and all, but we're both kind of winners because at the end of the day, our charities are getting money no matter what. So how about we have a personal wager, too, to make it interesting?"

"Winning isn't interesting enough on its own?"

"Nah. I'd rather wager sexual favors," Duncan joked, and Beck felt his face flush. Honestly, he hadn't blushed this much since middle school. "No, really? Wait. Wait. I was kidding, but I can totally not be kidding. Are you up for that?"

He shouldn't be. Hadn't he just given himself a pep talk about getting over this crush? No-strings-attached sex was not going to help with that.

"Against my better judgment, yes," Beck said gruffly. Goddamn it.

"I'll take it," Duncan said, and he surprised Beck by leaning in and kissing him before zipping back to the stove to tend to whatever he had going there.

Beck was reeling from the light contact. It had been over almost as soon as it had begun, but it was different and more intimate than any kiss Beck had shared with anyone before. He wasn't used to teasing, soft touches like that. Or being kissed with no warning. It made his lips tingle.

"So how are we doing this?" Duncan asked as he took his place in front of the range again and checked the sous vide. "Winner chooses the favor?"

Beck felt dazed.

"Winner picks the activity," Beck said.

"Deal. Loser can't complain, though. I don't want you whining while I'm blowing your mind a second time."

He was in so far over his head with this. The right thing to do would be to tell Duncan he'd changed his mind and extricate himself now. They could bet money, or a meal at a fancy restaurant. Or even some humiliatingly public boon, like posing in front of the Bean wearing a suit made out of lettuce or something. Anything that didn't pull Beck further into Duncan's orbit.

He could say no. It would be the smart thing to do.

He always did the smart thing.

Usually.

"Deal," Beck said before he could talk himself out of it. Fuck everything. He'd deal with his hypothetical broken heart later. Odds were good Duncan would piss him off enough in the interim that his crush took care of itself, and then the bet would be casual sex, nothing more.

Chapter ELEVEN

"SO THE food for the switch-outs is in the warmer, which is right under the counter," Beck said for the fourth time, and Duncan wanted to scream in frustration.

"Yes. The food is in the warmer. The teleprompters are beside the cameras with the script. We face the camera with the light on it. Look up when I talk. Don't let my body block my hands when I'm demonstrating. I've got it, Beck. I've done this before, remember?"

Beck had been hovering for the last hour, giving tips about how to talk to the camera and how to follow the cues from the cameramen and the director. It had been cute at first, but now it was driving Duncan crazy.

"Yes, but when you did it before, we had a fucking script," Beck growled. He sighed, forcing himself to calm down. "I just want it to go smoothly."

The spike of irritation Duncan had felt during Beck's condescending lecture seeped out of him when he saw the small frown on Beck's face.

Duncan clucked his tongue. "Hey, I know. It'll be fine. Rehearsals went well, didn't they?"

They had. It was killing Duncan to keep getting up early every day, but he'd been in the studio at six yesterday morning to do a run-through of the show. There had been a few snafus with the pacing, but he'd worked with the scriptwriters and the producers yesterday, and Duncan was confident he could pull it off today.

"Rolling in five," someone called from off set. Duncan felt a wave of nerves crash through him, making his muscles tense and his stomach flutter.

It didn't help that Christian was sitting to the left of the main camera, watching everything with a smug look. Duncan wished he could ask him to leave; having him there was disconcerting.

Duncan felt a hand graze his lower back and disappear. "Ignore him," Beck said quietly. "Pretend you're talking to a group of people who are touring your kitchen or something."

It had been easier when Lindsay and Campbell had staked out spots next to the camera, but they were meeting with an investor right now. "Is that what you do?"

"Sometimes. It's old hat to me now, but it was terrifying the first few times. The writers even put in all my jokes and asides because I'd freeze up without the teleprompter."

"Is that why you've been so distant lately? Because I had them nix the script? You'll be fine, Beck. The best parts of the last show were the ones where we tossed the script and just talked."

Beck made a noncommittal noise that frustrated Duncan even more. He wanted to get back to the easy camaraderie they'd had before. He knew this had to be about the sex. It was one of the reasons why he never slept with coworkers. Too complicated. Too many people could get hurt. It had been stupid to break his rule.

The director was giving the countdown before Duncan knew it, and then the cameras were rolling. He felt a moment of panic sweep over him, but Beck was a steady, calm presence at his side, and Duncan settled into the cadence of the show.

"Thanks for tuning in to *King of the Kitchen*. If you joined us last week, you already know the format for the next three weeks is a little different," Beck said to the camera. "Duncan Walters is joining me for a culinary challenge—we'll be taking classic dishes and putting new twists on them. And then you will get to vote on whose dish you think was the best reinvention by making a small donation to some very worthy charities."

Duncan grinned. "Speaking of last week, I think it's well past time we find out who won the brussels sprout challenge. Bob? Can you join us here and do the honors?"

They'd planned to have Christian do it, but his face was still mottled with slow-healing bruises, so Bob had stepped in again.

"Well, it was a close race. I tasted both dishes after filming last week, and let me tell you, it was a hard decision. They were both fabulous," he said, smiling for the camera. "Thanks to our generous viewers, we raised more than twenty thousand dollars between the two charities."

Duncan couldn't help but gape. That was a lot of money for a small organization like Healthy U, and they were only one week into the month. He hadn't fully realized how much money he'd be bringing in for the charity.

"So. The official votes are all in and tallied, and last week's winner was—Duncan!"

Duncan pumped his fist in the air. "Never go up against bacon foam," he said to Beck, who smiled and offered him a hand to shake.

"I'm not out yet," Beck teased. "Thanks, Bob. Do you want to introduce today's dish?"

"I'll leave that to you gentlemen," Bob said. He gave Duncan an awkward half hug. "Congratulations on your win."

The camera panned, the light on the one next to it clicked on, and Duncan focused on shifting his gaze to it and smiling.

"Today we're taking on the classic dish asparagus in hollandaise," Beck said, and Duncan followed Beck's lead and bent to grab the first of the prepped dishes Andre's team had made.

"It's hard to reinvent something that's already delicious, but I'm game to give it a go," he said.

Beck pointed to the ingredients assembled next to a large stockpot. "I'll be making a roasted asparagus soup with a hollandaise crème fraîche."

"And I'll be making an asparagus pie a la mode with hollandaise ice cream," Duncan said.

"As you can see, Duncan's style of cooking is a little different from what we're used to here on *King of the Kitchen*," Beck joked. "Duncan has degrees in microbiology and chemistry, and he brings that into the kitchen. He specializes in something called molecular gastronomy, and it produces some of the most intriguing food out there right now. He taught us all about making a foam last episode, and he'll be walking us through a few new techniques here today."

Duncan looked at the camera and smiled. "Let's get started, shall we?"

Chapter TWELVE

"ARE YOU sure you want to do this? Even I don't want to be here, and he's my father."

Beck squeezed Duncan's hand and grinned at him. "I do 'meet the parents' well. Don't worry."

Duncan snorted. "You should put that on your Grindr profile."

"I don't have a—"

"Yeah, I know. I was kidding."

Beck side-eyed him. "Do you?"

"What, meet the parents well? I wouldn't know. I've never done it. Besides, it's not like this is actually a date. We're just telling him about me accepting a contract with the network."

"Have a Grindr account," Beck said flatly, his lips twitching of their own accord when Duncan took on an overly innocent mien. He shouldn't find it cute, but he did.

"Of course not," Duncan said, overplaying it so he looked absolutely affronted. He waited a few beats, until the point Beck was actually on the verge of apologizing, before he added, "I have a Tinder. Equal opportunity, you know."

Of course he would. Beck closed his eyes for a moment and forced himself to remember he was here for moral support while Duncan broke the news to his father that he was going to start developing his own cooking show for the network. He wasn't here because Duncan actually wanted them to socialize with his father like a couple. He was a colleague, not a date.

"Besides, I don't think you can call it 'meet the parents' if you already know him. Once you've helped someone clean blood off racquet strings, you're past the casual acquaintance stage." Duncan stopped at the hostess stand and offered the pretty girl a blinding smile. "We're meeting someone here. Has Vincent Walters arrived yet?"

The woman's eyes widened at the name, and Beck could tell the moment she realized who he and Duncan were because she flushed a pretty pink. No doubt the foodie gossip rags would be full of the story about how he and Duncan were being seen out and about together again. They'd stopped once the show started filming, but that hadn't ended the speculation in the press about their friendship.

Who knew, the two of them meeting Duncan's father at a fancy restaurant would probably spark all sorts of new rumors. He'd probably read on the blogs tomorrow that they were buying a house together in the suburbs or something. Lindsay had been bored lately anyway. Putting out those fires would give her something fun to do.

"He hasn't arrived yet, sir, but I can seat you if you like."

Duncan raised an eyebrow at her. "Do you typically seat patrons if their entire party hasn't arrived yet?"

"N-no."

"Well, I wouldn't want to get you in trouble. We're perfectly happy to wait at the bar until he gets here."

Beck didn't bother to even try to muffle his laugh as the woman stammered her agreement and pointed them toward the bar.

"That wasn't very nice," he whispered as they made their way over to a gorgeous mahogany hard-top table that wasn't claimed.

"Would you allow your host to seat a partial party at any of your restaurants?"

Beck grinned. "Nope."

"And I know Zane Miller has the same policy. It gums up the flow and is rude as hell." Duncan picked up the bar menu a passing waitress had left for them. "Hmm. Classic or experimental tonight? Though it looks like the trendy options aren't very exciting. How many reincarnations of a Pimm's Cup are we going to have to see before those die out?"

Beck settled onto the stool right next to Duncan—the waitress had only left one menu, so it only made sense to crowd in close— and perused the offerings. Duncan was right. Everything had candied flowers or other *en vogue* ingredients.

"I'll have a Vieux Carré. With Château de Beaulon if you have it, Hennessey if you don't," Beck told the waitress when she materialized a minute later.

Duncan snorted and shook his head. "So fucking fancy. Is the Flossmoor Station Iron Horse Stout on tap today?"

She nodded.

"That, then. Thanks."

"Why were you even looking at the cocktails if you were just going to order a beer?" Beck asked, rolling his eyes.

"Because I like to see what people are doing. And I don't think I like your tone," he teased. "There's nothing wrong with beer. It's not like I ordered a Sam Adams."

"See! You gave me shit for ordering top-shelf liquor in my drink, but you don't want low-bar stuff, either. It matters."

"I don't see how you can actually taste the difference when it comes to cognac that's mixed with other things. I mean, why spend the money on higher-quality cognac if you're going to mix it with bottom-shelf rye?"

A cough from behind them made them both turn around, and Beck watched Duncan's eyes light up as he threw his arms around the man who'd interrupted.

"I would never serve bottom-shelf anything, you plebeian. You know that. You're the one who picked out the local beers, after all. Though I stock Sam Adams and whatnot because we do have some patrons who like it."

"Because they've never tried a nice small-batch local beer," Duncan groused. "Beck, this is Zane. This dive is his place. Zane, this is Beck Douglas. I wasn't sure if you two had met before or not."

Zane gave Beck an appraising look before offering his hand. Beck shook it, studying him with equal scrutiny. He'd heard of Zane, but he'd never tried his restaurant before. Even though food was his business, Beck didn't get a chance to eat out around Chicago very often. This place had been on his short list of restaurants to try, so he'd been glad when Duncan said it was where he met his father for dinner once a month.

"We haven't had the pleasure, but I've heard a lot about him," Zane said before turning his attention solely on Beck. "Duncan's never brought a plus-one to his standing I-can't-kill-you-because-we're-in-public dinner with Vincent. I kind of want to sit in, to be honest. You must be all I've read about and more if you've captured Duncan's attention."

Either Zane was a jealous ex-fling, or he and Duncan were closer than Duncan had let on, because the interest in Zane's voice was pointed.

"We're not dating," Duncan said with an annoyed huff. "And besides, he's a special snowflake."

Beck recoiled a bit but kept himself from fidgeting by curling his toes in his shoes. It was an old trick of his, honed during Christian's interminable speeches and employed in all of the boring restaurant audit meetings Beck had to endure now. It also worked to help him keep his expression neutral when he wanted to frown or flinch. Duncan's casual dismissal of the idea that they could be dating made him want to do both.

Duncan's denial got a smile out of Zane. "He does appear to be." The waitress brought their drinks, placing them on the high top with extreme care because her boss was standing right there. "I'll leave you to your fortifications. I saw Vincent for lunch a few days ago. He's livid about that show of yours. You're going to need them."

He excused himself after patting Duncan heartily on the back and left them to their drinks. His warning had brought Duncan's frown back. Beck nudged him with his knee under the table.

"I'm sure it won't be that bad."

Duncan huffed. "Oh, it won't be. It'll be worse. That's how things go with Vincent."

Beck wasn't sure what to say to that, so they sat in silence, sipping their drinks, until the host from earlier came over to get them.

"Mr. Walters has arrived. If you'll follow me," she said, her face still a bit flushed.

They gathered up their drinks and let her lead them to a table set into a bit of an alcove near the back. Duncan let Beck in first before he slumped into a seat in the high-backed velvet booth directly across from his father.

"Vincent," he said, his voice even and detached.

"Mr. Walters, nice to see you again," Beck said, holding his hand out.

Vincent shook it and winked at him. "Call me Vincent. After all, my own son does."

There was a slight edge to his voice that belied the easiness of his wink, and Beck felt Duncan tense up slightly next to him.

"I apologize for being late. I got caught up in the kitchen at Goût and got away a little later than I'd have liked."

"It's no problem," Beck assured him, when the silence from Duncan made it clear he wasn't going to be answering.

"So things have been going well with the two of you, I see," Vincent said, and Duncan sat up even straighter, the tightness of his lips becoming more pronounced.

"Maybe we should order before we start talking shop," Duncan said, his tone clipped.

"I wasn't aware there was much shop to be talked, but as you wish." Vincent's gaze turned shrewd as he looked at the two of them.

"Actually, no." Duncan looked up from the menu he'd been studying. "Maybe we should do this before we order."

"Do what?" Vincent asked, his eyes narrowing. "Don't tell me you're going to leave the kitchen to work on that show permanently."

Beck tried not to recoil at the condescending way Vincent referred to *King of the Kitchen*, but it was hard. He knew a lot of chefs thought working in television was below them, and he'd even had a clue Duncan's father would be one of them because of the absolute glee Duncan had taken in signing his contract, but he hadn't realized quite how much disdain Vincent had for it.

"Actually, something like that. And, thanks for asking, it's going really well," Duncan said flatly. "And there's nothing to say I couldn't do both, like Beck does. He manages several restaurants and is responsible for most of the content of the show."

Beck's pulse jumped at the pride and affection in Duncan's voice as he defended him.

"What, then? Are you finally ready to take the helm at Goût? I'll rescind my offer if you mean to try to do it and the television show. No offense, Beck, but a chef needs to be fully present to do his food justice. You're talented enough to oversee Goût, but that's not a part-time job, Duncan."

Duncan scowled. "I've told you I don't want that job. I don't want any job from you. I don't know how I can be clearer than that, Vincent."

Duncan's tone was more irritated and angry than Beck had ever heard it before, but Vincent didn't seem the slightest bit surprised to have it directed at him. Beck had assumed Duncan's animosity toward his father was playful, but apparently it wasn't. There wasn't anything jovial or teasing about the way the two of them were squaring off over the table. No wonder Zane had them sit at the alcove table. This was quickly becoming a scene.

Diffusing fraught situations was one of Beck's specialties. He had ample opportunity to practice his diplomacy whenever Christian was around. His uncle was brash and opinionated, two things that didn't mix well when other strong personalities like celebrity chefs and food critics were involved. Beck spent a lot of time smoothing ruffled feathers.

He reached out without thinking, resting a hand on Duncan's shoulder. There wasn't anything intimate about it—it was friendly, a gesture Beck had made with Campbell a hundred times before. But it caught Vincent's attention, and his amused-but-beleaguered expression soured.

"So that's how it is," he muttered, shaking his head. "Duncan, I thought you were past that phase."

Beck let his hand drop, but Duncan grabbed it and tugged him closer, until the only thing he could comfortably do was put his arm around Duncan.

"Phase? My fascination with deep-fat frying everything was a phase. My obsession with punk music was a phase. My sexuality *is not a phase*. You know that."

Beck's eyes widened as he watched Vincent's cheeks begin to get ruddy. He looked halfway to a stroke.

Vincent scoffed. "Your sexuality? Please. We both know this is nothing more than a cry for attention, just like that busboy you—"

"You have no right to talk about that at all."

"No right? It was my restaurant, Duncan! My employee! My goddamn walk-in freezer!"

Duncan seemed to sink into himself instead of lurching into the fight like he normally would, and Beck couldn't help but think he'd never seen Duncan like this. Duncan was a bit shorter and quite a bit leaner than Beck was, but he'd never looked small before. Sitting here getting berated by his father was making Duncan *less* somehow, and Beck wasn't going to let anyone reduce Duncan's sarcastic and ebullient self into this.

"Am I to infer that were Duncan and I to tell you we were dating, it wouldn't be a happy revelation?" he asked, his tone careful and bitingly polite.

Vincent turned his razor-sharp glare on Beck, but Beck didn't so much as blink. He didn't have any history with this man—Vincent could do as he pleased, and it wouldn't affect Beck whatsoever. He'd dealt with bigots before, and while it wasn't pleasant, he was secure enough in his own sense of self-worth that he wasn't going to let someone like Duncan's father tear him down. And he'd damn well do his best to make sure he didn't get to tear Duncan down, either.

"This isn't your business," Vincent snapped. He dropped his napkin on the table and started to slide out of the booth. There really wasn't a way to do that with dignity, and Beck allowed himself a tiny smile as he watched Vincent struggle to get up.

"It's very much my business, sir, given that I'm the one you seem to think is dating him," Beck answered pleasantly. "If there's anyone at this table whose business it *isn't*, I'd say it's yours."

Vincent was nearly purple by now, and there was no way other diners hadn't noticed his raised voice. "I warned you if you didn't stop with this foolishness I'd cut you out of the business," he said, pointing a finger at Duncan.

Duncan flinched, none of his usual bravado surfacing. He'd heard Duncan go toe-to-toe with Vincent on the phone before, and he'd seen a lot more backbone than this out of him when they'd met up for racquetball. Beck guessed it was the topic that had Duncan so withdrawn. There was clearly a lot of history there, and while Duncan seemed to have no problem standing up for himself against Vincent when it came to his career and the kitchen, there was no sign of that here.

"Respectfully, not five minutes ago Duncan made it clear to you he doesn't want to be part of your business. I'm starting to see why."

Duncan snickered at Beck's subtle jab, and Beck scooted as close as he could get, keeping his arm squeezed tight around Duncan's shoulders.

Vincent ignored Beck, his gaze locked on Duncan. "I've excused a lot of things from you. Your attitude. Your insistence on getting a useless degree. Your love of whatever trend-of-the-moment is coming through the kitchens. But this isn't something I can excuse, Duncan. You have to make a choice. Do you want me in your life or not? Because I won't stand here and watch you throw your life away with trash like this."

That got Duncan fired up. "You don't get to call him trash," he spat, regaining some of the color he'd lost when Vincent had started his rant. "You don't get to call him anything. Beck is a better man than you'll ever be, and I don't want you talking about him at all."

"He's luring you into perversion—"

"It's not a perversion to be attracted to someone of the same sex! It's natural. It's who I am," Duncan said hotly.

Beck squeezed his shoulder, glad to see the Duncan he knew resurfacing.

"It is not who you are. It's who you're choosing to be because it makes the most waves at the moment. You date women, Duncan. Your dalliances with men are an abomination manufactured solely to spite me. I know you think I failed you as a father, and maybe I did. But going against God and nature isn't the way to punish me for that."

Beck choked on a laugh. It was inappropriate as hell to find anything about this amusing, but he couldn't help himself. Vincent really thought Duncan's attraction to men was some sort of revenge plot? Did he really believe half of the things that were coming out of his mouth? Sure, he'd read interviews here and there where Vincent credited his success to his strong faith, but somehow Beck had missed the right-wing Bible-thumping undertones. Christian referring to him as a zealot made so much more sense now.

Beck's shoulders started to shake as he failed to keep his amusement under wraps, and a second later Duncan joined in. The two of them couldn't stop, feeding off each other and Vincent's apoplectic anger at their hysterical laughter.

"This is not a laughing matter. This is an affront to God—"

Someone must have complained, or maybe he'd been watching the table, expecting trouble, because Zane materialized and took Vincent by the elbow before Vincent could finish. "You're either going to have to sit back down and be civil or go back to my office and cool down," he said. "The middle of a restaurant isn't the place for this."

Duncan and Beck's laughter trailed off, though Beck could see Duncan was still grinning.

"We're done here anyway," Duncan said, more cheerful than Beck had heard him sound all day.

"Circumstances being what they are, we won't wait for the check. Please make sure our server and the bartender split whatever's left," Beck said, handing Zane two fifties to cover their drinks and hopefully make up for some of the hubbub they'd caused the waitstaff.

"Duncan, if you walk away, I won't pursue you like I did last time," Vincent warned.

Duncan scoffed. "Last time I was seventeen and living with you. I didn't have a choice. But you know what? I do now. And I don't know why it's taken me this long to realize that. Good-bye, Vincent."

He stood, pulling Beck behind him, and the two of them walked out of the restaurant. There were a few glances from curious patrons, and at least one person took their picture, but Beck didn't care. He'd never considered himself much of an activist, though he'd had his photo taken for the NOH8 campaign when it came to town a few years ago, and there had been a few LGBT magazine features on him over the years that had turned a few heads and set some tongues wagging in the culinary world.

But the thought of seventeen-year-old Duncan dealing with the kind of vitriol Vincent had tossed at him tonight made Beck's blood boil. He'd never experienced anything like that. All his run-ins with bigots and homophobes were limited to viewers who took offense at his sexuality or alpha males who wanted to make a point. He'd never even considered what it would be like to get that kind of reaction from your own family. It broke his heart. It also made him determined to start doing something about it. He had a little influence and a fair amount of money, and he'd be damned if he wouldn't put it to good use protecting kids from that kind of treatment. He couldn't turn back time and save Duncan from his father, but he could help another kid in a similar position.

Duncan held his head high and kept his pace relaxed as they made their way out of the restaurant, but as soon as the valet brought Beck's car, all of the fight and pride went out of Duncan, and he collapsed into the passenger seat in a heap.

"I'm sorry you got dragged into that," he said softly. "Thanks for going along with it. I shouldn't have implied we were dating, but when he jumped to that conclusion…."

"It's fine. I'm sorry your father's such an ass." Beck reached out and grabbed Duncan's hand, squeezing it hard before letting go.

Beck chanced a glance over at Duncan and was pleased to see him looking worn out but not beaten down like he had been when Vincent had started in on him.

"Is this going to cause problems for the show?"

Beck furrowed his brow, trying to sort out Duncan's question. "Your father being a reprehensible homophobe? No, I don't think so."

Duncan's shoulders slumped. "No. The part where he erroneously outed us as a couple to an entire restaurant."

Beck laughed, even though there wasn't anything remotely funny about this. It was like being stuck in a nightmare, though not for the reasons Duncan seemed to be worried about. "Are you kidding me? That's going to be gold for ratings. Viewers are going to be thrilled our 'bromance' has turned into a romance."

"Oho, the real reason for you wanting to fake date me comes out. You just wanted to make sure everyone stopped using that word," Duncan teased.

"Yes. Forget that I'm hot for your nubile body and your acerbic wit. It's because of that," Beck said, his lips quirking up into a smile when Duncan reached over and smacked him. "Hey, driving!"

"I'm the sarcastic asshole in this relationship. You're the pedantic asshole. Stop infringing on my milieu."

"So we're an asshole version of the odd couple?" Beck whistled. "I like it. Sounds like the perfect concept for a new show to me."

"Ah, yes. Assholes in Love. Catchy. Though that might be more reality television fodder than a cooking show subject."

It was closer to the truth than Beck liked. His crush on Duncan wasn't dying off like he'd hoped. If anything, it was getting worse. Now that Beck had a better understanding of why Duncan was so oriented toward casual relationships, he couldn't really blame him. If he'd grown up with a parent who openly hated his sexuality, he might have a hard time with dating and commitment, too.

Beck swallowed back all the words threatening to burst out of his mouth. This wasn't the time to unload his feelings on Duncan.

"Should we stop somewhere to get something to eat? Now that my righteous indignation has worn off, I'm kind of hungry."

Duncan laughed. "Oh, absolutely. We're not too far from Sunrise Cafe. Let's stop there and infiltrate the kitchen."

Beck's lips twitched. He hadn't realized he'd been driving out of the city. He'd just been focused on getting Duncan away from that scene. "Will you make me eggs Benedict?"

"No way, buddy. I gave you the chance at my eggs Benedict once. It's on you that you passed it up. Your loss."

"You probably make it with McCormick's powder in a kitchen that rushed. I doubt I missed anything life affirming."

Duncan swatted him again, but Beck was braced for it this time. Without taking his eyes off the road, he caught Duncan's hand and held it against his chest. He wasn't trying to hold his hand. It was purely self-defense.

"Don't think I don't see what you're doing, trying to goad me into making it for you," Duncan said.

"Did it work?"

Duncan pinched him, and Beck let him go, rubbing ruefully at his chest where Duncan had managed to get not only some skin but a healthy bit of chest hair too.

"That's not a no. You're totally going to make me eggs Benedict."

Chapter THIRTEEN

STEPPING INSIDE the back door of Sunrise Cafe felt like coming home. The second he slid his key into the lock, Duncan felt some of the tension that had been coiled in his stomach all evening release.

He'd texted John to let him know they were coming, and Duncan grinned when he saw a pair of his old chef's whites hanging on a peg near the door.

"Still slumming it as Charlie, I see," Beck said with a grin when Duncan pulled on the embroidered shirt.

"Maybe Charlie is my real identity and Duncan is the farce," Duncan said. He couldn't hide his smile when Beck buttoned it for him and smoothed the shoulders.

"You want something? John never throws anything out. I don't think any of mine would fit you, but he's bound to have a pair or two that would."

Beck smirked and shook his head. "I thought you were cooking for me?"

Flirting with Beck was the perfect balm for how tired and angry his father made him. Usually, Duncan moped for hours, if not days, after a big blowup with Vincent, but tonight Beck had him feeling almost like his old self in no time. Duncan wasn't sure if it was because having Beck by his side during the whole thing made him feel better, or if it was because there had been an air of finality to today's fight that hadn't been there before. Vincent certainly seemed like he was washing his hands of Duncan, and even if he wasn't, Duncan was ready to cut the cord himself.

"Still want eggs Benedict, or should I fix you up two eggs over easy, bacon, and whole wheat toast?"

Beck gaped at him. "We haven't had breakfast together before. How do you know my order?"

Duncan gave his hands a good wash and tied an apron over his jeans. He tossed another one to Beck, who obediently put it on. The kitchen was suspiciously empty, which probably meant John had sent whoever was on shift home, knowing Duncan would want to cook for a few hours. He wasn't going to let Beck stand by and watch him—not that he thought Beck was any more capable of that than Duncan was himself. Being in the kitchen was kind of like a drug. A very addictive one at that. The pure joy Duncan got from spending a sweaty shift in a busy kitchen wasn't something he found many other places.

"First of all, that's not true. Our first civil conversation occurred over breakfast at my house, remember? And secondly, it's what you ordered when you came into the diner the first time we met."

Beck's eyes widened. "You remember my egg order? Are you some sort of line-cook savant?"

Duncan snorted. "No, but if I ever have to have business cards printed, I'm totally using that as my title. I like it." He grinned at Beck. "I remember your egg order because it was so out of whack with your fancy suit."

He hadn't been in the kitchen at the cafe in a few months, but nothing had changed. John had always talked big about all the changes he was going to make when he inherited the place, but if he'd implemented any of them yet, they weren't obvious to Duncan.

He stuck his head through the pass-through and saw John leaning up against the counter, chatting with a waitress Duncan didn't recognize. There weren't any customers, which wasn't surprising. This was kind of a dead time for the diner.

They'd been meeting Vincent for a late dinner, and it had taken awhile to get over to the cafe after they'd decided that's where they wanted to go afterward. It was well past the dinner rush, but in an hour or so, the diner would get another influx of customers when the shift workers were off for the day and anyone who'd been out at the bars would be looking for something greasy to soak up the alcohol.

"You going to make me cook for my dinner?" Duncan called out, grinning when John flinched before he whirled around.

"Of course I am, you bastard! No free rides here." John reached through the pass-through and grabbed Duncan by his bicep, squeezing just hard enough to hurt. "Sandra, this is Duncan. He used to cook for us before he got too big for his britches."

Duncan laughed. "As if. I've been too busy lately with places that, you know, pay me in things that aren't hash browns."

John pointed at him. "Lies."

"Maybe I could balance the books at Brix if I paid the staff in potatoes. Tell me more," Beck said. He held out a hand. "Hi, I'm Beck."

John looked irritated at the greeting, but Duncan was pretty sure he'd seen Sandra swoon. Beck was a charming motherfucker, when he wanted to be.

"We've met," John said, giving him the briefest handshake possible. "You hold the world record for the best tipper this cafe has ever had. Feel free to come back and be an ass anytime, as long as you always tip like that."

Duncan scowled at John, but Beck laughed it off.

"To be fair, it wasn't totally my fault," Beck said.

"I claim most of the blame, actually," Duncan said wryly. "I was being a dick that day."

"Oh, was it a day that ended in *y*?" Beck asked, his tone bright and cheerful.

Duncan squirmed out of his grip and elbowed him lightly in the stomach. John was laughing out loud, and Sandra looked torn between laughing and fleeing. They were a lot to take in for a stranger.

"I changed my mind. You're welcome anytime," John said, and this time he actually did sound welcoming. "Especially if you're cooking. You up for a shift? I was down a guy tonight anyway because Ernie called in sick, and Stephen's anniversary is today, so I took pity on him and sent him packing when Duncan texted you two were on your way over."

Beck looked down at his apron and shrugged. "Sure."

It had been a long day, and the emotional scene with Vincent hadn't helped much. They were going to need some sustenance before cooking for a rush. Duncan moved over to the walk-in, pulling out eggs, cheese, chorizo, onions, garlic, peppers, a container of ranchero sauce, and a fat stack of corn tortillas.

They didn't offer chilaquiles on the menu, but it was easy enough to slap together with the ingredients they kept on hand for huevos rancheros. Duncan squirted some oil on the cooktop and dumped a generous portion of the chorizo onto it. He grabbed a spatula and started a pile of veggies cooking next to it. The perfume of garlic and onions wafted up from the sizzling cooktop, and Duncan breathed it in, his shoulders dropping a bit more at the familiar scent. He was almost back to normal. A good hard shift slinging eggs and bacon would fix him right up.

And as a bonus, he got to watch Beck struggle along through it right beside him. While a lot of the basic skills were the same, diner cooking and haute cuisine cooking were totally different animals. He was looking forward to seeing how Beck did.

"So we won't get busy for another hour or so," Duncan said as he used the spatula to break up the cooking chorizo and move it around the cooktop. The onions and peppers got another squirt of oil and a similar treatment. "You want to poke around and familiarize yourself with the kitchen? John keeps a binder of recipes somewhere in the office if you want, or we can double-team things and you can be in charge of eggs and protein, while I put everything together since I know the menu."

"Here I thought we were taking things slow, but on our first official fake date you're asking me to double-team. Nice."

Duncan poured a healthy dollop of the ranchero sauce on the chorizo, noting that he'd have to start a fresh batch before the rush hit because they wouldn't have enough to get through the breakfast shift tomorrow with what was in the fridge.

"I have a feeling you'd keep things interesting enough I won't really want to bring in anyone else," Duncan teased.

"Have you?" Beck asked, his voice a little strange.

Duncan turned around, wondering if the thought of a threesome was really that disturbing for Beck, but the slight glaze of sweat over his brow made Duncan reevaluate. Clearly Beck was not disgusted by the thought. Interesting.

"Double-teamed someone? No," he said, raising an eyebrow in challenge. "But have I been double-teamed?"

Beck outright choked at that, and Duncan grinned in triumph.

"Actually, the answer to that is also no. But it's a fun thought."

He laughed at Beck's indignant huff at being teased and turned back to the cooktop. The veggies were nicely softened and starting to caramelize, so he folded them into the chorizo mixture. He pushed it off to the outer edge of the cooking surface to keep warm while he fiddled with the salamander to make sure it was at the temperature he wanted to broil.

"Make yourself useful," Duncan said, tossing the tortillas to Beck. "Quarter those and fry 'em up."

He half expected Beck to balk at the order, but Beck washed up at the sink and set about following the instructions. Neither of them had their own knives with them, and Beck made a face before selecting one and slicing through the tortillas.

He couldn't even make fun of him for being a snob, because Duncan totally agreed. The kitchen was clean and serviceable, but the knives made Duncan want to cry every time he saw them. They weren't up to his standard, though to be fair, his standard was far above what a kitchen like Sunrise Cafe needed.

Beck didn't need any instruction to work the fryer, which was also impressive. Not that it was rocket science, because it wasn't. But it was an older model and probably different from the state-of-the-art fryers Beck was used to, so to see him handling it like the expert he was sent a thrill up Duncan's spine.

It was ridiculous to find competency attractive, but there it was.

Beck had been quick to come to his defense when Vincent had jumped to the wrong conclusion, and Duncan hadn't missed the careful way he'd worded his responses. He hadn't said they were dating, but he had made it clear it wasn't an offensive suggestion. It was something to think on. Maybe everything would blow over and nothing about the fight would come out tomorrow, but Duncan wasn't going to count on that. When it came to the press, he'd learned that lucky breaks rarely came around. They'd have to talk to Lindsay about their strategy, but he was wondering if maybe Beck might be someone he'd like to actually date instead of just pretend with.

Would that be something Beck wanted? Duncan would venture to guess the answer was yes. Would it be shitty to ask him out? Was that overstepping? Beck's silent treatment after their romp in the shower had sent the crystal clear message that he wasn't interested in casual, so Duncan had backed off because casual was all he did. But Beck hadn't totally pushed him away, and he'd stuck up for Duncan tonight in a way that no one ever had before. Did that mean Beck would be up for dating, if

Duncan could get there himself? Ugh, he couldn't deal with this tonight. One existential crisis at a time.

By the time Duncan had the salamander roaring and an ovenproof dish ready to go, Beck had finished and had a crispy pile of tortilla chips ready for him. They worked together, layering the chips with more of the ranchero sauce and topping it with crumbles of feta. It should have been queso fresco, but John was a Neanderthal who refused to order it even though the kitchen staff probably made chilaquiles for themselves at least a few times a week.

Duncan popped the dish in the salamander to broil and grabbed the eggs. "Scrambled or fried?"

Beck squinted his eyes as he thought. "Fried, but over easy. I like a runny yolk because it makes the chilaquiles creamier."

The more Duncan learned about him, the more he was becoming convinced Beck might actually be the perfect man.

Duncan cracked a few eggs on the cooktop and pulled the dish out of the salamander. The cheese was browned and the chips were slightly burnt on the edges, exactly the way he liked it. He added in the chorizo and veggies and smothered it all with even more of the ranchero sauce, topping it off with the eggs. The dish was screaming hot, so he laid down a towel on the tiny table in the back before settling the chilaquiles on it.

"Dig in," he said, rustling up two forks and handing one to Beck.

"We're eating in the kitchen? Isn't that a health code violation?"

Duncan winked at him and reached up, pulling the curtain he'd helped John install years ago. It separated the kitchen from the table area, which was just outside the office.

"I don't think that's up to code," Beck teased.

"Never had an inspector complain," he said. "And besides, you wouldn't want to do this in full view of the restaurant." Duncan leaned in and gave him a kiss, lingering a bit. It was sweet and lazy, not the hurried, lust-filled kisses Beck was used to. It was nice, though.

"What was that for?" Beck asked thickly, when Duncan let the kiss end and sat back down.

"To thank you for what you did with Vincent," Duncan said with a shrug. "For not running the other way. For sticking around and agreeing to help me cook in a greasy spoon all night just to make sure I'm okay."

It was hard to tell in the fluorescent-tinged room, but it looked like Beck was blushing. He dug into his food with more concentration than was strictly necessary. It was kind of adorable, which was an odd thought because Duncan didn't think he'd ever classed anything other than baby pandas and kittens as adorable before.

"You don't need to thank me for that. Surely there are tons of people in your throng of admirers who would have done the same."

"I don't know where you are getting this idea I'm some kind of culinary rock star with a different groupie in my bed every night," Duncan said with a snort. He took a bite of the chilaquiles, burning his tongue a bit. "I'm not, P.S.," he said after he swallowed the too-hot bite.

Beck took a bite and chewed, his expression thoughtful. "The feta isn't as bad as I thought it would be."

"Right? Though it would be so much better with queso fresco. I'll have to make this some time for you and do it up right."

Beck shot him a sappy grin. "I'd like that."

Duncan laughed. "Careful or I'll think you're one of those groupies you seem convinced I have. Besides, you have your own groupies, Beck. When tonight's fake-dating story hits the blogs, middle-aged women's hearts across the country will break."

Beck pointed his fork at him. "You're an ass."

"But you're not contradicting me! I'm right!" Duncan crowed.

"*King of the Kitchen*'s demographic does skew to the middle-aged range, but it's pretty equally distributed among men and women. And I'm pretty sure the viewers all know I'm gay, anyway. That photo spread I did last year for *Out Magazine* ended up everywhere."

It had. Duncan had a copy on his phone. The photographer's playful use of the chef's hat was particularly inspired. Duncan had been sure at the time there had been ample Photoshopping, but now he'd seen Beck naked himself, he could attest there hadn't been. Beck's body really was that cut.

While thinking about Beck naked was entertaining, they had more important things to talk about. Duncan had put off explaining Vincent's tantrum for long enough. He wanted to get everything out in the open before the late-night rush started so it wasn't hanging over his head while he was cooking.

Having the food between them helped. Most of the important conversations in Duncan's life happened over a plate of food. It gave him something to focus on and a reason not to make eye contact, which he knew was classic avoidance, but he didn't care. He'd never had an easy time expressing his emotions, so Duncan figured whatever crutch helped him through it was valid. Plus the chilaquiles were good, and he was starving.

"I figure I owe you the story behind Vincent's meltdown. You could probably find some account of it somewhere online, since the Internet never forgets anything, but I'd rather you hear it from me," Duncan said finally.

"You don't owe me anything," Beck said, his voice earnest. "Seriously. And I won't go looking up old articles about you. I respect your privacy, Duncan. I understand what it's like to have a bunch of people watching you and waiting for you to mess up."

Huh. Duncan had never thought about it, but he supposed Beck was right. If anyone could understand what it felt like growing up sharing the limelight with a celebrity chef, he supposed Beck would be it. He'd dealt with a lot of the same things himself over the years.

Except the homophobia and bigotry. Christian was a hardass, but he'd always made a point of getting involved with LGBT causes and showing support for Beck whenever someone small-minded tried to make an issue of his sexuality.

"Well, I want you to know," Duncan said, forcing himself to make eye contact. Beck was looking at him full of compassion and encouragement, and it was almost too much to take in. Maybe he was falling for Beck. Was this what being in a relationship felt like? Knowing there was always someone on your side who would back you up and help fight for you when you couldn't do it yourself?

"Anyway, you probably know I started working in Vincent's kitchens as soon as I was old enough. I really enjoyed it, even though he and I have never gotten along. The summer I was seventeen, he'd promoted me to prep, and I was really excited about it. The head prep chef at the restaurant was ridiculously attractive, and he and I had this flirtation going on all summer. I learned a lot from him too. He was one of the most influential mentors I'd had, other than Vincent himself.

"That summer was also around the time I was figuring out I was bisexual. I'd lost my virginity to a girl the year before, and it had been awesome, but the more time I spent with the prep chef, the more I realized I liked guys too. He was gay, and we got involved. Nothing too heavy. There weren't any declarations of love or anything like that. Just light stuff, fooling around, having fun."

Beck nodded. "I think we've all had a relationship like that."

"Exactly. But we weren't smart about it, and one night after hours, Vincent walked in on us in the walk-in freezer. I've never been so scared in my life. I actually thought he might kill the guy."

"Was he a lot older?"

Duncan shook his head. "He was twenty. So a little older, but it wasn't like he was forty with a family or something. His age wasn't the part that had Vincent frothing. He went ballistic because I was with a guy. It was a lot like what you heard from him today, but with more cursing and a lot more promises of eternal damnation and hellfire."

Duncan hadn't told anyone about what had happened. Not even his mother. Duncan had been so ashamed of it for so long that telling anyone felt like it would make things worse. And it wasn't like he was blameless. Yes, Vincent's reaction had been over the top, but they *had* been at work.

"So what happened after that?"

Duncan shrugged. "He fired Kevin. Made sure to bad-mouth him enough that no kitchen in Chicago would hire him. I don't know where he went—if I'd been able to, I'd have gotten as far away from Vincent as I could. I don't blame Kevin for disappearing and not looking back."

"But you couldn't because you were a minor."

Duncan hummed in agreement. "I was a minor. It was almost the end of summer break anyway, so I went home to my mom and ducked out of the last few weeks in the kitchen. By the next summer, I'd finished high school and been accepted to college across the country, so I arranged an internship with a molecular gastronomist out west and spent my summer there. My mom wasn't pleased, since I think she liked having me less than an hour away in Chicago for the summers, but things between me and Vincent had gotten so bad, I guess she knew not to push it."

"How?"

"He started sending me Bible passages, and he offered to send me to one of those reprogramming camps. My mom didn't let him do that, of course, and by then I was eighteen and he couldn't have made me do anything. But he apologized, and she kept urging me to forgive him, and when I came back this time, I caved and started having dinners with him when I was in town."

"That's what Zane meant by your standing date?"

"Yup. Public place to minimize scenes, and we never, ever talk about my sexuality. Until tonight."

"Until tonight," Beck echoed quietly. "I'm sorry I brought that on."

"I already told you not to apologize. I mean, we aren't dating. He jumped to that conclusion, and that's on him."

"And when the story about us dating hits the press? What's he going to do then?"

Duncan blew out a breath. The brick in his stomach returned full force. "I don't know."

Beck smiled grimly. "And what are you going to do?"

Duncan shrugged. He wanted to laugh this off, but the moment was too important. "Tell them the truth? That I do like men and don't agree I'm going to hell for it? That you're attractive as fuck, and I'd love to date you if I knew anything about dating?"

Beck's eyes widened. "Seriously?"

"You know you're gorgeous."

"Not that," Beck said dismissively. "Did you really mean you'd like to date me?"

Duncan swallowed hard. "I think so? I wasn't kidding when I said I don't date. I have this hard and fast rule not to mix business and pleasure, after what happened with Kevin. And I'm almost always working, so that eliminates most of the pool of people I could have a relationship with."

"And what changed? If you never get involved with someone you work with, what was that in the shower at the studio?"

"A mistake," Duncan answered honestly. He didn't like the way it made Beck shrink in on himself, but he wasn't going to lie. "I was attracted to you, and I thought I could get it out of my system with a quickie. And I was wrong. But I didn't want to mess things up even more by getting into any sort of relationship with you, given my history."

"Your history of not dating?"

"Exactly. You're someone special, Beck. I don't want to hurt you, and I can't promise I wouldn't. It's all new territory for me."

"Shouldn't you let me be the judge of what I get into? I'm a big boy, Duncan. I've had my heart broken before and lived to tell the tale."

Before Duncan could respond, John rang the bell in the pass-through. "Hate to break up what sounded like a delightfully terrible conversation, gentlemen, but we've got an order in."

Duncan squared his shoulders and smiled at Beck. "Hold that thought, okay?"

THE LATE-NIGHT dinner rush at the cafe ran until about three in the morning, and he and Beck had stayed until the next shift came in at four. They were both bone tired, but Duncan didn't want to leave things the way they were.

Beck didn't seem to want to, either. "Come home with me? We have to be at the studio in five hours anyway. May as well be together."

"I'm kind of all talked out," Duncan warned. He'd talked more about feelings in the last few hours than he had in the last year, and he didn't think he had much more in him. But he did want to be with Beck. There was something comforting about being close to him he couldn't quite explain, and going home alone after a night like tonight seemed like a bad idea.

He fell asleep somewhere between getting in Beck's car in the suburbs and arriving at Beck's building downtown. He didn't remember any of the drive, so it must have been pretty soon after they'd started their drive into the city. Duncan didn't know where they were, but waking up in a garage as spacious and well-lit as this one meant it had to be somewhere nice.

"C'mon, you can sleep more upstairs," Beck murmured, pulling him out of the car.

Duncan felt pliant from his catnap and a little drunk with exhaustion. He let Beck drape an arm around him to guide him toward the elevators.

"And if I don't want to sleep?" he challenged, looking Beck up and down with his best leer.

Beck hesitated, then shuffled him into the elevator and hit the button for the top floor. Swanky.

"If you don't want to sleep, we don't have to. But I'm going to be honest with you. I'm not looking for another casual fuck."

Beck's tone was even, but his expression was tight. Duncan could imagine what it was costing him to have this conversation, and he hated knowing he was responsible for that hurt. Duncan swallowed and nodded. He'd felt terrible after Beck had started avoiding him after they'd had sex at the studio, and he had no intention of putting Beck in that situation again. "I can do that. I mean, the not-casual thing. At least, I think I can. I can try."

Beck was quiet for the ride up, and for a moment Duncan wondered if he'd fallen asleep. But he looked over and saw Beck watching him, his expression thoughtful.

"Okay," he said when the elevator doors opened. "Okay."

As soon as Beck closed his apartment door behind them, Duncan lunged forward and caged him against it, kissing him hungrily. He'd never had sex where feelings were involved, beyond mutual admiration and friendship, and it was a bit of a shock to his system to find it felt different. He was more invested, and there seemed to be more of a weight to the touches they exchanged. It was a whole new world of sensations.

They left a trail of clothes to Beck's bedroom, and by the time they were standing in front of the bed, they were both naked.

Beck's eyes swept down Duncan's bare chest, traveling over the flat planes of his stomach and lingering at the trail of wiry hair that led down to Duncan's half-hard cock, which twitched under the scrutiny.

"Still time to change your mind," Beck said, his voice strained.

Duncan angled his neck so Beck could press a row of kisses along his jaw. He canted his hips forward, rubbing his body against Beck's, their erections brushing against each other.

"I regret nothing," he said with a laugh when Beck's hands ghosted up his sides, tickling him.

After a brief fondle that had Duncan protesting when it stopped, Beck rested his other hand on Duncan's hip and urged him down onto the bed. Duncan made a questioning sound, but before he could say anything, Beck was on his knees, feet slipping on the hardwood floor as he moved, mouth joining his hand on Duncan's erection.

Duncan's head slammed back against the mattress, and he was suddenly very, very grateful Beck had had the foresight to guide them to the bed.

Beck's teeth nipped lightly at the head of Duncan's cock as he drew his head back, tongue laving over the abused flesh in a way that made Duncan's eyes roll back in his head.

A spit-slick finger slipped between Duncan's cheeks, rubbing small, delicious circles against his entrance. Duncan lost his train of thought, his focus on the sensations now as Beck took him deeper into his mouth. Duncan whimpered and forced himself up on his elbows so he could watch the way his cock disappeared into Beck's mouth, pink lips wrapped over sharp teeth as he bobbed up and down on Duncan's length.

Duncan shifted, moving his feet farther apart to give Beck better access. He saw Beck's dimples flash as he smiled around the cock in his mouth, and it was nearly enough to send Duncan careening over the edge. He blinked furiously, not wanting to miss a moment of the deliciously erotic picture Beck made as he sucked him off. God, had it been like this when he'd sucked Beck off at the studio? No wonder Beck had looked downright pained—it was the most delicious kind of torture, different from any blowjob Duncan had had before. There was an extra spark with Beck he'd never had with any of his other partners, and the result was amazing.

Beck barely breached Duncan's entrance with his finger, and the sting of it brought Duncan back from the edge a bit. Duncan lamented the lack of lube as Beck's finger retreated, continuing its massage of his hole from the outside, and all Duncan could think about was how much better it would be if they did have the lube. It could have been Beck's cock instead of his finger—

His orgasm crested without warning, and it was all he could do not to pump furiously into the tight heat of Beck's mouth as he came, his hands buried in Beck's mop of hair. He was vaguely aware of someone moaning, and it took a moment before he realized it was him.

Duncan lolled against the bed for a moment, coming down from his orgasm, so he didn't notice Beck fisting himself roughly until he was nearly done, the sound of his palm moving over flesh unmistakable even though Duncan's eyes were closed. He pried them open enough to watch as Beck stroked himself, half-kneeling, half-crouching at the edge of the bed. Realizing he was about to miss his chance to reciprocate, Duncan grabbed Beck under the armpits and tried to haul him up the side of the bed. It didn't work—Beck was solid muscle—but Beck took the hint and climbed up. Duncan shifted around until he was face to face with Beck's erection, so close he could feel the heat of it even though he wasn't touching it.

He licked at the thin skin of Beck's inner thigh, drawing a long groan out of Beck. Duncan buried his nose in the crease of Beck's hip, his tongue tracing a path downward until he could stretch his lips around Beck's sac, drawing one of Beck's balls into his mouth to suck.

Beck's hand came up and wrapped around the back of Duncan's neck, lightly enough he could shirk it off if he wanted to but showing Beck's impatience all the same. Duncan grinned, letting Beck's sac slip out of his mouth, and licked a stripe up his cock, his tongue delving gently into Beck's slit when he got to the head.

Beck's quiet gasps and groans as Duncan swallowed him down were enough to have Duncan wishing he could get hard again. He was enjoying the heavy weight of Beck in his mouth. Duncan teased him, his mouth moving up and down Beck's shaft at a languid pace.

Beck stroked a thumb down Duncan's jaw, his hips canting forward and threatening to choke Duncan as he desperately searched for more friction. Duncan relented, bringing a hand up to wrap around Beck's cock, pumping it as he bobbed his mouth up and down the length of it. The response was immediate. Beck's legs started to shake, and when Beck's eyes slid shut, Duncan closed his own and sped up his strokes, taking Beck as deep as he could without losing his rhythm or letting go of the base.

When Beck's cock started to pulse, Duncan didn't back off. He suckled at him until Beck pushed him away, letting the softening cock slide out of his mouth and fall against Beck's thigh.

"So that happened," Duncan began, stopping when Beck opened an eye and elbowed him hard.

"Don't ruin the afterglow. Panic later."

"I'm not going to panic, I—"

Beck rolled over and manhandled Duncan out of the bed, marching him toward the bathroom. It was gigantic, because of course it was. Everything in Beck's apartment screamed money, and the en suite was no different. Even the shower was opulent—how could one person need that many showerheads?

The snarky comment he'd been planning to make died away when he stepped under the spray. His own shower required a minimum of five minutes to heat up, but Beck's was scalding hot right away. The multiple heads felt like heaven, and even when Beck pushed his way in behind him, there was plenty of space to share.

He could hardly keep his eyes open, especially when Beck started shampooing his hair. It felt more intimate than anything else they'd done, and Duncan relaxed into the sensation. He was dead on his feet and barely able to help dry himself off when Beck rinsed both of them off and stopped the water.

Duncan let himself be guided back to bed and arranged easily until they were spooning.

"This okay?"

Beck's question had Duncan reeling. *This* was what he was going to ask about? "I'm breaking all my rules for you," Duncan muttered sleepily.

If Beck had any response to that, Duncan didn't hear it. He was out like a light.

Chapter FOURTEEN

BECK HALF expected Duncan to be gone in the morning, but when his alarm went off two hours after they'd gone to sleep, Duncan was still sprawled across his bed, snoring.

If they didn't leave soon, they'd be late for the morning read-through, but Beck was sorely tempted to let it slide and snuggle back in beside Duncan. They deserved to sleep in after how crazy last night had been.

Unfortunately, Beck's life never worked like that. He was always overscheduled, so he knew if he let himself lapse this one time it could easily turn into a habit. He poked Duncan in the side, but Duncan mumbled something unintelligible and rolled away, taking all of the blankets with him.

He looked so young with his face lax in sleep. Not that he usually looked old; he didn't. But Beck wasn't used to seeing Duncan's face at rest, and it made him look different. More vulnerable and less defensive. Duncan wore his over-the-top expressions like a shield, Beck was coming to realize. Kind of like how he hid behind a mask of polite indifference whenever he got flustered, except the exact opposite. Duncan was the clown, the one who always went for the laugh. Or, at the opposite end, the hot-headed guy who waded into things that were over his head in the moment.

Beck heard the front door open, and a second later, Lindsay called out.

"Beck? You'd better be dying, you asshole! I drove all the way over here because you wouldn't answer your goddamn phone!"

Shit.

Duncan hadn't woken in the commotion, so Beck slipped out of bed and grabbed his robe, tied it tightly around himself, and eased the bedroom door shut behind him. No good would come of Lindsay knowing—

He stopped dead as he turned the corner to the living room, where Lindsay was kicking what was obviously two different sets of clothing into a large pile.

Well, fuck. There was no way she wouldn't figure out who the T-shirt on top belonged to. It didn't take a genius to realize they only knew one person who'd be caught dead in a T-shirt with a smirking rolling pin and the caption "Bakers do it for the dough."

"Really, Beck? I have to come tearing over here because you can't be bothered to pick up the phone because you're still in bed with Duncan?"

He grabbed the pants he'd been wearing last night and dug his phone out of the pocket. It was nearly dead and showed ten missed calls from Lindsay, plus two from Christian and one from Campbell. Fucking hell. It was barely seven.

"So I'm guessing the blogs got a hold of Vincent's rant?" he asked, dropping his phone on the side table and padding to the kitchen. If he had to be up, there was damn well going to be coffee.

"Of course they did. It's made national news. Someone took a video, and it's already been shared more than 500,000 times on YouTube."

Oh God. Duncan was going to flip his shit.

"Of what, exactly?" he asked, not wanting to disclose more than he had to. Who knew what had gotten picked up.

Lindsay opened the laptop she'd been clutching to her chest and put it on the counter while Beck poked at his coffee machine.

"Why don't you go get Duncan so you can both see this?" she asked.

"Because he's sleeping, and there's no reason to ruin his day until he gets up," Beck snapped. "Show me the damn video."

It was grainy, obviously shot with a camera phone from a few tables away. Lindsay cranked the sound on the laptop, and even then it was hard to distinguish Vincent's voice from the din of the restaurant itself. They'd caught him at the peak of his rant, and even with the poor lighting and zoom, it was easy to see how red his face was. Beck and Duncan looked flushed too, but nowhere near as badly as Vincent.

It only lasted thirty seconds and consisted mostly of Vincent waving his hands angrily and Beck putting his arm around Duncan, but the stony look on Beck's face and the absolute misery on Duncan's didn't leave much question as to whether or not Vincent was angry with them.

"There are a few blogs with transcripts. I'm guessing either from someone who was there or someone who's better at lip-reading than I am," Lindsay said. "I'm kind of hoping they're wrong, actually. Did he really say those things to Duncan?"

Beck gritted his teeth and poured them cups of coffee. He added creamer and a generous sprinkling of sugar in to his and handed Lindsay's over black. "What, that gays are an abomination and he'd disown him if he didn't give up this gay phase? Yes, he did. He's a vile human being."

Lindsay looked sick. "How's Duncan?"

"How do you think? He's going to be a hundred times worse when he finds out this is all over the place," Beck growled.

"Hey, I didn't have anything to do with it. I'm the one who woke up to two calls at five in the morning asking for the network's comment on your relationship."

Beck grimaced. "So that made it too?"

"What, the part where you—hold on, let me find it." She flipped between tabs until she came to what she wanted, then read off the screen. "'A source in the crowd said *King of the Kitchen*'s Beck Douglas tossed Vincent Walters's words back at him and protectively wrapped around an obviously distraught Duncan Walters to shield him from both his father and onlookers.'"

Beck choked on his coffee. "No! I didn't. Well, no." He shook his head as he combed his memory of last night. He'd put his hand on Duncan's shoulder for support, and Duncan had been the one to pull his arm around him so it looked like they were embracing.

"Beck, I need to know. Are you and Duncan dating?"

Beck picked up his spoon and stirred his coffee, watching the milky liquid swirl around. "Maybe?"

Lindsay made a frustrated noise. "I can't work with 'maybe,' Beck. I need a yes or a no. I have to issue a statement, both from the network and from you, and maybe even from Duncan if he wants me to. Vincent's people are going to be all over this soon, if they aren't already. They're going to spin it as a misunderstanding between father and son and ask for the media and fans to stay out of it. Is that what you want to happen?"

Beck ran a hand through his hair. "It's not my place to say, Lindsay! This is his life. I don't get to decide those kinds of things for him. Personally, I'd like the entire world to know what a horrible, flaming bigot his father is. I want people to boycott all of Vincent Walters's restaurants. I want Big Gay to get out there and leave horrible reviews on his Yelp pages. It's petty, but I do. I hate what he's done to Duncan, the way he's made Duncan ashamed of who he is."

Lindsay clucked her tongue. "So burn him to the ground? I can do that."

"No!" He squeezed his eyes shut, wishing he was still curled up in bed with Duncan. It would have been nice for them to have had this conversation with each other before he had to have it with someone else. "It's up to him."

"Then wake him up, Beck."

He took a deep breath and counted to five before responding. "No. He's going to wake up to what might be one of the worst days of his life. He was mortified people overheard Vincent last night—he's going to be absolutely gutted that it's on the Internet. So I'm letting him sleep."

She sighed. "Fine. We'll do our part, then. How involved are you with Duncan?"

He snorted. "Obviously, I slept with him."

"Oh really," she said flatly.

He looked up and glared at her. "Twice. At the studio a few weeks ago and then here last night."

She squinted at him. "Was it terrible?"

"What? No!"

Her brows furrowed, and she leaned forward and rested her head on her fist. "Well, that's usually the only reason two consenting adults avoid each other like the plague after knocking boots, which must have been what caused that rift between you after the first show."

"It was great. Is that what you want to hear? Too good, because I thought it meant more than it did, but it was a casual thing for him. So I've been avoiding him because I'm in a little over my head and I don't want it to bleed over into the show. And then things happened last night and here we are."

"So what are we looking at here? Do you *want* to be in a relationship?"

He looked up and sighed. "I don't know? I told him I couldn't do casual, and he said okay, but we haven't talked about it yet today."

She nodded. "All right. First order of business, DTR."

"DTR?"

"Define the Relationship," she said with exaggerated slowness.

"Well, excuse me for not using chat-speak like an eleven-year-old girl," he snapped.

"Second order of business," she continued like he hadn't interrupted, "come up with a media plan for all the contingencies."

"Can I seriously not let this play out on its own without you and your lackeys getting involved?"

"No, you really can't." She sighed. "Look, I'm sorry. Dating's hard. I get it. Shit, I can't keep a guy around for more than a few dates, so maybe I don't get it. I don't know. But the point is, you and Duncan are in the public eye. And what's more, you're in the public eye together, representing the network. So if two of my costars tell me they're going to start dating? You bet I need a plan. Even more so when the public gets ahold of that information. I need to know if you want to confirm or deny the story to the public. I need to know what to do if you break up. If Duncan was a chick, I'd need a plan for what to do if he got pregnant, so you can be thankful we're leaving that one out."

Beck sighed and rubbed his face. "I know. I just—I like him. He's ridiculous and kind of obnoxious, but I like him."

Her frown softened. "He's obviously into you, Beck. I know the two of you bicker constantly, but I really do think it's flirtatious. And both of you are know-it-alls, but that's not something that's going to change." She laughed when Beck made an outraged noise. "I've seen him with people he doesn't like. My father, for one. He goes all quiet and tense. You should have seen him that morning when they went toe-to-toe. I thought he was going to bore through the table with the force of his glare. It's nothing like how he acts around you. I'm pretty sure you two will work things out."

"And if we don't?"

"And if you don't, I'll have a media plan for that," she said sassily, ducking when he tossed a paper clip at her. "Can we get Duncan up now?"

"No need," Duncan said, shuffling into the kitchen. "You're not exactly quiet. Lindsay has a voice that, shall we say, carries."

She stuck her tongue out at him. "Are you calling me shrill?"

"No, but I'm not contradicting you, either." He poured himself a cup of coffee and dumped half the sugar shaker in it before stealing Beck's spoon to stir it. "Hit me with it."

"I could just be here for breakfast," she said.

"Or you could have come in forty minutes ago shrieking the place down. I heard a lot of it. Including you trying to save me from this for a bit, which I appreciate," he said to Beck, pressing a kiss to Beck's temple.

Beck nearly melted with relief when he felt Duncan's hand intertwine with his. He squeezed, locking their fingers together.

"Yesterday's blowup with your father is probably going viral today," Lindsay said bluntly. "Someone recorded it, and it's on YouTube. We can't do anything about that," she said, holding up a hand when Duncan opened his mouth. "What we're looking at is damage control. What do you want officially out there from the network, from Beck, and from you? I can help you with all that."

Duncan looked down and swallowed. "The video—"

"Pretty much," Beck said, not wanting Duncan to have to say the words. "It has everything important."

Duncan's shoulders slumped. "And people are saying?"

Lindsay cringed. "That Vincent Walters is a homophobic asshole who doesn't deserve a penny of their money in his fancy restaurants. That Beck Douglas and Duncan Walters should be ashamed of themselves and listen to Vincent, because he's a God-fearing man who's looking out for their souls, and no one should watch *King of the Kitchen* because it promotes sodomy. It's all over the place."

Jesus. Christian was probably having a fit over that. He was always supportive, but he hated it when the show or his restaurants got dragged into things. Then again, he *really* hated Vincent, so maybe the fact Beck was in the news because he'd gone up against him would actually make Christian happy. It was hard to say.

"What do you want to do?" Lindsay asked softly.

Duncan hadn't raised his gaze from his untouched coffee. "Issue a statement, I guess. Tell them that after a lot of thought and years of soul-searching, I've decided to cut ties with my father once and for all. That his bigoted views are backward and hurtful, and apologize to anyone who was hurt by them."

Beck squeezed his hand.

"And about your relationship with Beck?" Lindsay prompted.

Duncan did look up at that, his eyes meeting Beck's. "I said I'd give it a go last night. You still up for that?"

Beck's stomach swooped. "Yeah?" he asked, watching Duncan carefully. "If you're sure, then, yes."

"So were you or weren't you meeting up with Vincent to tell him you two were dating?" Lindsay asked.

"We weren't. We weren't even dating till just now, really."

Lindsay cooed. "How precious. Now. Moving on. I need to know what you want people to know, what people don't already know about this clusterfuck that you want them to continue not to know, and what I need to watch out for."

Beck groaned. "That could take a while."

Lindsay took out a notebook and uncapped a pen, then looked up with an expectant smile. "Good thing I blocked out my entire morning, then."

Duncan finally took a sip of his coffee. "I'm not going to like this, am I?"

"Not even a little bit," Beck confirmed grimly.

Chapter FIFTEEN

DUNCAN HAD hoped once he and Beck issued a statement, things would die down. He and his father were chefs, for Christ's sake. Who the hell cared about them? Beck was on national television, so Duncan understood his popularity. But Vincent didn't even have restaurants outside the Midwest. Why would anyone in California or New York care about him?

But apparently they did. Or maybe the viral video of a fundamentalist father berating his bisexual son hit the right notes at the right time, and it didn't really matter who Duncan and his father were, only that they'd fought over his sexuality and it had been caught on camera.

A week later, it still hadn't died down. Duncan was getting calls from the *Today Show* and *Ellen* asking him to come on and speak, and Vincent's business manager had frozen all of Vincent's restaurant social media accounts because of all of the attacks on him. Public favor was mostly with Duncan, though there had been a few right-wing talk show hosts who'd congratulated Vincent on doing what was right and disowning his son over his sexual proclivities. A lot of the early backlash had been split, but now it was heavily slanted toward Duncan.

He'd had to make the drive downstate to talk to his mom a few days ago because she'd been getting calls from the media too. He'd been forced to tell her the whole story, and it had been terrible. The good news was she wasn't going to be guilting him into reconciling with Vincent again. He'd never heard some of the words she'd used come out of her mouth before, but suffice it to say she was horrified when she heard what had happened with the prep chef when Duncan was seventeen, and equally angered to hear what Vincent had said to him at Zane's restaurant.

Beck had come along with him, and that had been terrifying too. Laying himself bare for his mother and bringing a significant other home for the first time were two nerve-wracking experiences he'd like to never have to repeat.

He and Beck had taken the morning off just to have an hour or two to themselves. Or rather, Beck had taken the morning off. Duncan was still subbing in at Bar Rio, but that didn't involve any kind of managerial tasks, so his mornings and afternoons were his own. He'd spent most of them tagging along with Beck over the last week, hiding from reporters in Beck's office at the studio or the kitchen at Brix.

It should have been a recipe for disaster. Starting a relationship amid a media blitz and public scandal was crazy enough but then spending practically every day together? A few weeks ago Duncan would have felt nothing but pity for the poor soul who found himself in that situation, but now he was actually enjoying himself. Not the media parts, but the Beck part. Spending time together doing inane things, cooking simple meals at Beck's before they crashed for the night, waking up insanely early in the morning so Beck could get to work. Duncan had jumped into the deep end, and much to his surprise, he was swimming along just fine. They were heading into the studio to film in about twenty minutes, and he was actually looking forward to it. The director didn't allow any interruptions while they were filming, so there could be no reporters calling or even well-meaning friends checking in. He was more than ready for the break.

"You're good with the script? I don't want you ad-libbing the intro," Lindsay said, typing furiously on her phone. Her office had been working overtime to keep up with all the influx of interview requests and other things since the scandal had hit. There had even been a query from another network about him and Beck doing a reality TV series about their relationship. Ridiculous.

"Yes, I've already signed in blood that I'm going to stick to the intro," Duncan grumbled.

The writers had worked with Lindsay to put together a few-sentence statement thanking fans for their concern and asking for their understanding. He didn't think it was going to do much good, but it certainly couldn't hurt.

"If you don't want to do it, I can," Beck offered. He rested a hand on the back of Duncan's neck, and Duncan relaxed into the warmth, letting it leach tension out of his shoulders.

"No, I can do it. And then we'll cook," he said, offering Beck the artificial smile Lindsay had forced him to practice earlier while she'd drilled him on the carefully worded statement.

"Nice," Beck said, his lips curving as he fought a smile. Duncan was cute even when he was being petulant.

"We all set?" Bob asked, scanning the sound stage.

Beck nodded. "Yeah. Did Christian say he wanted to announce last week's winner or are you doing it again?"

"I'm going to do it because I've done the others. We decided consistency was best," Bob said.

Duncan doubted that was how the conversation had gone, but more power to Bob if he had the balls to stand up to Christian. Though he'd risen in esteem in Duncan's eyes over the last week. Not only had he had Lindsay issue a statement from him supporting Beck and Duncan's fledgling relationship, he'd also offered Duncan a job heading up one of his restaurants. Duncan had turned him down, but it had been a nice gesture.

The director clapped. "We're on in three, two, one, go!"

"Thanks for tuning in to *King of the Kitchen*," Beck said. Duncan grabbed his hand under the counter, and Beck squeezed back. "We're into week three of our cooking challenge, and things are getting interesting."

The camera panned a bit, and Duncan made sure he was standing on his mark. "Before we dive into that, I wanted to take a few minutes to thank viewers for their concern over the last week. Beck and I appreciate all the kind notes you've sent us. While your support means the world to us, we're asking for privacy at this time. It's not easy to start a relationship, and that goes double for doing it in the public eye," Duncan said with a self-deprecating grin.

They'd decided not to mention Vincent or even address the altercation at all, though it was unlikely any fans of the show had missed it. Still, Lindsay said keeping the message positive was the way to move past it, and Duncan had very little positive to say about his father.

"And you don't have to worry about our relationship affecting the competition, because I'm not going to take it easy on him just because he's cute," Duncan added, winking at Beck.

"I resent that. Maybe I'm the one taking it easy on you."

Bob laughed and stepped between them, resting a hand on each of their shoulders. "Before we get started today, I wanted to announce last week's winner. Duncan took the prize the first week, and last week they both had strong dishes, but the audience liked Beck's the best. So you gentlemen are neck and neck going into today's challenge."

Beck took a regal bow, and Duncan laughed and swatted him lightly. "Congratulations," he said.

"Thanks," Beck said, grinning ear to ear. "Today we're taking on shepherd's pie, also known as cottage pie. For anyone not familiar with this hearty meal, it's usually a meat pie filled with vegetables and topped with a crust of baked mashed potatoes."

Duncan sat a finished shepherd's pie out on the counter with a *thunk*. "When Beck says hearty, that's code for *heavy*. Did you hear that thing when I put it down? It weighs a couple pounds."

"And you'll be changing that, I assume?" Beck asked, glancing over at him.

"I will. Today I'll be making a beef in the sous vide, which is a style of cooking that allows meats to retain all of their natural juices and cook beautifully, and I'll be pairing it with potatoes espuma and red wine caviar."

Beck's brows rose. "Red wine caviar?"

"You'll have to wait and see with everyone else."

"Fair enough. I'll be lightening up this classic dish by turning it upside down. Instead of a topping of mashed potatoes, we'll be putting some beef medallions in a crunchy potato basket and adding in a carrot puree and a nice red wine sauce."

"A basket? Is that another name for a bird's nest?"

"Pretty much."

"I like it," Duncan said, bobbing his head. "So let's get started. We'll get our beef lightly seared on the outside and then packed up and into the sous vide, which uses an immersed heater to bring the water to a gentle and constant temperature that lets the beef cook slowly and evenly."

He checked the sous vide and added the beef, already sealed in the plastic bag, into it. "Now, an espuma is just a different type of foam, one with a bit more texture. Think of it kind of like a warm mousse. While I get the potatoes going for that, Beck's going to tell you about his baskets."

He watched Beck grate potatoes and get them onto the baking sheet, molding them around ramekins so they'd have the right shape. When Beck moved on to cooking his carrots and getting his beef medallions in the pan, Duncan grabbed his red wine and the ingredients he needed for his "caviar."

"Right. So this red wine caviar is molecular gastronomy at its easiest and most impressive. Anyone can do this at home if they have the right ingredients. We're using a good red drinking wine and two chemical additives that will help us shape it into tiny spheres that look like caviar and will pop on your tongue when you eat it, releasing the wine. Those are calcium chloride and sodium alginate."

"Bless you," Beck teased, and Duncan scowled at him.

"Whoever told you you were funny was lying, Beck," he said. He turned to the camera. "We shouldn't encourage him. Now, as I was saying, this is incredibly simple. We need to have a bowl with eighteen ounces of water ready for this, which Beck will fetch for me in penance for his terrible joke, while I show you what to do with the wine.

"We'll mix the sodium alginate in our wine, being careful to get it nicely combined because it likes to clump," Duncan narrated as he whisked the powder in. Beck set the bowl down next to him. "Thanks, you're forgiven," he said, laughing when Beck shook his head in exasperation. "We'll mix the calcium chloride in the water. It's going to help our little caviar pearls form when the wine hits the water."

He loaded up a small syringe with the wine and held it over the glass. "The height you drop this from and how much you put in at once determines the shape and size of your spheres. Try to be as even as you can with your amounts because these look most impressive when they're all the same size."

He dropped a bit of the wine into the water, and it beaded up right away. He followed it up with a few more to show the process, then put the syringe aside and used a strainer to take the spheres out of the bath.

"We'll rinse these and then they're ready to go."

Beck reached in and popped one from the finished pile in his mouth. He shuddered a little when it burst on his tongue. "I don't know why I wasn't expecting it to taste like wine, but it does. It's kind of like—did you ever have those fruit snacks as a kid?"

Duncan laughed. "Gushers?"

Beck pointed and nodded. "Yes! A similar mouth-feel experience."

"I suppose so. And that's a good warning too. These look like candy, which can be good if you're using the technique to spherify veggies to sneak them in so your kids will eat them because they look cool. But we didn't cook any alcohol out of this, so this red wine caviar isn't something you want your kids eating."

While Beck was busy assembling his potato baskets, Duncan pulled his beef out of the sous vide. He had one under the counter ready to slice, so he brought that out. "The meat is tender and soft but cooked perfectly," he said, showing the cutting board to the camera when it panned closer.

"Ah, but it's not caramelized and seared to perfection on the outside like this," Beck said, showing off his beef medallions. Duncan had to admit they looked pretty good. "We'll pull these carrots and stick them in the blender with a bit of beef stock to puree, season it up and we're ready to go over here. How are you doing, Duncan?"

"Getting ready to make our potato espuma," he said. "The key here is to mash our potatoes as well as we can, and then we're going to run it through a chinois, which is just a fancy strainer, to get it as fine as possible. Then we're going to add in cream and season the potatoes, and we'll load it into our siphon to create our espuma."

The foam was thick and exactly the way he wanted it, and Duncan grinned up at the camera. "We'll top that with our beef slices and our red wine caviar, and we're done!"

He put his plate next to Beck's with a flourish.

"It's almost too pretty to eat," Beck said, looking at Duncan's plate.

"And how do I eat yours? Cut into it, or pick up the basket?"

Beck snorted. "You're a heathen. Cut into it, you Neanderthal!"

They each took a bite, and Duncan was surprised at how flavorful Beck's beef medallions were. He'd have to give him this one—he hadn't accomplished that kind of complex taste with his sous vide. Not that he'd tell the audience that.

"All right, we're out of time for today. Thanks for inviting us into your kitchen, and don't forget to vote!" Beck pointed at the counter where the information would be edited in. "The numbers and URLs for our charities are on the screen right now. And this week there's an added twist—you can also vote for what classic you'd like to see us take on next week. Voting on that runs through Tuesday, so make sure you go online and make your preferences known. See you next week!"

As soon as the camera turned off, Duncan grabbed another bite of Beck's beef. "This is delicious."

Beck smirked. "I know. But I think you're going to win with your fancy red wine caviar." He poked at one and it rolled off the plate. "I think I prefer Gushers."

Duncan laughed. "Me too. But this is classic modernist cuisine, so I couldn't resist."

"So you're not going to call me old-fashioned because I prefer to drink my wine instead of chew it?"

"Nah. I happen to agree on that front."

"Do you want to go grab dinner?" Beck asked as they made their way back up to the offices.

"Can't. Navien has something that sounds horrendous. Thrush? I don't know. It involves her nipples and it's because of the baby and honestly I cut her off before she could explain because I'd rather work three twelves than know anything about it. I'll be closing for her tonight instead of over at Bar Rio."

Beck grimaced. "Understood. See you tomorrow, then?"

"Bright and early," Duncan groused. The early morning meetings were killing him.

Chapter SIXTEEN

"SO WE let the audience vote on the dish this week," Lindsay said, and from the way she was fidgeting, Beck knew he wasn't going to like where this was going.

They'd talked about this at the last programming meeting. He and Duncan had introduced the idea on the air. The last show was going to be live so votes could be taken while they were on the air, and the winner of today's challenge would be announced at the end.

Since it was the last one, they'd opened it up for viewers to vote on a list of four choices for what the dish would be. They'd picked something obscure Beck wasn't familiar with, but it hadn't been a big deal. The prep kitchen had made it a few days ago, so he and Duncan could taste it before they started planning their own menus.

"I was there when that happened, yes," he said to her. "And?"

Lindsay pressed her lips together, smothering a laugh. "Well, Bob thought we'd liven things up a bit this week and go with a theme for the set decorations."

That didn't sound too terrible, so there had to be another shoe to drop. Lindsay's eyes were sparkling with an unholy light that did not bode well.

Before she could say anything else, Carlie swept into the room with colorful bundles of fabric in her arms.

"We have two options. You can either have them match," she said, wiggling one set of fabric, "or you can have them in different plaids," she finished, waving the other, more colorful pile.

Lindsay clapped her hands. "Ooh, I don't think they should match. I mean, it's a competition, right? So they ought to look like they're from different clans."

Beck narrowed his eyes, focusing in on the fabric. They were plaids, like Carlie had said. The fabric was thick, but he couldn't figure out what they were. There were also a few of the show's standard chef's jackets tossed on top of the pile.

"I thought you might want to see how they looked together before you made a decision," Carlie said. She dumped the fabric on the conference room table and spread out the plaids. They were kilts.

What the hell?

THAT HAD been three hours ago, and no amount of arguing had dissuaded Lindsay from insisting he wear the thing. Which was how Beck came to be standing in the middle of the studio wearing what amounted to a heavy woolen skirt, held up by a thick leather belt that had a sheathe for a sword, which Carlie had stuck a whisk into.

Duncan had missed the morning meeting because he'd been covering a shift at John's cafe. Christian had been livid, but by this point, it didn't matter. They'd done all the planning for the episode, and Duncan was comfortable with how things worked in the studio. They'd done the dry run and gone over their marks and cues the day before.

The big change was the fact that they were actually going to be live, but that didn't affect Duncan or Beck. They'd been filming that way all through the challenge—the technical teams were the ones who would have to worry about getting graphics on the screen on time and manually handling camera fade-outs for commercial breaks.

But missing the meeting also meant Duncan had missed the wardrobe reveal, so when he walked onto the set a mere hour before filming, he was noticeably taken aback by the sight of Beck standing there in a kilt.

"You-you… it's a…."

Beck crossed his arms and gave Duncan an unimpressed look, and Duncan promptly burst into a fit of laughter.

"Yuck it up, because Lindsay made sure there's one for you too," Beck said dryly. He held up the kilt he'd stashed under the counter.

While Beck's kilt was a sedate blue-and-gray plaid, Duncan's was an over-the-top kelly-green-and-yellow number with enough decorative buckles to make him look like a Goth leprechaun.

Duncan's laughter stopped abruptly, his eyes traveling over the garishly colored kilt.

"Beck," Duncan pleaded, contrite. "I'm sorry for laughing. Let's talk about this. Clearly Lindsay has lost her mind."

Beck agreed, but he'd lost that fight. Nothing for it now but to put up a united front.

"The viewers wanted a theme show," he said with a shrug. "It's not like you're a stranger to wearing silly things."

Duncan looked down at his T-shirt, which had a very alarmed-looking bunch of cartoon vegetables in pirate costumes sailing in a potato skin boat, with a leek in the crow's nest and the caption "Captain, there's a leek in the boat!" underneath.

"This is not silly," he whined.

Beck held the kilt out to him. "Think how nicely it will go with this."

He'd saved his coup de grace for last, knowing it would work as well on Duncan as it had on him when Lindsay had used it.

"I doubt your charity needed the extra five grand anyway," Beck said, dropping the kilt on the counter.

"You have *got* to be kidding me," Duncan said with a groan. "The network is ponying up more money for us to wear these monstrosities?"

"Actually, the manufacturer is ponying up the money, so you'd better refrain from calling it a monstrosity on the air. But, yes. If we wear them during the show, our charities get an extra five grand. So suck it up, buttercup."

Duncan glared at the vibrantly hued pile. "Why does mine practically glow in the dark and yours doesn't?"

"Because I was here on time?"

Duncan turned on the megawatt smile that had fans so convinced he was the ultimate playboy. "Trade?"

Beck pretended to think it over before shaking his head. "Not on your life."

"Ass."

"Go get changed. Andre wants to go over our marks with us."

Duncan sighed loudly but grabbed the kilt and stomped backstage. It was an amusing sight. Totally worth the embarrassment of being in a kilt himself.

ACTUALLY, IT was kind of comfy. The stage was pretty hot, thanks to all the lights and the cooktops, but the kilt was keeping Beck quite comfortable. Not that he'd admit it to anyone.

Beck puttered around the set with Andre, figuring out where he'd need to switch out pans for shots and getting his timing down. There would be a clock just for him offstage, but that only helped if he knew what marks he was aiming for. Andre was great at his job and had supplied him with a sheet that listed what prepped items he had on hand and what time he needed to make the magic switches, so it would be seamless for the viewers. It was like having the stage direction part of the script without any of the dialogue cues.

A month ago the thought of hosting a show that way would have given him palpitations, but ad-libbing alongside Duncan was easy. Viewers had commented on how much more at ease he seemed and how much more fun the shows had been since Duncan joined, and Beck agreed. He used to hate filming days, and now he looked forward to them. It would be hard to adjust to the old routine once Duncan's four-show contract was up.

Duncan rejoined them a few minutes later, and Beck barely had time to admire the way the kilt draped over his hip bones—and accentuated the stupid T-shirt he'd kept on—before Andre dragged Duncan away to go over his cues.

In the whirl of activity before filming started, Beck didn't have a chance to talk to Duncan much. It wasn't until they were getting the one-minute countdown to the intro that he noticed how much Duncan was fidgeting with his kilt.

They were shoulder to shoulder at the counter, and Duncan's constant movement was distracting.

"Stop pulling at it!" Beck whispered, and Duncan dropped his hands guiltily.

"It's itchy," he whined.

"It's wool, of course it's—" Beck broke off, his gaze shooting to Duncan's waist. He leaned in closer, his shoulders brushing the tray Duncan was carrying. "Tell me you are wearing something underneath that, Duncan."

Duncan cringed.

"I am definitely not wearing anything underneath this." Duncan shifted again, his cheeks flushing. "Not one of my better ideas, I'll admit."

"Oh for Christ's sake," Beck muttered, his gaze drawn to Duncan's long, slender fingers, which had begun to inch their way to the front of his kilt so he could pull the fabric away from his skin again.

"It seemed like a good idea while I was up changing in your office," Duncan said.

Beck blew out a breath, his lips quirking. He didn't know if the thought of Duncan naked in his office or the thought of Duncan bare under the kilt was the more arousing picture, but both were having an uncomfortable effect under his own kilt.

"Shit," he breathed, studying Duncan's kilt intently. It brushed his knees and was perfectly proper. Nothing was showing that shouldn't be, and no one would have any idea he had nothing on underneath.

"Oh God. Stop watching me like that. You're making it worse," Duncan groaned. He gingerly pulled the kilt fabric away from his crotch, which only called attention to his half-hard cock.

"Well, stop messing with it."

"We're on in fifteen, gentlemen," the director called out.

Beck looked up, finding the right camera, and shuffled over a few steps so his knee was touching Duncan's. Duncan shivered slightly next to him. "This is going to suck," Duncan said under his breath.

In so many ways. "Probably so," Beck muttered back.

"In five, four, three, two, one, and we're rolling," the director called out.

Beck pushed thoughts of Duncan's dick out of his mind as best he could with the man standing right next to him, and smiled at the camera with the blinking red light. They were live.

"Thanks for tuning in to *King of the Kitchen*. This week we're continuing our chef challenge with Duncan Walters, who's best known for his forays into molecular gastronomy," Beck said. "And I'm Beck Douglas."

"Who's known for his rakish good looks as well as being one of the youngest chefs to take home a James Beard Award," Duncan put in.

Beck elbowed him. "Says the two-time Zagat 30 Under 30 winner," he teased. "If you've been watching the last three weeks, you know we've been recreating classic dishes. Last week we asked the audience to vote on the dish we'll take on today. So we're ending our month-long challenge series with cock-a-leekie soup, which is, unofficially, Scotland's national soup."

Duncan stepped out from the counter and spread his arms wide, the camera zooming in while he twirled around dramatically. Beck chanced a quick glance at him, relieved to see nothing seemed out of place now.

"The good people at Great Lakes Kilts upped the ante this week by offering us five thousand dollars for each of our charities if we wore the lovely kilts they provided," Duncan said. He rejoined Beck at the counter and threw his arm around him. "Quite a deal, because this is comfortable enough I'd have worn it for nothing," he said.

"But don't tell that to the Great Lakes Kilt people," Beck added with an exaggerated wink. "We do thank them for their generous donations. And we thank all you viewers for voting with your dollars as well. So far in the challenge, we've raised forty-four thousand dollars for Waste Not, Want Not, and forty-eight thousand for Healthy U—"

"Which means I'm *winning*," Duncan crowed.

Beck turned and scowled at him playfully. "Which does mean he's ahead, but I'll remind him this isn't over yet."

"So let's get started on today's challenge so I can bring my record to three to one," Duncan said, clapping his hands together.

"Traditional cock-a-leekie soup is a hearty chicken-stock-based soup with leeks, chicken, and rice, flavored with thyme. It's sweetened and thickened a bit with prunes, which is going to be an unusual flavor profile for our American viewers," Beck said.

"Prunes add more than just sweetness. There's a complexity of flavor there that really works in a savory dish," Duncan said. "Today I'm recreating this dish as a napoleon with homemade brown-rice crackers, crispy fried leeks, a thyme and smoked chicken puree, and pickled prunes."

Beck wrinkled his nose and shook his head at the camera. "Pickled prunes and chicken puree—I have this one in the bag, folks! Today we'll be stuffing a quail with leeks, rice, thyme, and prunes. Quail is similar to chicken, with a rich meat that is flavorful but not as fatty as duck. Ours will be crispy and delicious thanks to a generous basting with butter and chicken stock as it cooks."

And they were off. It wasn't quite the thrill of cooking a dish from start to finish in the kitchen, but it was close. There was the undeniable rush of trying to stay on pace, since they had to keep talking as they worked. It was surprisingly hard to talk about one thing while cooking something different. It had taken Beck months to master it—but of course, Duncan had taken to it naturally.

That was a good thing, though, because it made the time on the sound stage so much easier. There was never any dead air or awkward transitions because they kept up their joking and teasing as they went, easily filling any holes.

Plus, having a cohost who filled half the time with his own dish made the cooking part a breeze. It was handy to have the cameras cut away to zoom in on something Duncan was working on while Beck was switching out pans or pulling things out of the refrigerators and warmers hidden under the counter.

The hour flew by, and before he knew it, Beck was offering up a forkful of quail for Duncan to try.

He watched Duncan's lips close around the fork, and the twinkle in Duncan's eye was the only warning something was coming before Duncan moaned dramatically. Blood rushed to Beck's cock, which had behaved until now.

"I have to admit, that's good," Duncan said after he'd swallowed. "Though everything Beck makes is good. I never hesitate to put anything he's offering me in my mouth."

Beck choked on the bite of napoleon Duncan had given him. The double entendre had been perfectly timed for his swallow. Duncan grinned innocently at him and handed Beck the bottle of water a stagehand tossed him.

"Thank you," he choked out after he'd swallowed down a drink. "Despite the fact that it went down the wrong pipe, I did like it. The tart sweetness of the pickled prunes complemented the smoky chicken, though you're never going to convince me meat should be pureed."

Duncan laughed. "It's all about subverting expectations. Your brain expects certain foods to have certain textures, and when we play with that, you experience taste on a different level."

"I'll have to take your word for that, given you're the one with multiple science degrees," Beck said. The director gave him a cue, and Beck pointed downward, knowing the voting information would be popping up on the viewers' screens. "Sadly, you don't get the chance to taste these, but you do get to vote on your favorite. As we have in weeks past, we're letting you vote with your wallet. You have the numbers and URLs to call, text, or donate online. To vote for Duncan's napoleon, use the information here to donate to the Healthy U. To vote for my stuffed quail, use the information over here," he pointed toward the left side of the screen at the director's cue, "to vote for Waste Not, Want Not."

"No matter which of us wins this week's challenge, the big winners are these two amazing charities. The work they do is so important, and we're humbled to be working in support of their efforts," Duncan said. "Of course, that doesn't mean I wouldn't love a win. Because this napoleon, come on. Clear winner."

Beck rolled his eyes and shook his head fondly, looking at the camera. "That's it for today's challenge episode, but Duncan and I will be back in an hour to announce the winner. That means you only have until eight Central to get your vote in by calling or going online to donate to one of these charities. Thanks for inviting us into your kitchens, and we'll see you after *Cooking with Joy* is over in an hour!"

They both smiled at the cameras until the blinking light went out. "That's a wrap!" the director called.

Beck jumped when Duncan grabbed his ass, the unexpected contact making him spill his bottle of water.

Stagehands rushed forward to help him clean it up, and Beck's cheeks flushed hotly. "You're an ass," he whispered to Duncan, who'd danced out of the way of the spill. Beck's kilt was now wet down the front, making the heavy wool stick to his boxers and frame his cock uncomfortably.

It hadn't lessened his erection, which was a problem in its own right, now that the kilt provided nowhere to hide.

"Well, my work here is done," Duncan said with a shit-eating grin. He gave Beck's groin a pointed look and winked. "See you later."

Beck grabbed one of the kitchen towels he'd used to sop up the counter and held it over his crotch, hoping anyone who saw him would think he was embarrassed about the wet patch.

Everyone seemed to want to talk to him about the show, though, so he wasn't able to follow after Duncan. It took him a solid ten minutes to work his way through all the teasing about the kilt and the congratulations for a successful filming.

Not having Christian on the set today had everyone's mood elevated, it seemed. Beck could hear the boisterous laughter from the sound stage fade as he made his way down the corridor, blood pounding as he thought about Duncan naked underneath his kilt. It had killed him to be waylaid by crew members who needed things from him while Duncan had slipped off the sound stage, but he knew Duncan would be waiting for him somewhere. He'd been just as affected by the hour of teasing as Beck had, so there was little chance he'd leave without Beck.

He'd gotten through the show by focusing on the cooking and banter. Now, though, he had nothing to distract him, and his erection grew full force, despite the discomfort of his wet underwear.

The locker room would be busy this time of day, so Beck ran up the two flights of stairs to his office. As he'd thought, Duncan was there waiting for him. Beck made sure to lock the door behind him so there was at least the illusion of privacy. Half the staff had a key, so it wouldn't actually keep anyone out.

"I can't believe you were freeballing that entire time," Beck said, breathless from the run up the stairs and his anticipation.

He crowded Duncan up against his desk, kissing him and bringing a hand up his leg and under the kilt. True to his word, Duncan was completely bare. Both Beck and Duncan groaned as Beck's hand slid over soft skin.

Having sex at the network seemed to be becoming a habit, and it was terribly unprofessional. All of the work Beck had put into his reputation didn't hold a candle to how desperate he was to get more than his hands on Duncan's bare ass, though.

The possibility of being discovered only added to the excitement. Beck had heard illicit trysts were intoxicatingly exhilarating, but he'd never been with anyone who was worth the risk before Duncan. He managed to get under Beck's skin in a way no one else ever had.

Duncan squirmed out of his hold and turned around. "I thought you might like it if I bent over—" He rested his elbows on the desk, planting his feet as far apart as he comfortably could. "—and did this."

He reached back, flicking the rough material of the kilt up and exposing his ass. Beck hissed out a breath at the sight. He brought his hands up and glided his palms over Duncan's skin, tracing the curve of his ass. The skin was reddened and irritated from the rough wool, and Beck did his best to soothe it with soft, gentle strokes.

"Yes," Duncan breathed, his head dropping to the messy, paper-covered desk as he pushed his ass farther into the air.

Beck wished they had time for more than a quick romp. He'd like to keep Duncan splayed out over his desk like this, eating him out until he begged and moaned, and then fucking him open right there.

They hadn't done that yet, but Beck's office in a busy building wasn't the place to try it.

Beck ignored his own throbbing cock, focusing on the teasing caresses making Duncan shiver and twitch. Each sweep of his hands dipped a little lower until finally his thumbs brushed up against Duncan's sack, making Duncan cry out softly.

"Shit, we shouldn't be doing this. We have to go back on the air in forty minutes," Beck muttered. "I can't believe you talked about blowjobs on the air. This is your fault."

Duncan turned around and smirked. "I did not. I talked about loving all your food. You should thank me."

Beck gave Duncan's ass a firm tap with his palm. "Did you say thank you or spank you? Because I don't think thanks are in order."

Duncan laughed and wriggled against Beck's palm. "I'm open to a spanking."

Christ.

"We'll table that," Beck said, his voice hoarse. He'd never experimented with anything other than run-of-the-mill sex, but he was learning nothing about Duncan was average.

"You should table *me*," Duncan said, pushing back against Beck's groin suggestively. "Except without the kilt, because wet wool is not sexy."

"Your puns aren't sexy either," Beck sniped, but he stepped back to comply anyway. He pushed his wet underwear down over his hips and stepped out of them, following with the kilt.

He aligned his hips with Duncan's exposed ass, pleasure skating through him as his clammy skin came into contact with Duncan's warmth. Duncan rocked back obligingly, grinding against him.

Duncan tilted his head, looking back at Beck. "I don't suppose you have any lube?"

"This is my office! Of course I don't have any lube."

Duncan made a *tsk*ing sound and shook his head. "Well, it would come in handy right about now, wouldn't it, Judgy Judgerson?"

Beck leaned forward and buried his face against Duncan's T-shirt, muffling his laugh. Encouraging Duncan would only make things worse.

"You're a celebrity. Surely you have something. Eye cream? Can't have bags on national television."

Beck nipped at Duncan's back through the thin material. "I do not wear eye cream. And I'm not a celebrity."

"You just play one on TV?" Duncan teased, his shoulders shaking with laughter.

Usually talking in bed turned Beck off, but going back and forth with Duncan was actually a turn-on. Who knew?

Beck pressed forward, silencing Duncan's giggles by easing his cock into the cleft of Duncan's ass. Duncan wiggled his hips encouragingly.

"Lotion? Expensive olive oil from advertisers trying to woo you? Anything?"

Beck huffed out a laugh that turned into a moan when the head of his cock slid against Duncan's ass. "No one tries to woo me. Check the top drawer. Lindsay gave me some kind of lotion last winter because she said my cuticles were atrocious, whatever that means."

Duncan leaned forward and eased the drawer open. "Like you don't get a manicure every week. I know your type," he said, shimmying in triumph when he found a bottle of lotion. "It'll do."

"The kitchen is murder on french tips," Beck said, grinning when Duncan burst out laughing again.

He took the bottle from Duncan and squirted a generous amount in his palm. At least Lindsay had had the foresight to give him something unscented. He lubed his cock up well with it and without warning thrust forward, dragging his cock along the underside of Duncan's sack.

"Shit," Duncan whined.

Beck pressed forward again, biting his lip when Duncan responded by squeezing his thighs together and making the friction even more delicious. Beck gritted his teeth, steadying himself by placing a hand against the rough wool kilt that covered Duncan's lower back, and struggled to angle his thrusts upward ever so slightly so he maximized the contact with Duncan's balls. Duncan bucked back against him, groans muffled by the pile of paperwork he was resting his head on.

"Shh," Beck hissed. When Duncan quieted, Beck started to move again, thrusting at an almost frantic pace. He couldn't reach Duncan's cock from their awkward position, but he could feel Duncan stroking himself, his body jerking against Beck's as he pleasured himself.

Beck squeezed his eyes shut, hand fisting in the fabric of Duncan's kilt for leverage. Duncan's breathing was loud in the small office, and it went particularly ragged for a second before it stopped, Duncan's body tensing as he came.

Beck pulled back, and fisted himself roughly for a few strokes before coming across Duncan's reddened ass cheeks, perfectly framed by the kilt.

"I wish you could see this," he said, dragging a hand through the mess. Duncan looked so perfectly debauched, legs spread wide, Beck's come dripping down the curve of his ass, ridiculous kilt still hiked up.

"Maybe next time. How much longer do we have?"

Beck looked at the clock hanging by the door. "Twenty minutes, and we still have to get through makeup."

He was pretty sure the crew would know exactly what they'd gotten up to on their break, but there wasn't anything they could do about it. Beck grabbed some tissues from the box on the desk, wiped the come off Duncan's ass, and cleaned himself up too.

"For the love of God, please put your boxers on before we go back to the studio," he said.

"And if I said I didn't wear any today?"

Jesus. Duncan was killing him. "I have a spare pair in my gym bag. You can wear those."

Duncan groaned. "Wearing your underwear on national television seems like a good way to end up back here in another hour. I have mine," he said. He dug through a pile of clothes on Beck's chair and shimmied into them under the kilt.

"Hey," Duncan said as they were hustling out the door. "Remember our bet?"

"Our bet?"

"Winner gets to ask for a sexual favor?"

How had Beck managed to forget about that? "Yeah?"

Duncan grinned. "Nothing. Just reminding you," he said, palming the front of Beck's mostly dry kilt as he moved through the doorway.

Chapter SEVENTEEN

DUNCAN STILL couldn't believe he'd lost today. Beck's food had been good, but his had been *amazing*. And to make matters worse, even though they were technically tied on number of challenges, Beck had pulled ahead in the money, so Bob had proclaimed him the overall winner.

"Are you still pouting?" Beck pressed his fingers into Duncan's cheeks and forced his lips up into a smile. "Face it, Middle America just wasn't ready for pickled prunes and pureed chicken."

"But it was inspired! And the texture was perfect."

Beck dropped his hands and pressed a kiss to Duncan's forehead. "It was pretty awesome. Maybe if they could have tasted it, you'd have won."

Duncan wrinkled his nose. "Don't pander."

"You'd rather I tell you my food won on merit? Or should I tell you the truth, that even though your food was very well thought out and impeccably executed, it wasn't something that could be recreated in home kitchens, which is what viewers are really looking for?"

Duncan's lips twitched up on their own this time. "Who even says things like 'impeccably executed'? What are you, a *New York Times* food critic?"

"I could be. You never know. Critics usually go in disguise," Beck said, tilting his nose up into the air.

"Trust me, you'd never make it as a food critic."

Beck frowned. "Are you insulting my palate?"

"No, I'm paying you a compliment, asshat. You're too pretty to be forgettable. You wouldn't be able to blend, and I bet you get special treatment because of that jaw."

Beck looked affronted. "I do not get special treatment because of my *face*."

"Are we seriously arguing about your level of hotness? Is that a thing we're doing? Because you're going to lose."

"Of course we're not, because that's stupid!"

Lindsay breezed into the break room and poked Duncan in the side. "He's right, it's stupid," she said. She fed a handful of quarters into the machine and did a little dance when the Flamin' Hot Cheetos dropped into the bin. Beck wasn't sure why she ever worried they'd be out of stock—she was the only one who ate them because the rest of the building had actual functioning taste buds. "And Duncan's right too. You're just too beautiful for words, Beck."

She popped an alarmingly red Cheeto into her mouth and pointed the bag at Duncan, who grimaced and shook his head. "More for me," she said with a shrug. "Anyway, you're a hottie, darling. I should know because my department opens your mail. You get asked out all the time. There have even been marriage proposals."

Duncan crowed gleefully. "Have there been dick pics? Make my year and tell me yes, Lindsay. Tell me yes."

Lindsay smirked. "No, but I wouldn't be so smug. We're getting mail for you now as well. 'Is Duncan single?'" she said in a singsong voice. "'Would you consider doing a show where Duncan and Beck auction themselves off for charity?' and my favorite, several variations on 'are Duncan and Beck secretly a couple?' Won't have to bother answering those now, I guess. Cat's out of the bag on that one."

Duncan looked over at Beck, who had gone scarlet at Lindsay's last taunt. "Doesn't count if the question comes from Beck," he teased.

Beck seemed to flush even darker, which Duncan wouldn't have thought possible.

"Like you wouldn't pay good money to a charity if it meant you could get in his pants," Lindsay shot back.

Duncan bit his lip like he was considering the question. Then he reached into his pocket and pulled out his wallet. "Not that I need to enter a contest to do that, but how much are we talking here?"

Beck remained silent, but Lindsay cackled. "Well, it would be an auction. I bet some of his backers have pretty deep pockets."

Duncan snorted at her word choice. He'd like to be a backer for sure.

"Well, keep me on speed dial if you ever decide to pursue that particular suggestion," he said, leering suggestively at Beck before winking at Lindsay.

"I totally don't need any details," she said with a laugh. "And while it may not be a dating auction, you *will* be getting a call from the network about that show Bob was talking about, Duncan. I'm sure of it."

"And when I do, I should tell them I negotiate through you, right?"

She grinned. "Damn straight. I'll look out for you, baby."

"As well as you look out for me?" Beck asked dryly. "Where was this concern for your charge when you whored me out to this one?" he asked, pointing at Duncan.

"This worked out perfectly well for you, don't pretend otherwise," she said. She crumpled up her empty bag of radioactive Cheetos and tossed it in the garbage. "It's not my fault you had a public fight with someone you'd had a crush on for years. I'm glad it all worked out, though."

She blew them a kiss and traipsed out, leaving both of them staring dumbly in her wake.

Duncan whirled on Beck. "You had a crush on me? Seriously?"

"Whatever. It was a food crush," Beck muttered, looking down.

"That is such a lie. You hate my food," Duncan said, eyes widening. "Wait, do you still? I mean, I know we're involved, but do you still have a crush on me? Should I be waiting for Campbell to pass me a note?"

Beck's jaw tightened. "Don't."

"Don't what?"

"Don't be a jerk about this."

Duncan scoffed at that. "It's like you don't even know me. I'm a jerk about everything, Beck! This can't be news. And I'm going to milk this crush for all it's worth."

"I don't have a crush." Beck looked adorably flustered, and Duncan couldn't stop himself.

"I know I'm new to relationships, but I think that's kind of how this works. You have a crush on me, I have a crush on you; we're together."

Beck was fighting a grin, his face a complicated mix of indignant and amused. "I don't have a crush on you anymore."

"You don't? Has the fire gone out of our relationship already?" Duncan teased.

"No, you idiot. Crushes mean light feelings. I'm not crushing on you anymore because it's more than that. You're frustrating and you can be a real dick, but I think I'm falling in love with you."

Duncan's breath caught. He wasn't sure how to respond, so he fell back on his old standard, humor. "I'm sorry, all I heard was the word 'dick' and the word 'love.'"

Luckily, Beck seemed to get that it was too heavy for him at the moment. "I do love your dick," he said solemnly, nodding. "And probably the other parts of you too."

Duncan laughed. "I love your dick too," he said. "And I'm getting there on the rest. It may take a while, but I'm getting there."

Beck beamed. "We should celebrate."

"Celebrate our mutual love for each other's dicks?" Duncan asked, skeptical. "What would we do, get a cake? Can you imagine the look on the baker's face when we ask for the inscription 'Congrats on falling in love with my dick'?"

Beck's laugh was infectious. "No. I mean, let's go do something to celebrate. I won, and I want to claim my prize."

"Oh. Sex. Yes. Let's."

Beck shook his head. "No. We said the winner gets to choose, and I choose a date."

"A date?"

"Yes. We've never actually had one. Do you realize that? So I want to claim my prize and take you out. Like, really out. Not to one of Christian's restaurants or somewhere we know the owners. Someplace where we can have dinner, the two of us, without interruptions. Like a real date. I want to show you off."

That actually sounded pretty amazing. Things had been so hectic for the last month. Having a relaxing dinner would be awesome, and Duncan felt an undeniable thrill that Beck wanted to make their relationship public. It already was, to some extent, but this was different. This was doing it on their own terms, and that made a world of difference.

"You realize nothing's going to be just the two of us for long, right? We're bound to get noticed, and I plan on being all over you. That's what dates are for, right? There are going to be people who want to get the first picture of us out on a real date."

Beck quirked a brow at him. "So you're in?"

"I'm all in," he said.

Beck swept him into a kiss, leaving Duncan breathless when he pulled back. "From what Bob said about the audience participation today, we may be offered a contract together. That would mean working together permanently. I know you have reservations about that. You still in for this?"

Duncan wasn't sure where he was going careerwise. His family life was in shambles. He hadn't returned calls from most of his friends for the last few weeks because he'd been so busy. Basically, everything was up in the air and nothing was certain.

Seemed like a great time to take a huge leap and start something new.

"I told you once that I seem to be breaking all my rules for you. I'm still all in," he said, laughing when Beck moved in to kiss him again.

Recipes

BRAINSTORMING ABOUT what kind of food Duncan and Beck could make for the shows and writing them in the kitchen was honestly the highlight of writing this book for me. I love to cook, and I especially love experimenting in the kitchen. Sometimes things don't go as planned, and my family ends up eating cold cereal for dinner, but other times new favorites are born from my mad-scientist approach to cooking.

Here are a few of the dishes Duncan and Beck made in *King of the Kitchen*, including Duncan's red wine caviar for those of you who are feeling adventurous. I'll admit that one takes some doing and includes specialty ingredients you have to order off the Internet, but my son and I had a blast trying to get it just right!

REFRIGERATOR VELCRO FRITTATA

This can be made with pretty much anything in your refrigerator, which is what makes it such a versatile recipe. It's great for breakfast, but it's also perfect for dinner alongside a fresh salad and some crusty bread.

I've purposefully left this open for you to use whatever type of vegetable, protein, and herbs you have on hand. You really can't go wrong!

Ingredients

- 8 eggs, beaten
- 1/4 cup of milk
- 2 ounces of cheese (Parmesan, Mizithra, or gouda are my favorites, but use what you've got)
- 1 1/2 cups of cooked vegetables, chopped (squeeze moisture out of high water content veggies like spinach)
- 3/4 cup of cooked meat, chopped (beans also work)
- 1/2 teaspoon ground black pepper
- 1/2 teaspoon kosher salt

- 2 tablespoons unsalted butter or olive oil
- 1 tablespoon fresh herbs, chopped or 1/2 tablespoon dried herbs

Preheat oven to 350F. Combine eggs, salt, pepper, milk, cheese, and herbs in a bowl.

Heat a 10-inch nonstick oven-safe skillet over medium heat. Add the butter or oil, then sauté the veggies and meat until warm. Pour in the egg mixture and stir until evenly distributed. Cook for 4 to 5 minutes, using a spatula to push back the edges as they start to solidify so the egg mixture from the middle can reach the edges to cook.

Put the pan in the oven, uncovered, and bake for 12 to 15 minutes or until the middle is set. Let cool for a few minutes after cooking and cut into wedges to serve.

BECK'S BRUSSELS SPROUTS WITH BALSAMIC REDUCTION

Ingredients

- 1 pound brussels sprouts, cleaned and trimmed
- 1 pint grape tomatoes
- 3 tablespoons olive oil
- Kosher salt
- Ground pepper
- 1/2 cup balsamic vinegar

Preheat oven to 400F.

On the stovetop, bring the balsamic vinegar to a gentle simmer and let cook uncovered, stirring often, until the water cooks out and it reduces by about half. It should be a syrupy consistency that sticks to the back of your spoon or spatula when it's ready. Take it off the heat and set aside. (This makes enough to barely coat the brussels sprouts. If you really like balsamic glazes and want a thicker one on the sprouts, start with a full cup of balsamic vinegar.)

Slice brussels sprouts and grape tomatoes lengthwise (through the stem). Discard any yellowed leaves on the outside of the brussels sprouts. If you want extra-crispy bits (my family's favorite part!), then pull the larger brussels sprouts apart. Toss with the olive oil and distribute evenly on a heavy sheet pan. Arrange the sprouts and tomatoes cut side down for maximum caramelization. Sprinkle with a generous amount of kosher salt, and pepper to taste. Roast for twenty minutes, taking the pan out halfway through the cooking time to check for burning, and stirring if necessary.

The brussels sprouts are done when they have a nice caramel color. Ovens (and sprout sizes) vary, so keep an eye on them and adjust the cooking time as necessary. When they are finished, toss them with the balsamic reduction and serve.

Duncan's Red Wine Caviar

You can make this with any liquid that isn't overly acidic. Most red wines will be okay, and if you're trying it with juice, then apple and grape are a good place to start. You'll need chemicals to make this work, and there are a lot of molecular gastronomy sites that sell them. I recommend getting a kit if you want to experiment— that way you have everything you need to play around and see if you want to invest more money on tools and larger amounts of the chemicals later.

In addition, you will need some special tools: a syringe, plastic pipette, or drinking straw, and a slotted spoon or small sieve.

Ingredients

- 1 cup wine or juice
- 1/3 teaspoon sodium alginate
- 2 1/4 cups of water
- 1/2 teaspoon calcium chloride
- Food coloring to suit (optional)

Put the wine or juice in a bowl and add a drop or two of the food coloring if desired. I've found that I like the extra depth of color food coloring can bring, but it's not necessary. Sprinkle the sodium alginate in and immediately stir vigorously with an immersion blender as the alginate tends to clump. If you don't have an immersion blender, you can use a regular blender instead. Blend until the alginate is thoroughly incorporated.

Pour the water into a wide bowl and whisk in the calcium chloride. It takes a bit of time to dissolve. Once it has dissolved completely, take your dropper and suck up some of the juice or wine mixture. Gently drop beads of it into the water. If you are using a drinking straw, keep your finger over the top to control the drops.

Let the drops sit for no longer than a minute and then gently fish them out with the slotted spoon or small sieve and rinse them carefully with cold water.

Please note that since these are not cooked, if you make them with alcohol you cannot give the caviar to children.

BRU BAKER got her first taste of life as a writer at the tender age of four, when she started publishing a weekly newspaper for her family. What they called nosiness she called a nose for news, and no one was surprised when she ended up with degrees in journalism and political science and started a career in journalism.

Bru spent more than a decade writing for newspapers before making the jump to fiction. She now works in reference and readers' advisory in a Midwestern library, though she still finds it hard to believe someone's willing to pay her to talk about books all day. Most evenings you can find her curled up with a mug of tea, some fuzzy socks, and a book or her laptop. Whether it's creating her own characters or getting caught up in someone else's, there's no denying that Bru is happiest when she's engrossed in a story. She and her husband have two children, which means a lot of her books get written from the sidelines of various sports practices.

Website: www.bru-baker.com

Blog: www.bru-baker.blogspot.com

Twitter: @bru_baker

Facebook: www.facebook.com/bru.baker79

Goodreads: www.goodreads.com/author/show/6608093.Bru_Baker

E-mail: bru@bru-baker.com

All Parker Anderson has ever wanted is to take over as CEO of Anderson Industries when his father retires. But when his father is ready to leave the company, he doesn't plan to pass the reins to Parker. Instead, he plans to sell the company, jeopardizing not only Parker's job but hundreds of others.

Parker finds an unlikely ally in Mason Pike, the company's resident IT guru. What starts as a flirtation takes them from coworkers to coconspirators in a plan to forcibly buy Anderson Industries out from under Parker's father. While they focus on the buyout, their budding romance has to be put on hold, but that doesn't stop them from flirting and teasing each other to distraction—and once their master plan comes to fruition, nothing and no one can keep them apart.

www.dreamspinnerpress.com

If not for his family and his Christmas tree farm, David Rochester would be a recluse. And Erik Shriver wouldn't know a quiet moment if it smacked him in the face. But now David's farm has brought them together. When Erik's flurry of bad jokes and frenetic energy sets David off kilter, his family notices and begins conspiring. They push David and a very willing Erik together again and again until David stops denying his attraction. But an almost-hermit and a soon-to-be-former club boy each bring baggage into a relationship. They'll have to take things slowly to find the middle ground between David's taciturn silence and Eric's boundless chatter.

www.dreamspinnerpress.com

The Magic of Weihnachten

BRU BAKER

American Walsh Brandt is happy when a promotion lands him his dream job and a quiet new life in Germany. Until December rolls around, when he realizes it's almost impossible to hide from the holiday season in Germany.

Dierck Reiniger is fascinated by Walsh's hatred of Christmas and makes it his personal mission to help Walsh enjoy Weihnachten and the German traditions he grew up with. Walsh has a great time getting to know Dierck—but he still isn't sold on Christmas, despite Dierck's efforts. Dierck's on the rebound, and he's determined to develop their physical relationship slowly, much to Walsh's frustration. It isn't until they're alone in a secluded cabin—hiding from the traditional trappings—that Walsh finally recognizes what the magic of the season can bring when spent with someone special.

www.dreamspinnerpress.com

ISLAND HOUSE

BRU BAKER

Dropping Anchor: Book One

Unable to move on after the death of his lover, British expat Niall Ahern clings to Nolan's dream of living in the Caribbean by moving to Tortola. Once there, he finds that not even the beauty of the island can fill the hole in his heart. Broke and spent in nearly every way imaginable, Niall wants out of the lonely, miserable, guilt-ridden life he's carved out for himself.

When Ethan Bettencourt, a wealthy tech guru, shows up in British Virgin Islands looking to purchase a second home, he gives Niall hope that he can move on. Both men fall hard and fast, but Niall finds piloting his yacht in the midst of a hurricane is nothing compared to weathering life's simple misunderstandings. As their troubles come between them, Niall is left to wonder if he and Ethan are over before they've begun.

www.dreamspinnerpress.com

Dropping Anchor: Book Two

When an inheritance fell in Ian Mackay's lap, he fled the high-pressure banking industry and didn't look back. Since then, he's spent four years living carefree on the island of Tortola, his life a series of hookups and hanging out with friends.

After his best friend moves to Seattle and gets married, Ian finds himself lost. His unapologetic existence doesn't hold the same appeal, and he wonders if he's throwing his life away. After visiting Niall in Seattle, Ian decides to stay, but that means taking his life off hold and finding a real job. Meeting Luke Keys, who is about as far from a player as possible, isn't the plan but might be just what Ian needs. Luke and his values intrigue Ian, and he pursues Luke ruthlessly until Luke agrees to a date.

Their courtship sweeps Ian off his feet, and when the relationship gets complicated, Ian has the chance to cut and run. Habits born from years of being on his own are hard to shake, and self-proclaimed playboy Ian must decide if love is worth fighting for.

www.dreamspinnerpress.com

BRU BAKER

PLAYING HOUSE

BOOK 3 IN THE DROPPING ANCHOR SERIES

Dropping Anchor: Book Three

College sweethearts Frank and Warner have been together for sixteen years, married for eleven. Having grown up in a freewheeling hippie environment, Frank thinks their structured life is great, although lately he and Warner have fallen into a rut. Frank isn't concerned; it's what happens to old marrieds. Frank's blindsided, though, when he finds Warner looking into adopting, and Frank realizes just how not okay things really are.

Frank doesn't want kids. They bring chaos and unpredictability. He had enough of that growing up. Trying to salvage their relationship, Frank and Warner reach out for help. In the process of marriage counseling and working through their differences, Frank discovers his rigid adherence to schedules, anxiety attacks, and host of personality quirks are actually markers for Asperger Syndrome. With the help of a psychologist, Frank's life gets easier, and he realizes a future with children isn't as unfathomable as he once thought.

Through it all, Frank is stunned by how much making a family with Warner has boosted the intimacy between them. It's taken thirty-five years, but he's finally got a handle on life, and the future looks even better.

www.dreamspinnerpress.com

Waiting
for the
Moon
and You

L.J. LaBarthe

www.ingramcontent.com/pod-product-compliance
Lightning Source LLC
Chambersburg PA
CBHW060100260626
47160CB00005B/1729